Uma Lohray holds a law degree from one of India's premier national law schools. She has worked with a leading law firm and media house as legal counsel. She writes for passion.

A daughter of scientist parents, Uma grew up in Pune, Hyderabad and Ahmedabad. She practised in New Delhi as a lawyer. She married a fellow 'suit' and they slung backpacks around the world together.

Her itch to write was kept at bay by the balm of routine. She slowed down to cherish her newborn as the world slowed down to save itself from the pandemic and realisation struck her like a kick on the backside: her novels would never write themselves! After a year of dandling her infant, dealing with Covid, sweating out practising yoga postures and clacking away at her ancient but trusted MacBook, *The One-Way Ships* was born.

Uma lives in New Delhi with her husband and a five-year-old son, and travels to the mountains every single time she can.

THE ONE-WAY SHIPS

UMA LOHRAY

Om Books International

First published in 2025 by

Om Books International

Corporate & Editorial Office
A-12, Sector 64, Noida 201 301
Uttar Pradesh, India
Phone: +91 120 477 4100
Email: editorial@ombooks.com
Website: www.ombooksinternational.com

Sales Office
107, Ansari Road, Darya Ganj,
New Delhi 110 002, India
Phone: +91 11 4000 9000
Email: sales@ombooks.com
Website: www.ombooks.com

Copyright © Uma Lohray 2025

ALL RIGHTS RESERVED. This is a work of fiction. Names, characters, places, and incidents either are the product of the author's imagination or are used fictitiously. Any resemblance to actual persons, living or dead, events or locales, is entirely coincidental. No part of this book may be reproduced or transmitted in any form by any means, electronic or mechanical, including photocopying and recording, or by any information storage and retrieval system, except as may be expressly permitted in writing by the publisher.

ISBN: 978-93-6395-774-9

Printed in India

10 9 8 7 6 5 4 3 2 1

Dedication

To SD

my constant companion through every chapter,
on and off the page

PROLOGUE

20 June 2000
Marlow, Buckinghamshire

Rashmi stepped out of her cab, her gaze sweeping over the crescent of sleepy cottages huddled around a lush park. The town exuded a careful charm, presenting a curated portrait of English pastoral life as if for a postcard for one to collect. She imagined its denizens rising gently to cups of Earl Grey tea steeped just so, navigating unhurried days of modest exertions and looking forward placidly to the annual regatta. The exaggeration brought a smile to her lips. The townsfolk would gather in faithful answer to soft chimes of church bells on Sundays; children familiar with the sound since their days in cradle would spill on to the fields after school, their laughter threading through the still air—or so Rashmi's imagination insisted.

So this is where you made your last home.

The train journey from London Paddington had felt like a passage through time. The countryside had whirled by like pages from a charmingly illustrated book, with picturesque cottages nestled among rolling hills, serene lakes mirroring the skies, and Elizabethan mansions that stood as solemn witnesses to centuries gone by.

Yet, had it been up to Rashmi, she would never have known Asha's name. Marlow would have remained just a word, a distant pin on a map. But this day had earlier been marked for something else. The smart kurta she wore had been chosen for an occasion of far greater consequence—a formal interview that had been fixed after months of waiting. A British parliamentarian of Indian descent, rumoured to be a rising contender for the post of prime minister, was to be her subject. It had been a stroke of journalistic inspiration, an idea that had taken months to conceive, shape, and turn into an opportunity.

The interview would have finally cast her as a serious journalist after three years of fluff pieces, like 'The Urban Dweller's Best Friend. Find Out Which Pet Suits Your Lifestyle' and 'Cargo Pants or Capris? Unlocking Fashion Trends This Y' for *Interludes*, a flimsy supplementary edition to *The National Standard*. The editor had even promised that this time her piece would not languish in the margins of *Interludes*. It would have graced the pages of *The National Standard* itself, with all its weight and legitimacy.

Rashmi had aligned her shots with precision. There was no chance she could be replaced, sidelined, or undermined on this assignment. Her cousin Koel, or Kuki, as the family fondly called her, was marrying a Londoner this summer, and Rashmi's parents had been relentless in coaxing her to reserve holidays for the occasion. Initially resistant, she had grudgingly given in and soon recognised the opportunity hidden in the guise of obligation. A week in London, hosted by her relatives and funded by her parents, could be turned into a career-defining move.

Her research had been immaculate. She had studied the arc of her interviewee's meteoric career with almost obsessive diligence: the migration of his grandparents from East Africa, his glittering academic record, the formative years as an investment banker, and his deliberate, methodical pivot to British politics. Every detail had been committed to memory, every quote dissected and annotated. This interview was to be her masterpiece, and when he would rise to claim the office of prime minister, media houses would clamour to syndicate her foresight.

Yes, she had already felt like a celebrity journalist, entering her office building at ITO, New Delhi, that morning, only four days ago. She breezed through meetings, disarming adversaries with sharp quips, and even deigned to join the post-lunch chatter with the 'fossils', a term of endearment (and mild disdain) the younger recruits used for the senior employees. Some of the fossils seemed genuinely pleased with her, their goodwill evident in the way they asked questions, while others slyly slid their shopping wish lists into the conversation. Rashmi noted their requests with good humour, mentally categorising them into broad themes: cosmetics and confectionery. This was not her trying to keep everyone happy, this was just her feeling happy. Her flight to London was scheduled for early next morning. Maybe she'd even buy something for her editor this time—a bottle of traditionally distilled gin or a wedge of raw-milk cheese, a nod to his affected connoisseurship. But Debendro Bagchi, her editor-in-chief, had an unparalleled talent for squandering the good favour of his team no sooner than he managed to earn it. It was no different this time.

As Rashmi refreshed her inbox one last time before packing up for the day, a new email appeared with the ominous inevitability of a storm cloud. In telegraphic fashion, it read:

RR, London assignment transferred to Madhav Sarin.
Sorry. PFA the dossier with your new assignment.
Bagchi

Rashmi blinked at the screen—once and then twice—till the meaning settled in like an unwelcome guest. Then the rage started to boil. Her pulse quickened as she clicked on the attachment, a dossier on her 'new' assignment.

She skimmed through the contents, getting angrier by the word. It was regarding a fluff piece about some elderly woman of Indian origin, once an ayah in England, who had been given some local award by a band of bumpkins somewhere she hadn't heard of. Despite the utter disbelief at the turn of events, her instinct for thoroughness kicked in—and that only stoked her indignation further. She looked up the woman's name online. The search yielded two meagre articles from websites she had never heard of, each parroting the same scant 300-word biography.

Her colleagues were packing up for the day, their chatter and laughter spilling into the hallway. Rashmi had planned to join them, indulge in a few drinks, and head home to pack in her typical last-minute fashion for her 3 a.m. journey. But now, there was only one thing to do: bring battle to Bagchi.

She spotted his shiny pate hovering behind the frosted glass of his cabin, bobbing slightly as he simpered at an intern's feeble jokes. A teacup dangled from his hand, half-raised to his lips. Rashmi yanked her thick notebook from her drawer and stormed across the hall, the sound of her heels ricocheting off the walls. She pushed open the door with the force of an invading army and turned to the intern. "Please leave. This is urgent."

The minion vanished before the teacup could even reach Bagchi's saucer. He had barely begun to arrange a conciliatory smile before Rashmi slammed the notebook on to his desk, the thud loud enough to make him recoil. He opened his mouth, spilling out half-formed justifications not to Rashmi but to the poor, trembling teacup in his hand.

"Bagchi-da, look at me!" she barked, her voice sharp and cutting. "Who is this Madhav Sarin? Did you just snatch my brainchild, my months of planning, and hand it over to some random guy?"

Her tone cracked like a whip, and Bagchi instinctively shrank behind his desk, a turtle retreating into its shell.

"Rashmi," he began weakly, "I—I knew you'd be upset! I didn't want to…"

"*Of course*, I'm upset!" she growled, eyes blazing. "You are *not* doing this."

"I never would have!" he remonstrated, waving his stick-thin arms as though fending off an unseen swarm of flies. "It wasn't I! It was a call from the senior editors! The *Standard* people! Had it been *Interludes*, I would have put my foot down, you know that!"

"You have no foot to put down! No spine either!"

The confrontation dragged on, stretching into an hour of verbal sparring. Bagchi squirmed through a litany of justifications: "He's had more experience with high-profile interviews. He'll bring a depth of perspective", along with similar half-hearted platitudes.

It was only after some well-placed threats that the truth came tumbling out: Madhav Sarin was a prized recruit poached from a close competitor, and was currently vacationing in London during his pre-joining period. The London assignment had been dangled as a golden opportunity to sweeten the deal.

"And you thought, 'Let's snatch this girl's assignment and hand it to the pro!'" Rashmi's voice rose with every word. "Because clearly, I couldn't have done justice to *my own assignment*, right?"

Bagchi flushed a deeper shade of pink, his discomfort palpable as he shoved the printout of the dossier defensively across the desk. "I know it doesn't seem fair, Rao, but it's out of my hands. I've tried my best to give you a decent replacement."

"*Really*!" Rashmi laughed bitterly, looking away for a brief moment before turning her disbelieving gaze back to him. "You took away my potential British PM and handed me ..." she concluded throwing her hands up in exasperation, "... a *baai*!"

Bagchi flinched but held his ground. "Look, Rao, it could be an interesting interview. You can mine first-hand insights into the British Raj."

Rashmi stared at him for a few seconds with silent disbelief. "I'm waiting for the part where you tell me how this makes any sense."

"Rao, I won't force you to do this assignment. But I will say this: Read the proposal once. Attend your cousin's wedding, take some time to think about it, and if you still feel it's beneath you, don't do it. But this is where things stand—it's management's decision."

Rashmi glared at him, her contempt scalding and silent. Without another word, she turned on her heel and left, the sound of the door being slammed echoing through the office. She hurriedly cleared her desk with shaking hands and tore a part of the dossier while shoving it angrily in her bag. Before her composure cracked, she effected a hasty exit and stepped into the office cab. The silence in the vehicle was only broken by her soft sobs all the way home. Her parents had left for London a few weeks ago, so now she was to bear her sorrow in solitude.

The flight to London was a blur. Her thoughts were bitter, her grief only interrupted by exhausted bouts of sleep. In the quiet, half-conscious space between wakefulness and sleep, she dreamt of Madhav Sarin. Her subconscious had its own interpretation of him: a vulture morphed into a thin, cackling human. His face was hollow, with dark circles under his eyes, his head beginning to bald from years of sleepless frustration. She pictured him sitting at Bagchi's desk, pecking at gory scraps while Bagchi, inexplicably dressed as the office peon, Ayodhya-ji, served tea to the office. The absurdity of it all was almost too much—almost.

The nap calmed down her nerves, and a kingly meal paired with champagne soothed the edges of her distressed mind. By the time she finally stepped out into the cool, refreshing London air, she felt decidedly better. The festive atmosphere further lifted her spirits. Meeting her cousins, hearing Kuki's jubilant recounting of her love story to a rapt audience, and the distant murmur of her uncles huddled in corners, safely removed from their wives, and sipping Black Dog and dissecting Indian politics—it all felt oddly comforting. Her aunts badgered her with incisive questions about her non-existent love life, grandparents pleaded with her in injured tones to get married before they passed away. These bizarre spectacles at the family gathering helped push her disappointment to the back of her mind. Later that night, though the tiredness of jet lag weighed heavily on her, Rashmi glanced at the torn dossier still in her bag.

Bagchi had a thousand flaws, but he certainly knew how to put together his dossiers. It far surpassed the web pages she had found. Her interviewee, Asha, was a woman in her late eighties, born and raised in pre-independence India. She had worked as a 'baby ayah' in the homes of British families, caring for their children. Now living alone in Marlow, Buckinghamshire, Asha had dedicated her life to uplifting women without means, following years of rehabilitating ayahs at the Ayah Home in Hackney, London. Through her personal contributions, she had supported ayahs from India, China, Sri Lanka, and Indonesia. Recently, Asha had been honoured with a local award.

It might be an interesting interview, though perhaps better suited for a fresher, she thought, stuffing fruit cake in her mouth as she turned the last page. A domestic help with a vantage point into the inner workings of the British elite—it was undoubtedly an interesting story. Given her humble beginnings, how did Asha gather the wherewithal to contribute towards the welfare of other ayahs in her time? Rashmi suspected Bagchi had deliberately given just enough information to make the assignment seem like an enigma—something to keep her curious.

There was no doubt that this woman had led an interesting life. A quick look at Marlow in the tourist guidebook had given her the briefest glimpse into the town's charm. The countryside was picturesque, and the commute, shorter than the one from her office to her home back in India, was practically a breeze. The interview would likely take no more than an hour and a half—plenty of time to tick off a few tourist spots before heading back. The blush pink kurta had been staring at her from the suitcase, mocking her with its uselessness.

So, here she was, in Marlow, chasing not the future, but the faint echoes of a life already lived.

Taking a deep breath, she flicked on her 'journalist vision' and began scanning her surroundings. She noted the house before her—a charming structure with a sloping brown roof and crisp white panelling, giving off an aura of quiet elegance. Juliet balconies overflowed with bright red flowers, and the front porch housed a neat cane table and two small chairs beneath a dainty wind chime that clinked softly in the breeze. The garden was immaculate—pink geraniums lined the perimeter, while freshly planted tulips added a splash of colour to the flower bed. The whole scene radiated a sense of warmth, an understated allure that Rashmi hadn't anticipated.

She rang the bell and waited. When a minute passed with no response, she reached for the bell again but halted at the sound of the door unlocking. A petite, slouched figure appeared behind the netted safety door. Her face, wrinkled and fair, was framed by short, silver hair that seemed to shimmer in the light. Rashmi hesitated, suddenly unsure of how to broach the purpose of her visit. The face, hesitant at first, broke into a small, kind smile.

"Yes, my dear?" The voice that followed was delicate, tinged with an English accent.

Rashmi found herself fumbling for words. "Err ... I'm here for Ms Asha. I'm Rashmi Rao ... from India," she said, instinctively joining her hands in a namaste. "I'm a journalist with *The National Standard*," she continued, pulling her ID card from her bag. "Our office had reached out to you for an appointment, I believe," she added quickly, unsure if Asha would remember. "I should have called before."

Asha narrowed her eyes, considering the words before a gentle chuckle escaped her. "Oh, yes ..." she said, unlocking the safety door with a careful motion. "I had agreed to this day and time, Ms Rao, but old age doesn't let me remember things very well." A mischievous glint sparkled in her eyes. "I'm afraid my hands aren't ready for a handshake," she added, raising her right hand to show that it was covered in some sort of dough.

Rashmi smiled back, amused by the unexpected humour, as she was ushered inside. The kitchen was just a few paces away. Asha led her through a brightly lit foyer into the heart of her home.

"Today is the day I make cookies for the month, so we may have to talk while I work," she announced, her voice as warm as the kitchen around them. "But you're most welcome to eat as many you want," she added with a wink.

Rashmi acknowledged the offer with a smile and perched on a stool by the kitchen counter, while Asha bent to check the cookies in the oven. Despite appearing somewhat frail at first look, the woman moved with a grace that belied her years, each action deliberate and purposeful. The rimless glasses perched on her nose seemed to magnify the attentive gleam in her eyes as she checked the oven's temperature. Beneath her flowery apron, adorned with fluffy bows, Asha wore a black polka-dotted shirt and white trousers, an ensemble that hinted at a sprightly personality.

Rashmi's gaze drifted around the kitchen, drinking in and processing the details. This was no Indian home transplanted into England, she decided; it was distinctly English. The decor bore no trace of an Indian household. The walls were covered in pastel green and cream striped wallpaper, giving the space a calm, soothing quality. The air smelled of cinnamon, ginger, and butter—no hint of masala or incense here. No pictures of gods, no altar for prayers. It was a home woven entirely from the fabric of English life. Through the window, she could just make out the backyard garden beyond, a neat row of hyacinth bulbs just beginning to bloom in the soft sunlight.

Soon, Asha placed a plate of fresh cookies and a cup of warm milk on the counter and joined Rashmi at the table, settling into a chair with a contented sigh. Rashmi hesitated out of a habitual politeness before reaching for a cookie. She noticed Asha was watching her with keen eyes, taking in some details herself.

"You know, dear, I have had two or three interviews from our local newspapers after that award. I have to be honest, I did not like them much. I was going to decline this one too, but that bizarre man from your office simply would not leave me alone the past two days!"

Rashmi chuckled at the image of Bagchi hounding Asha grimly, following the heated interaction they had.

"I'm sorry," she said, her smile warm. "Journalists can be like that sometimes. But you won't find me annoying, I promise." She infused her voice with sincerity. "And congratulations on the award. I've only gathered a little about your work so far, but I'm eager to learn more from you. In fact, I've been looking forward to meeting you. I've never met anyone with such an adventurous history from the British era," she added, weaving in a touch of flattery.

Asha observed her for a moment, her eyes soft yet perceptive. She gave a small, unfathomable smile before replying, "Well, dear, I don't know what brought you all the way from India for this story. Our generation did have lives worth talking about, I suppose, but those were different times. Maybe you should talk to your grandparents more."

Rashmi raised an eyebrow, intrigued. "Well, mine didn't travel abroad in those times. I understand that our culture would have ostracised anyone who crossed the seven seas," she replied, the slight edge of challenge evident in her voice. "Was it the same for you?"

Asha chuckled lightly, taking another cookie. "Oh my! Has the interview already begun, dear?" She looked over at Rashmi with amusement.

"Not if you don't want it to," Rashmi replied, her tone easy but firm. She detected the undercurrent of resistance.

"Mine is a long story. I'm not sure your questions will do justice to it. This is what I told the others who came along. They still preferred to stick to their questions, so I answered only what they wanted to know, nothing more. I'll do the same with you—yes, it was taboo in our days to travel overseas and unheard of for a girl."

Rashmi took a moment to process this. It was clear she was dealing with someone who wouldn't be easily led or have terms dictated to her. Asha was someone who wouldn't appreciate her story being reduced to a series of questions. Rashmi decided to follow her instincts.

"Actually, Asha, you're right. There are specific things I want to know, but more than that, I want to hear your story as you lived it. So, let's do away with the questions."

Rashmi set aside her notes and pulled out a recorder, aware that her training would make it difficult to let go of the need to intervene or steer the conversation. But for once, she was determined to just listen.

Asha's smile widened, a gleam of approval in her eyes. "Aren't you brave?"

Grinning, Rashmi leaned back in her chair, her focus entirely on Asha.

In the background, the oven ticked softly as Asha began to unravel her story, letting the threads of time unwind before Rashmi's attentive gaze. And Rashmi let her recorder play its part.

1

I was born and raised in the hills of Pauri Garhwal. I don't remember my mother, but I was told she was a pious and kind lady. She sadly passed away during my birth. My father, however, was a constant presence, warm and doting, and I miss him even today. When I was five, he decided to move to Simla after securing a stable job at the post office. I grew up in a close-knit neighbourhood, surrounded by children—some of whom went to school, while others worked to help their families make ends meet. My father, despite the challenges, made sure I went to school, though it was a little later than most children of my age group. I remember feeling proud of him for this, as not many girls had that privilege at the time.

He cooked for me, did the dishes, and tucked me into bed each night, weaving stories of the Garhwali forests and the grand epics of the Pandavas from the Mahabharata. He spoke of the creation of the universe, of gods, and their manifestations. Everything had a story, he would say, be it the mountains that cradled us, the rivers that wound through the valleys, the squirrel that scurried up the deodar trees. My young mind, full of wonder, soaked it all in. Those stories have stayed with me, woven into the very fabric of my being, and even now, when I think of my father, I remember them—not just as tales but as a reflection of the love he gave me. Even today they remind me of what parental love felt like—a love that spoke in soft touches on the head, in the warmth of his chest as I nestled close, and in the soothing cadence of his voice that made me feel secure and safe.

I have come to realise that the most profound kind of love is the one that is given freely, simply because you exist. A parents' love asks for nothing in return, it has no reason. When you become a caregiver, you long for that kind of love again, but it's something you can never truly get back. It is the quiet ache of growing up.

My childhood, though simple, was filled with the warmth of such early memories, all of which I carried like a resilient candle in the storms that were to come. Simla, towards the end of the 1920s, was a town filled with Englishmen who, after collecting sufficient leaves and funds, would flee from the searing heat of the plains to spend the summer in the cool embrace of the mountains. Those who had no families, or whose families had been reduced to a memory from England, would travel to Mussoorie on sick leaves, and pass their days playing cards and smoking cigars at the Himalayan Club, recovering from whatever affliction the Indian heat had dealt them. But there was another group of English people who came to Simla each summer—the grass widows, a term I came to understand as I grew older. These were women whose husbands, stationed far away in the plains, could not join them, or could only do so once they were granted leave. These women, stranded in a foreign land, waited—some for their husbands, some in hope of respite for their children from the ravages of the Indian climate, but all for a life that had been put on hold.

They lived isolated lives, their world revolving around their homes, their servants, and the strange customs of this country they could never truly call their own. They became fixtures in the town, these Anglo-Indian women, and Simla catered to them. Shops stocked the things they needed—everything from bonnets to brandy, guns to tea. The local *durzee* reproduced the latest English fashion for them, and the town, in its own way, treated them with a mixture of deference and indulgence. They were a part of the landscape, and yet they were always set apart.

As a child, I had little to do with these women, but I was keenly aware of our differences. They seemed to live in another world—their food, their clothes, and their pale skin set them apart from us. I was fair-skinned as well, and my father dressed me well, so I remember moments when some of the British men and women would offer me sweets. But my friend Jitu, the boy who lived next door, was darker-skinned and often ignored or shooed away. As soon as they left, Jitu would throw me to the ground, snatch the treats from my hands, and devour them. He didn't even enjoy them, but he would eat them voraciously all the same.

As I grew older, that initial curiosity cooled into indifference. There were places in Simla where we were not allowed to go, and even the briefest of eye contact from the natives was avoided by the Anglos. Their carriages would clatter through the streets, and we, the locals, would quickly hop aside to make way. I came to understand that while some of them may have been kind, most regarded us with disdain or utter indifference even as they took our city as their home. Simla was theirs, and we were only supposed to exist at the edges of it.

Life began to shift irrevocably the day my beloved father fell ill. I was fourteen, still innocent in many ways, and understood little of the gravity of his sickness, except that the doctor in Ripon could not treat this deadly disease called tuberculosis. It was a cruel and unforgiving disease, they said. On the morning of 14 August 1928, it took father away from me. Before he passed away, my father arranged for Jitu's father to send telegrams to our relatives, entreating them to come and oversee his last rites.

No one came. I refused to undo my braid—the last one my father had tied for me. I wouldn't let them take him away. I wouldn't let anyone touch his charpoy, because that was where he had sat for the final time. I stared at his old chappals, their worn soles a faint echo of the rough brown feet that had once filled them. I wouldn't wash any clothes lest they lose his smell. His shawl, his hair oil, his rings—I clung to these things, desperate to hold on to him just a little longer.

Jitu's mother, with her loving but strict presence, guided me through those initial days of grief. She cared for me as a mother would, her sternness never overshadowing her kindness. Jitu's father took care of the final rites. If my father had harboured hopes that his missives would conjure a caregiver for me, I am glad he passed away still waiting. It was a hope that died with him. The unfamiliar distant relatives remained unfamiliar to me. I was left to Jitu's family, which consisted of his parents, two married sisters who lived in villages a few hours away, and dear Jitu, who wouldn't leave my side through all of this.

"Munni? Munni?"

I woke with a start. The darkness inside the hut clung to my senses, I was barely aware of where I was.

"Munni!"

It was Jitu's voice, insistent and urgent. I scrambled out of bed, fumbling in the dark for my chappals. Jitu would not stop knocking. I opened the door, still half-dazed.

There he was, leaning against the door frame, hiding something behind his back. His eyes sparkled with mischief as he tilted his head, a half-smile tugging at the corners of his mouth.

"Who sleeps at this hour, Munni?"

"Is it morning already?" I blinked at him, confused. "But I just had lunch..."

"You've been sleeping since lunch? It's dinner time. Amma's made Bichchhu Ghas."

He presented a plate of saag made from the nettle, wrapped in a thin cloth. I inhaled a whiff of mustard oil and garlic from the preparation. It conjured an image of Jitu's mother, or Amma as I had taken to calling her, working away in her kitchen, her face set in its usual stony expression. She spoke little but cared in her own way, perhaps moved by the loss of my mother when I was just an infant. Jitu had inherited her sharp features, but his dark skin came from his great-grandfather, marking him since his birth as an outsider in our little Pahadi neighbourhood. Jitu had learnt to live with it.

"I should really start doing something," I murmured, embarrassed. It had been over two weeks since my father died, and I had still not found the strength to do anything beyond exist.

"You should," Jitu replied, "but not because you can't accept our food. Amma says it's no trouble to cook for one more. You can join us for meals anytime. You barely eat anything these days."

His words were simple, but they carried with them a warmth that made my heart ache. I smiled weakly as tears welled up in my eyes.

"What would I do without you all?" I whispered, my voice trembling.

He wiped my tears away with the rough heel of his hand, his touch more comforting than I could ever explain. "Don't be stupid," he said softly. "Kaka would have done the same for us."

He pulled me unsurely into a half-embrace. I could feel his yearning to somehow comfort me, but I could barely breathe with the weight of my grief pressing down on me. We pulled away awkwardly, the silence between us heavy.

"Why don't you eat?" he asked. "I'll get my bedding from inside and keep you company for dinner."

"You don't have to do this, Jitu. It's a chilly night. You might catch a cold, and then I'll have to nurse you back to health."

"At least you'll have to move a limb, lazy girl," he teased, a grin spreading across his face as he turned and walked away.

From that day on, Jitu or his father slept outside my hut every night, keeping watch, making sure I felt safe. What more family could I ask for?

The first night, we shared dinner in the warmth of the small fire that flickered in the corner of my hut. Between bites of the leafy greens Amma had prepared, we talked—not of the sorrow that clung to every moment but of lighter things—of the time we'd sneaked into Thandi Sadak to buy Jitu's beedis when he could scrape together the money.

"But you never bought anything," he teased, laughing. "Are you going to take your pocket money to the grave?"

"I used to save up, so I could buy one of those precious stones from Mulberry's. But now ... I think I've grown out of that fascination."

"Rubbish! You couldn't have!" he shot back. "Chamoli mausi says that a woman can never have too much jewellery. But I should make it very clear to you that if you marry me, I'm not buying you any jewellery. You'll be the one to buy it for me!"

The sheer absurdity of it could not be denied a laugh. So I laughed. "Oh yes! I'm clearly the seth-ji here!"

We both chuckled, the sound ringing in the stillness of the night, the kind of laughter that feels like a balm on a raw wound.

Jitu lay down to gaze at the stars above us and sighed. "I always thought you were destined for something more, Munni."

"What more?" I asked, not stopping my meal.

He sat up, his eyes earnest. "There's something in you, unlike the rest of us. I guess Kaka raised you better than anyone else raised their child."

I scoffed and nudged him playfully. "Hey! I'm going to tell on you to Amma. Let's hear what she has to say to that!"

That night, after dinner, we were gently scolded and sent to bed by Jitu's father. Aside from the moments Jitu saved for me, those days were painful and paralysing. As the world continued its endless motion, I was still trapped in my grief, unable to see the path ahead. I used to go to bed thinking that I'd go to Thandi Sadak, which *they* called Mall Road, and get a job with a local shop. I figured I could easily get one, given my knowledge of calculations and elementary understanding of English. However, I slept every night holding myself tight, crying to sleep. Each morning I would wake up with a headache and the day would pass by leaving me panic-struck, unable to move or breathe as my heart tore itself with anxiety and panic. I would try to steal some sleep as a palliative, sealing myself to the noise of the village coming to life outside, all the while wishing for the pain to stop.

Day after day passed in a haze, leaving me without any clear vision of my future or the prospect of a job. The dinner-time conversations with Jitu were the only respite in my otherwise desolate existence. He would tell me everything—what happened in school, updates on the townsfolk, or anything to pull me away from the weight of my own life. Often, he urged me to return to school and take on a part-time job, suggesting it might help me rebuild my life. I passively entertained the idea, but doubt always followed close behind. How would things play out? Was I becoming dependent on Jitu's family? If so, it felt as though I needed to give something back—to contribute, not just receive. The growing awkwardness settled like a heavy cloud over me.

One evening, after our usual conversation, Jitu stood to leave.

"I've been asked to bring vegetables from Chamoli mausi's house," he said. "They've got too many, and Amma wants me to get them before they go to the neighbours. You go to bed, okay?" He squatted by the handpump while I finished washing my plate.

My head throbbed, the silence around us suddenly feeling too loud. I didn't know what to say.

"Munni, just run inside and grab my bedding," he continued, as he started jogging away. "Chamoli mausi's house is uphill, so it'll take me a while. Amma will want to lock the door. Just leave the bedding near your door when you get it."

I nodded absently, watching him disappear into the darkness of the gully. I made my bed and, feeling the weight of my own weariness, went through the back door of Jitu's house to avoid disturbing anyone. The night lanterns barely flickered, casting long shadows as I tiptoed outside. All of a sudden, I could hear raised voices of Jitu's parents.

There was a frustrated, cracking voice, wracked with pain and bitterness. "You think I don't sympathise with her? I've cooked and offered all I can, but for how long? I've been skipping a roti every night for Jitu for God knows how long. Now ... with all this, how are we to manage any more."

That was met by an angry, blustering reply. "Not now! Just ... not now."

The words sliced through the quiet of the night. I froze, my entire body rigid with fear, my heart pounding so loudly I feared they might hear it. I slipped out of their house, my breath shallow, and ran back to mine, the sound of my footsteps muffled against the earth.

Once I locked the door behind me, the floodgates opened, and I cried—harder than I had in the past days, harder than the misery of the past week had ever made me. I wept into my pillow, the raw grief of my situation overwhelming me. A thought crossed my mind: being an orphan meant living a life of humiliation and dependence, and this marked the beginning of that phase for me. My head ached as the tears flowed, and eventually, exhaustion overcame me. I fell asleep in the cold, the weight of my sadness pressing down on my chest.

But the next morning was different. I woke up early, before the sun had even begun to break the darkness. I sat in prayer, my heart heavy, summoning the courage and resilience to face whatever life had in store. For the first time in days, that first act of discipline gave me a fleeting sense of power.

I made certain decisions. I would no longer accept food from Jitu's house. I respected his mother deeply for all she had done, but last night had made me realise something: misfortune was not mine alone in this world, adults were susceptible to it too. The burden of hardship was not only on me. I could no longer impose on their generosity.

I also decided that I could not let another day pass without finding work.

With this new-found resolve, I dressed in my best clothes, forced a smile on to my face, and set out for Thandi Sadak. I moved from shop to shop, inquiring about job opportunities. Some of the shopkeepers were old acquaintances of my father's, which made the task feel doubly embarrassing. But I didn't let that stop me. By noon, my stomach began to growl with hunger. I went home for lunch, finding some buckwheat flour and sugar in the kitchen. I made rotis, sprinkling sugar over them. I set aside a few for dinner and set out again, more determined than I had felt in days.

The day wore on, and though the work was exhausting, I felt a strange sense of accomplishment. I had navigated the world on my own, at least for some part of the day. There was enough flour at home for a couple more days—but what would I do once the ration was exhausted? I didn't want to think about it. Not yet.

I remember how each step felt so heavy that day, the weight of my body and my thoughts dragging me down. The thirst that rose in my throat seemed endless, and yet, in the moments when the weight of my task felt too much, I'd stop and look out at the view. The valley stretched out before me, the snow-clad mountains glittering in the afternoon sun. It was the same view I had passed by every day on my way to school, but it felt different now. The view was the same, but I felt like a stranger.

Turning away, I sought comfort in the crowds that had begun to gather outside Christ Church. Gentlemen in starched shirts, ladies in their finest, children laughing in the warm sunlight. The scene was so familiar, and yet it felt foreign. Rickshaw pullers in their turbans and constables in their uniforms waited nearby in eager attendance.

My pitch shifted slightly with every shop I visited, but rejection came in every form. Restaurants had no need for an additional cleaner; women didn't wait tables back then. Bookshops, grocery stores, and cloth shops had no openings for assistants. The sting of rejection had become familiar by the evening. I thought then of Amanullah Khan, silver-bearded and portly, one of the most renowned and preferred durzees in Simla at the time. In my childhood, I was somewhat intimidated by his booming voice and bushy eyebrows and avoided his shop, though my father always had a salaam and a smile for him, especially when Khan's aged father had still been around, and used to perch outside his son's shop. Khan's father had been well known in the town, even before Amanullah rose to fame as a durzee. My father had told me of their history, of how Khan's father had once worked as a driver with the legendary Mail Tonga

Service—a fleet of two-wheeled carriages pulled by Kabuli ponies, delivering mail, parcels, and passengers through treacherous mountain weather. The service had ceased when the Kalka–Simla rail was inaugurated, and Khan's family had settled in Simla. Khan's father was welcomed in the community that respected his tireless service and legendary strength. Khan had made good of his father's social capital in his own career as a seamster, working tirelessly through his life. Now he had a team of seamsters and embroidery artists who exclusively served the memsahibs of Simla. Some spent hours in the verandahs of British officers' quarters, carefully stitching away on their Singer machines. Khan had built his reputation over decades, guarding it fiercely, hovering over his workers, swooping down on any mistake with wrath.

It was worth a try. I quickly prepared my pitch, hoping he might offer me something. I was skilled at hand embroidery, painting, and sewing. Though I didn't operate machines, I was a quick learner and fairly dexterous with my hands.

I found him seated inside his narrow shop, flanked by two rows of men working on machines. He looked oddly like a sultan holding durbar with his courtiers. Short and plump, Khan had a face that could shift from thunderous fury towards his workers to obsequious courtesy towards his memsahib clients in an instant. A sturdy turban encircled his head like a fortress, and his silver moustache and fluffy beard completed his commanding appearance. I walked in, tried to steady myself, and stood before him.

"Chacha … can you spare a minute or two for me?" I asked.

He looked up from his sewing machine, his thick eyebrows raised in inquiry. Noticing an unfamiliar face, his eyes softened and a curious "hmm" emanated from his beard.

"My name is Asha. I'm good at hand sewing and embroidery. I need a job. Do you have anything for me, chacha?"

He seemed bemused and stood up. "Aren't you Clerk Sahib's daughter, my dear?"

I nodded.

"Oh my ... sit down," he gestured kindly, and after a moment, he added, "Are you doing alright, beti?"

"I'm as fine as an orphaned girl can be, chacha. But I need a job."

"I understand that, beti. But have you thought this through? Is this the kind of job you want?"

"I don't have many choices," I said, eager to convince him. "I can do basic calculations and manage the shop if you ask me. I understand a little English, so I could accompany your men to the memsahibs. I can sew and embroider well, and I pick things up quickly. If you need me to operate a sewing machine, I'm willing to learn."

He raised an eyebrow and smiled. "My, my ... what a clever little girl!" He gestured at his workers, who looked up and smiled in return.

I maintained a straight face, responding seriously, "Please guide me."

His smile faded, and his expression grew thoughtful. "Beti, let me tell you my thoughts. This profession is dominated by Muslim men. I'm not sure it's ideal for a Hindu girl. You'll need to think about how your society will see you."

"Chacha, it wouldn't be ideal for any girl of any faith to die hungry or fall into theft or beggary, would it?" I held his gaze, trying to keep my desperation in check. "I need a job to avoid those fates. The flour at home won't last the whole week."

Amanullah Khan's eyebrows rose, but he tried to reason with me again. "I understand what you're saying, child. But since you've come to me for help, I'll offer what help I think is best for you. Working here might not do you any good, but I have another offer—one that will pay you better and take care of your meals," he said, with a twinkle in his eye.

"Anything will do, chacha, as long as it's honourable."

The machines in the shop fell silent as the workers listened intently. Khan lowered his voice, signalling for privacy.

"Beti, one of the memsahibs I work for needs an ayah for her little girls. Do you know what an ayah does?"

I had a vague idea but wanted to hear it from him, so I shook my head.

"Ayahs are round-the-clock caregivers. You tend to the child, feed them, play with them, attend to their every need day and night. It's more challenging than the work you could do here, but it pays better, and I don't see any social complications. I know the memsahib personally. She may be a little impatient, but she's fair. She'll teach you whatever you need to know. She needs help urgently, and she doesn't want an older woman. She wants a baby ayah. Like you."

He looked around at his workers, catalysing them back into action, before lowering his voice again.

"I'll tell you something more, beti. Her child was getting too attached to Naeem-bi, the previous ayah. These children spend more time with their ayahs than their mothers. Naeem-bi is an old widow with grown children, and she handled the child better than the memsahib herself. This might work out for you. You're young, and you'll be no competition to the memsahib," he said with a wave of his palms.

I hesitated, unsure of the offer. He observed my hesitance and added gently, "You can always say *khuda hafiz* to them if you don't like it. You'll just need to do your best and collect your pay every month."

"Is this right for me, chacha?" I asked, more to myself than to him. "I don't know how I would feel about working in someone's house ... It's different from working in a shop, isn't it? I've never been at anyone's beck and call."

He looked down, his face softening. "You've never been an orphan either, beti. You take what life gives you. If you have doubts, you can keep trying for something else and come back to me if you change your mind."

I paused, but only for a moment.

"How much is the pay, chacha?"

And so my unexpected fate found me. Just like that.

2

After leaving Khan's shop, I wandered down Thandi Sadak a while longer, still hoping to find jobs that would suit me better. I stopped at every shop and office that seemed even slightly promising, steeling myself for the inevitable questions: *What skills do you have? How long can you work?* Each failed attempt stung—either the pay was too meagre to survive on or nobody wanted a girl like me.

In our community, women ruled their households with quiet authority, yet they were deemed unfit for work outside. A woman seeking a job in the marketplace was an anomaly—a curiosity born of misfortune. And I was hardly anyone's first choice: *too young, too inexperienced, and too vulnerable to the whims of marriage*. The only women I saw working were the shopkeepers' relatives, who slipped behind the counters with a sense of belonging I couldn't claim.

That evening, I pondered over my options. The rapidly dwindling contents of the kitchen jars demanded a decision.

I sat on the *khatiya* outside my house, trying to let the cool air clear my mind. I had avoided Jitu's amma's gaze, mumbling an excuse about having already eaten. Jitu had been out playing until late and had just got back. Instead of going home, he saw me and hopped on to the khatiya with his customary easy familiarity.

"Someone looks like they had a good day," he said, grinning widely.

"Achchha?" I asked, raising an eyebrow. "And how can you tell?"

"Well, anyone can tell. Your hair is neat, you're wearing something nice, and your eyes … err …" he hesitated, and then finished awkwardly, "they don't look tired."

I smiled despite myself. "I did have a good day, in a way. I found a job, or at least a way out. I haven't decided yet, but I'm considering it seriously."

Jitu sat up straighter. "A job? So soon? That was quick, Munni! What's the work?"

"It's a little unusual," I said, measuring my words. "A memsahib needs an ayah for her daughters—round the clock."

"Day and night?" His brow furrowed. "That means staying there all the time. What about school? How will you come to school if you stay there with the memsahib all the time, Munni?"

I looked away, the question striking deeper than I'd expected. "I suppose I can't go to school if I take the job."

He fell silent, and the weight of his unspoken thoughts hung between us.

"I need to support myself, Jitu," I said softly. "If this job means giving up school, so be it. Most kids here don't finish school anyway. We were just … lucky for a while."

"But have you decided," he asked slowly, "that you won't come back to school?"

I looked away. The confusion in his voice unlocked a hurt in me that I didn't want to explore any further any sooner than I had to.

"It's not a decision. It's my reality. Grieving over what I can't have won't change anything."

Jitu shifted uncomfortably, his usual buoyancy replaced by an unfamiliar solemnity. "You don't have to leave school. We're here to help you."

I shook my head, trying to not tear up. "No, Jitu. I can't depend on anyone. Do you even know what the school fee is? And it's not just that. This is how things are now, Jitu. Fate doesn't ask for permission. I have to be at peace with it. You cannot think of both of us in the same way any more."

My heart sank at the look of his face. I knew he meant well. It was I who seemed to have grown up and become a stranger overnight. He stared at the fading embers of the fire nearby, the orange glow reflecting in his eyes.

"If you take the job, will you still visit me sometimes?"

I smiled, trying to lighten the mood. "You're the Betaal to my Vikram. Do you think I could stay away for long?"

His grin returned, fleeting but reassuring.

That night, as I lay in bed, memories of happier times came unbidden. I thought of the evenings my father and I spent at Jitu's house, the warmth of shared meals and laughter wrapping around us like a blanket. Jitu's mother would call me in advance to help cook, her voice tinged with affection. I'd make pooris or bhang chutney, while Jitu swept the floors under her watchful eye. At dinner, his father would tease me, saying all the ghee I was eating would make me rounder.

Afterwards, Jitu and I would sit outside, chewing sweet tamarind and talking until the stars blurred in the night sky.

Our fathers would smoke *chillam* by the dying fire, their voices low and steady as they discussed the village's troubles, never worrying about their growing children being so close.

There would never be such dinners again. Jitu and I were finally grown up and I had no father any more. I couldn't hope that my days would be routine or go by a plan, and I had nobody to make plans for me. I took a deep breath and deliberately smiled to keep my panicked tears away and breathed softly until I wasn't clutching the sides of my bed any more. These thoughts had to be pushed out. I began counting my breaths till I fell asleep.

The next morning, I rose before dawn, the quiet house stirring something resolute within me. I prayed longer than usual, asking God to guide me—or at least to give me strength. Then I set to work: sweeping the floor, dusting the khatiya, folding clothes, wiping the mirror until it shone. The house looked better, though I wasn't sure if I did.

I dressed in my best skirt, braiding my hair with care. A touch of kajal to my eyes made me look almost composed. But something was missing. Just then my gaze fell on the peacock-blue stole hanging by the door. My father's last gift to me, given on my birthday the year before. I wrapped it around my shoulders while thinking of him.

On my way to Thandi Sadak, I was a bundle of nerves imagining everyone's eyes following me. Were they staring at the blue stole draped over my shoulders? Did they think it inappropriate for me to wear something so striking just days after my father's passing? I wasn't sure if I was even allowed to smile yet, let alone look presentable.

I diverted my attention to some shops. Morning rituals were a comforting constant across all kinds of shops: brooms sweeping away the remnants of yesterday, soft chimes of bells accompanying brief prayers, the fragrant waft of incense mingling with the earthy scent of *guggal*. Shopkeepers tucked away bites of breakfast behind their counters, readying themselves for the day ahead.

The Himalayan sun cast a gentle light over the valley, setting the vegetation aglow in a way that made my eyes sting, perhaps from more than just the brightness. I allowed myself to stand still for a moment and took a deep breath. *Things are changing*, I thought. A tingling sensation spread through my palms, the kind that comes when something dear is slipping away. Brushing the thought aside, I pressed on.

When I reached Amanullah Khan's shop, I found him perched on the edge of a charpoy outside, directing an assistant who was folding clothes with careful precision. His sharp eyes noticed me at once, and he welcomed me with a smile and a salaam, both of which I reciprocated.

"That colour suits you," he said, gesturing at the stole.

"Thank you, chacha," I replied, gathering my courage. "I've come about the ayah job. Is it still available?"

"Ah, good." He nodded approvingly. "I'm on my way to the memsahib's house now, beti. You can meet her and decide for yourself."

I sat on the shop steps while the old master tailor finished issuing his batch of instructions and deftly organising his bundles for the day. He handed me a paper cone filled with roasted peanuts as we waited, and I nibbled on them quietly, trying to settle the flurry of thoughts in my mind.

When he was ready, we set off, each carrying one of his large bags at my insistence. Despite his age, Khan moved briskly, stopping only to jot down an order at a garment shop and to purchase *choona* for his betel leaves.

The walk took us to a cluster of bungalows near the United Services Club. These grand houses, with their austere facades, held an air of mystery for us locals. They were inhabited by officers whose lives seemed worlds apart from ours, with men who smoked cigars and drank expensive liquor, women who danced in glittering gowns at late-night balls, and families that required constant care for their fragile health. I shuddered with sudden apprehension—I was entering a very different world, one that had hitherto been so inscrutable and aloof.

From the gate, the bungalow looked as immaculate as it was intimidating. The bars of the white gate gleamed. I pushed it open cautiously, following Khan up a ramp that curved gently to the freshly whitewashed house. Wild growths of moss, which once softened the stark walls, had been scrubbed away by an eager painter's brush.

I followed Khan meekly, trying to drive out my fear of entering this alien world. I caught up with him and matched his confident pace. He smiled paternally and said, "Beti, you don't need to take this job if you don't like it. But keep an open mind and try to like these people. If you can't like them, you won't be able to serve them. You do understand?"

He patted my shoulder as we approached the large wooden door at the entrance. He knocked on a side window, and a woman appeared, adjusting her dupatta before gesturing for us to circle to the back.

"We durzees usually work on the verandah," Khan explained as we made our way around the house, his tone now more business-like. "The memsahibs brief us about their preferences, and the job is done then and there. Of course, I always send my *chela*s but this memsahib specifically asks for me. Her name is Mrs Stager. She has two daughters who are four and six years old and a baby boy who's only a few months old. She needs you only for the girls, okay? She has a ... wet nurse hired for the baby. I believe that's what they call them."

I nodded and surveyed the verandah. It was spacious and shaded by a corrugated roof. I set down the bag beside Khan's and accepted a glass of water from the maid, gulping it down gratefully. She took the bags and disappeared. While we waited, Khan regaled me with stories about the trade of a durzee and their unique importance in meeting the whims of the memsahibs, who would loathe to repeat outfits at their frequent gatherings and demanded the latest modes and fashions before they became common.

I gazed at her, trying to study her demeanour and attire. She moved gracefully, neutrally acknowledging the deep bow and warm smiles Khan extended towards her. Her beige gown and tightly coiled bun lent her an air of quiet authority. Her pale complexion, accentuated by a touch of make-up, made her seem almost other-worldly. I realised I hadn't bowed, but by then she had sat down gracefully on a wrought-iron chair and gestured for us to take our seats. Her thin lips, pursed in a firm line, yielded no smile. I instinctively began to lower myself into a seat but halted midway, noticing that Khan remained standing.

The maid stepped forward, presenting a few of the memsahib's gowns, pointing out minor fitting issues. Khan listened intently, nodding and grunting his acknowledgement while mentally cataloguing each alteration. My gaze flitted between the two as they conversed in Hindustani. The few glances I stole carefully at the lady indicated that she understood much of what was being said despite not joining the conversation. The discussion ended with the maid handing over payment for the gowns, a meticulous transaction that felt like a ceremony of its own. Khan accepted the money with a slight bow, and then he turned to the memsahib and addressed her directly in English.

"Memsahib, this is Asha," he said, enunciating each word slowly. "She's in need of a job as an ayah. I'll be honest, she has not worked anywhere before, but she has a good heart. She is hard-working and will learn everything very quickly. Her only demand is a decent pay as she's in need of money and food thrice a day. If memsahib is kind enough, then half a day's holiday once a week would help her manage her own domestic affairs and enable her discharge her duties better. She'll be grateful, memsahib."

Mrs Stager looked amused. To be honest, I too was amused. I hadn't even thought of what to ask for, and Khan's seasoned petitioning on my behalf sounded too good to be true.

The memsahib raised her eyebrows and replied cuttingly, "She's never worked, so she doesn't know anything about the job. I'll have to teach her everything, which could very well be a waste of my time if she turns out to be lazy. And now, to top off the misery, she wants a holiday? Khan, this sounds like a rather strange proposition to me."

I caught most of her words except the word 'misery', even without Khan's translations. Before Khan could tug my stole in caution, I took a step forward and addressed Mrs Stager directly, my voice steady despite my racing heart.

"Not having prior work experience leaves me most mouldable, memsahib, perfectly suited to adapt to memsahib's preferences. I am an orphan in desperate need of a job, so I cannot afford to be lazy. Caring for little children is no easy task, and time off would allow me to maintain my health and serve your household better in the long run."

My words were confidently spoken and I watched the memsahib carefully as Khan translated, trying to sound apologetic for my forwardness. Mrs Stager's sharp expression softened slightly as her lips curved into a faint, almost grudging smile. She considered me for a moment before responding, "I'll give you the food and the holiday, but I'll pay you less than Naeem-bi for now. If I find your work satisfactory after a month, I'll raise your wages to match hers. I think that's fair."

My heart leapt with unexpected joy. It was happening! *Meals meant survival, and any earnings beyond that was a saving*, I thought to myself joyously. I could hear the triumph in Amanullah Khan's voice: "That sounds fair, memsahib!"

We stepped out of the bungalow, and the cool air hit my face as if urging me to wake from a dream. My mind was in a daze. Khan walked beside me, his cheerful voice booming out enthusiastic congratulations, punctuated with advice: how to carry myself, how to deal with the children, and how to navigate the unpredictable moods of the memsahib. I nodded occasionally, half-listening, as I tried to process everything that he had just secured for me.

I had become a servant, some would say. Yet for the first time in days, I felt unburdened of the suffocating dread that had gripped me. A cautious lightness began to seep into my heart, and I smiled back at Khan.

So began my journey as an ayah.

3

The next morning, I reported to work wearing my cleanest set of clothes and a look of determination that I hoped masked my nervousness. As I approached the house, I took in its details with fresh eyes. The lock on the heavy gate was rusted and creaked noisily as I strained to swing the gate open. The little garden beyond was alive with the dew-dappled freshness of a cold Himalayan morning. The myriad flowerpots glistened, frost-kissed. My spirits lifted momentarily at the familiar trilling of birds I had known since childhood.

I paused briefly at the curving stone path, taking a deep breath and offering a quick prayer before cautiously making my way to the back verandah. There, seated on a patio chair, was Mrs Stager, her pale hands deftly sewing initials on to a fine handkerchief. She put down her work abruptly as she heard my footsteps, rising to her feet with a glare that made my heart sink.

"You're terribly late!" she snapped. "I expected you at seven. It's eight now! Is this how you'll work?"

I reeled at her reprimand, embarrassment flushing my face as I understood her tone before my mind processed the English. I hadn't been given a specific time and had assumed that 8 a.m. would suffice, the same hour my father used to leave for work. But it seemed painfully obvious then that a household like this stirred far earlier. Struggling to summon my best English, I stammered out an apology and promised to arrive earlier the next day.

Mrs Stager seemed unimpressed but didn't linger on the matter. Instead, she briskly listed my duties. I was to feed the two girls, bathe them, dress them, and ensure they were ready for their home-school sessions each day. Beyond that, I was to keep them entertained during their free hours so they wouldn't disturb their mother and ensure they stayed within the bounds of the house and garden. Additionally, I was to assist the maid, Hameera, with odd jobs as per need.

As she rattled off the instructions, I tried to memorise them, each task adding to the weight of my responsibility. Still stinging from the embarrassment of my misstep, I resolved silently to prove myself capable. This was my chance, and I could not afford to fail.

I was curious about the girls, who were occupied in their home-school session until lunch. Mrs Stager informed me I was too late to meaningfully engage in their routine today. Instead, she instructed me to spend the remainder of the day observing the household's ways and begin my duties in earnest the following morning. She placed me in the kitchen under the supervision of Hameera, a gawky, dark-skinned Mohammedan woman of around forty, who was immersed in her cooking but nevertheless had a surprising amount of time to tutor me in household gossip and drink in my reactions with a sly, glittering eye.

Hameera carried herself with a curious mixture of deference and cunning. She obeyed Mrs Stager's instructions without meeting her eyes or offering a comment and allocated me a spot in the kitchen, far from the cooking area. My task was simple: stitching a running seam on a cotton quilt meant to replicate an embroidery style that Mrs Stager had picked up during the colonel's posting in Barrackpore, West Bengal. I vaguely remembered West Bengal from school and nodded.

Once Mrs Stager left, the quiet tension in the kitchen dissolved. Hameera broke her silence, leaning into a stream of small talk that seemed as natural to her as breathing. Squatting on the floor to marinate a whole chicken, she gave me a lingering, appraising look.

"Do you eat meat?" she queried, rubbing her pointed nose with her wrist.

I shook my head.

"Poor child! It's the best thing you'll ever eat," she declared with a dramatic shake of her head. "When they're done, we can have the rest,"

Her words landed awkwardly. I didn't like the thought of eating leftovers. A surge of dismay rose in me, and I was tempted to tell her I was different, that I wasn't a servant, just a victim of circumstance. But even as the thought crossed my mind, it left a bitter aftertaste. I felt ashamed of myself. Who was I to look down on her? Was my sense of distinction anything more than a stubborn refusal to confront my new reality?

Even so, I resolved to find a way to keep this line, however fragile, intact. I could choose not to eat leftovers from someone else's table. If needed, I resolved to bring my own lunch from home. True, there wasn't much left in the pantry, but even the spinach growing in our backyard would have sufficed for a week until my first wage arrived.

Hameera's untidily done kohl eyes rested on me again, her expression again at once detached and probing.

"They don't eat a lot of vegetables. I make myself some chapati every day. Shall I make some for you too? Now that there are two of us, you can take care of the *tarkari*."

"Oh? Do we get to cook our own meals?" I sighed in relief.

"Of course! There are Indian rations set aside for the servants. Memsahib wouldn't want to waste the meat she cooks with her expensive ingredients—unless, of course, there's too little left for another serving."

The hierarchy—so casually expressed—struck me. I nodded and managed a faint smile. "Chapati sounds good. I'll make the tarkari."

Hameera's face softened, her slyness fading for a moment as she busied herself with the chicken again. "Good girl," she said absently with a half-smile. "We have to look out for each other."

In a single instructive hour with Hameera, I absorbed more about the household than I might have gleaned in weeks on my own. Mr Stager's complete name was Colonel Edward William Stager. He was currently stationed in Secunderabad, a place I learned from the maid was blazing hot this time of year. Mrs Stager always preferred moving with her husband, but the heat of the plains had taken a toll on her health during her third pregnancy, prompting the colonel to move her to the hills to have baby Louis following the doctor's advice.

"Memsahib doesn't like being away from her husband," said Hameera knowingly as she went about chopping vegetables. "But what could she do? The colonel wasn't about to risk her health or the boy's. A son after two daughters is precious, you know."

I pondered that. So memsahibs too did as they were told?

"Memsahib has hired Bilkis as a wet nurse for the baby," Hameera said with theatrical shake of her head, her voice heavy with disapproval. "Bilkis isn't good pedigree, you know, but when it comes to their needs, the goras don't care about all this."

"What's a wet nurse?"

Hameera looked at me with surprise. "A wet nurse, like the memsahib has, are women employed to nurse the baby."

I was shocked at this unimagined mode of service. Could mother's milk too be a form of employment, a paid vocation? The thought unsettled me.

Catching the bewilderment on my face, Hameera leaned in closer, her voice dropping conspiratorially. "If they could, they wouldn't even raise their children, you know? They still don't, if you ask me. It's just the fear of losing their *angreziyat* that makes them keep their children close. They're not like us."

I mulled over her words, weighing them. Could it really be true? It was tempting to fall in with the intriguing notion that these people, so other-worldly and far removed from us, had turned even motherhood into a transaction. But some part of me baulked at the idea of accepting such an extreme assessment without the evidence of my own experience. Perhaps it was naive, but I wanted to understand these people for myself. I secretly resolved to make up my own mind in due course.

I picked up and catalogued details about the Stager children. The Stager girls were six-year-old Lily and four-year-old Poppy. Baby Louis, Mrs Stager's youngest, was about four months old. Poppy was supposedly a sweet child, as most toddlers that age are. Lily, however, had a reputation that seemed less endearing. According to Hameera, she was already "frosty like her mother" and "already on her way to becoming a *pura gora*."

They were home-schooled by Charlotte, the wife of a junior soldier currently stationed at Almora. It was common knowledge that Charlotte did not intend to live any longer with her husband, having discovered his infidelity, and had elected to live in dignified employment in India rather than go back to her relatives in England. She had been trained as a teacher, so she was highly sought after by British families marooned in India and desperate to provide their children with a semblance of an English education. There was something about Charlotte's story that lingered with me. What must it have been like, to decide to leave behind 'home' and forge a life for herself on her own terms, however difficult or unconventional, in a foreign land? I could sense that despite her grumbling, Hameera had a keen understanding of hierarchies and a firm belief in preserving them. In particular, she held her own views on the proper equations between Charlotte and Mrs Stager.

"I know that she is a teacher to the children, but she's also a woman without a husband, and ultimately a servant," she whispered with a quick glance towards the door. Her bulging eyes, set in her thin, dark face, seemed to burn with indignation. "Just because she's a gora, she shouldn't be sitting with the memsahib ordering me for tea, right?"

I felt awkwardly stuck between her indignation and expectation of kinship from me, and my own novice position in the household. Politely, I nodded and murmured words of agreement as I focused on my embroidery, hoping the topic would shift. The girls were released from their home-schooling session just before lunch. Hameera informed me that they were being escorted by Charlotte to a play date with other children.

"Gora kids don't play with all children. They have sharp divides even among themselves. Colonel saab's kids will only play with other colonel saabs' kids. Soldier kids? They stick to soldier kids," she explained with a certain relish.

I gathered that even a memsahib could not socialise with all memsahibs. From Hameera's stints at various English households, it seemed that wives of senior officers interacted only with their equals, unless exceptions were made for unique situations, like Charlotte's. This was news to me. It must be difficult for Mrs Stager and her children to find fulfilling companionship in a foreign land, mired in so many restrictions. According to Hameera, the girls would follow the fate of most English children born in India and soon be sent away to England to their grandparents for an English upbringing, unless colonel saab himself got transferred back home. The thought struck me as terribly sad. For all their privileges, these children were no freer than I was in charting the course of their lives.

I learned that Hameera, a widow with three children in their late teens, was remarkably industrious and had carved out a niche for herself in this unusual industry. Having grown up working for the British, she was adept at their ways, from managing the cleaning and upkeep of their households to mastering nearly all domestic chores. These skills, she confided with a smug smile, were significant assets in securing employment in English homes.

She had already married off her two daughters and was now saving for her future. "I don't want to depend on my son when he's married and has his own family to look after," she declared firmly. In addition to managing the household, she also served as an informal translator for Mrs Stager despite her rudimentary grasp of spoken English. "It's no good being dependent, bachche. Eat less, but eat off your own earnings. The world has no use for someone who can't fend for themselves. See what a place I've made for myself?"

By evening, I had completed my chores and prepared tea for everyone as per the memsahib's precise instructions. Tea was served in the garden, and to my surprise, Mrs Stager preferred for us to have it together. I sat by the stairs in the back verandah, nibbling a biscuit with my tea, while Mrs Stager enjoyed a slice of pie, and Hameera watered the garden after having her milk tea. The evening was serene, and it felt nice to share silence in that little private garden.

"Asha, would you mind being addressed as Ashley?" Mrs Stager asked suddenly, breaking the silence.

Startled, I looked up. Hameera's dupatta-clad head tilted towards me instantly.

"Is my name hard to pronounce, memsahib?" I ventured cautiously in broken English, trying to rely as little on Hindustani as possible.

Mrs Stager gestured to Hameera, who translated.

"Of course it isn't," she replied briskly. "But I'll be frank. One of the reasons I dismissed the ayah before you was her usage of Hindustani. I do not wish for the girls to pick up the local language. I don't want them addressing you with a Hindustani name.

"I expect you to join the home-schooling sessions with Charlotte to improve your English, and I want you to speak exclusively in English with the children. Charlotte told me the girls wanted to make 'rotis' during their play date a few days ago. This is unacceptable to me. They are to be raised like children of England, not like Hindoo children.

"You must be proper in your conversation with them, and refrain from sharing Hindoo religious stories, your opinions about us, or your views on anything Indian. Keep things clear and simple for them. Do you understand?"

I nodded quietly, drinking in the words and the meaning behind them. I wasn't Ashley, but clearly I would have to be.

Soon after, Charlotte and the girls appeared, walking up the pathway. I bowed deferentially to Charlotte, though she barely acknowledged it, and stole a curious glance at the children. The girls pecked their mother's cheeks before darting off to a corner of the garden where they had assembled a makeshift tent.

Charlotte seated herself beside Mrs Stager and said, "I'll ready them for dinner. Louis must be fast asleep by now, so you can rest a while longer."

"You're a saviour, Charlotte. I've spoken with the new ayah," Mrs Stager said, gesturing towards me.

"That's a smart move," Charlotte replied, settling into the garden chair and waving imperiously at Hameera for tea.

Hameera left for the kitchen, but not before shooting a sharp, resentful glance at the plants she had been watering moments earlier.

Fascinatedly, I watched the little girls play with their dolls in front of the little tent. They were dressed impeccably: knee-length blue frocks, socks running up to their shins, polished shoes and hair done neatly in braids and tied with ribbons. Lily, the older of the two, had recently lost a tooth. She smiled little and kept bossing her sister around. The younger one, Poppy, was very cheerful and didn't seem to mind her sister's bossiness. The older girl dictated the choice of games and dolls, while the younger one played along with joyful abandon.

I wasn't sure how to deal with the girls—whether I wanted to be their friend or their caretaker. One thing was certain, I wasn't to be their servant.

That night, I saw the light of a lantern from Jitu's house, but I couldn't make myself go and speak to him. I blotted out all thoughts and went to bed, determined to do my best the next day and change the lacklustre first impression I had given.

I reported to Mrs Stager's much earlier the next morning. Mrs Stager offered no remark and instructed Hameera to introduce me to the girls.

The nursery was located on the upper floor, a spacious attic-like room with a sloping ceiling. While slightly unkempt, it had a certain charm to it. A large window on the far wall let in soft, dappled light, filtering through the branches of a chinar tree just outside. Beneath the window frame sat a crowded, disorganised toy shelf. The room held two beds on either end, both with a messy heap of quilts and pillows.

The adjacent home-schooling room felt smaller and more practical. It was fitted with a tall cupboard stuffed with books, a blackboard, and a couple of tables and chairs arranged for lessons.

The girls had just woken up. Lily wore a grumpy expression that suggested she wasn't a morning person, while Poppy rubbed her eyes and smiled affably, her hair sticking up in tufts.

Hameera started to introduce 'Ashley' to the girls. She had just started with, "She's your ayah…" when I stepped in, determined to make my own introduction.

"We'll have plenty of time for chatting later," I said confidently, making an effort to keep my English clear and mixing as little Hindi as possible. "For now, let's get ready for school. Who wants to take a bath first?"

I clapped my hands together and smiled warmly, hoping to mask the nervousness. I waited anxiously—would they understand? Would they obey?

For a moment, the girls stared at me with curiosity, as if deciding what to make of this new presence in their lives. Then, to my relief, they hopped off their beds and stood waiting.

Both girls were truly poles apart in temperament. Poppy was shy in an endearing way, and not yet old enough to completely mask her curiosity. She didn't speak much at first but observed me with wide eyes as I buttoned her frock, her gaze quickly darting out of the window towards the chinar tree when I looked her way. When our eyes met again, I offered her a smile, and to my delight, it coaxed a giggle from her. Thus began a friendship.

Lily insisted on bathing herself, and I stood outside the bathroom, towel in hand, knocking periodically to keep her on schedule. She emerged with a sullen expression, clearly irritated by my attempts to hurry her along as I helped her dress. I quickly realised this approach wasn't going to win her over. I'd have to wake her earlier tomorrow to give her more time. When I tried to engage her by asking what she liked to eat for breakfast, she stayed silent, her demeanour unyielding.

In the first few days, it felt surreal to be so close and in physical contact with these little girls who looked so stunningly different from me—the pale skin, the freckles, the golden hair were all alien to me. But as the days passed, these differences melted away. They became, quite simply, two young girls in need of care and companionship. The nature of my position still weighed on me. What was I to them: an authority figure, belonging to a race ruled by theirs? Did they already understand the societal gulf between us? Would they look down on me, or did they not yet comprehend such distinctions? These questions were tangled in my mind, difficult and uncomfortable.

My relationship with Mrs Stager, however, was more straightforward. I couldn't make things work if I acted like Hameera, who avoided eye contact and carried an air of subservience around her. I decided I would maintain respect but not servility. To me she was the head of the household, someone whose instructions I would follow, provided she treated me fairly. So far, she had been distant but not unkind, and I could work with that.

She was unlike the Englishwomen Amanullah Khan had described to me. She didn't seem to care much for dancing, social gatherings or card games we associated with the British elite. The fancy clothes she commissioned from Khan were mostly sent away to relatives in England rather than worn at parties. She seemed to have no friends here, and letters from England were her only solace. I often saw her rereading those letters during siesta time, after she'd carefully pull them out from a recipe book in her wardrobe. The sight of her sitting quietly with those letters spoke of a profound loneliness, one I couldn't help but feel sorry for.

As days turned into weeks, I began to unravel the unspoken rules that governed the Stager household. Chief among them was the deliberate absence of any mention of Colonel Stager. His presence was a ghostly undercurrent in the house, acknowledged only in the way Mrs Stager would look away while reading his letters. If I happened upon her at such a moment, I instinctively knew to withdraw and pretend it never happened. She was fiercely protective of the image she had constructed: her children were to be impeccably behaved and unmistakably English, her embroidery flawless, her meals refined, her staff efficient, and her house pristine. Any disruption to this delicate balance frayed her composure.

In the early weeks, she watched me with an almost hawk-like vigilance. She scrutinised my every interaction with the girls, ensuring our conversations were purposeful and in English. She often appeared unannounced in the schoolroom, checking if I was attentive and making an effort to learn their language. When I faltered in grammar, she corrected me, but only in private, never in front of the children. She would silently observe as I embroidered her pillowcases, occasionally leaning over my shoulder to direct a minor adjustment. For all her reserve, I began to interpret these small interventions as her way of expressing approval, however indirectly.

My time at the Stagers' taught me several skills. I absorbed the rhythms of their daily life and the skills it required. I learned the intricacies of their preferred cuisine, from simple scones to more elaborate French dishes that seemed to hold a particular allure for Mrs Stager. She reserved the preparation of these meals, accented with white wine, a touch of her own sophistication, for herself. I would watch her intently as she narrated the recipes from her carefully maintained journal, committing each step to memory.

In the months that followed, my relationship with the girls progressed. Poppy looked for opportunities to rope me into her play. All she wanted was company. She'd invent elaborate tea parties, asking me to fetch her snacks, only to share them with her dolls before ceremoniously offering me an imaginary cup of tea. Sometimes it was still surreal to comb her curly golden hair—but then there would be an innocent smile as she turned her head and I'd be reminded that she was just a little girl, as I used to be. My heart would fill with tenderness and love. She would ask me my favourite colours and foods and made sure to incorporate these details into her games and when she 'cooked' for me.

She pined for Lily's attention, though Lily, reserved and independent, often preferred her own company. More often Poppy would have to be content with her dolls, most of whom were counting their last days despite being fairly new. When the two did play together, I noticed Lily's occasional protectiveness over her younger sister, especially when others were involved. I could tell that Lily wasn't comfortable when Poppy played with me. Sometimes when Poppy demanded a tea party to be set up, Lily would get involved and ask me to leave, which I did not mind as I had plenty of chores. While I detected insecurity, there was no contempt. I deemed it healthy for the girls' bonding.

Having grown up in isolation, Lily had much to learn about sharing, sportsmanship and manners. The sisters' games together were inevitably on Lily's terms. She would claim the best dolls and dictate the rules of play. Poppy seemed to have ever been the obedient sidekick, but had now began noticing the imbalance. She would complain sometimes about the unfairness, and even assert herself on occasions.

Their disagreements were usually settled by their mother, and I preferred not to intervene. Partly, I was unsure of how to handle such situations, and partly, I hesitated because I feared Lily might challenge my authority. What would happen if she refused to listen? What would my role in the household become if I was undermined?

Meanwhile, my role in the household continued to expand. Mrs Stager began entrusting me with responsibilities beyond the nursery. I escorted the girls to their play dates, ensuring my appearance was tidy and professional, not to impress Mrs Stager but to infuse a sense of pride and satisfaction in my own work. I sensed, however, that my efforts pleased her desire to always present an image of perfection in everything and everyone around her.

We'd go hiking on days the memsahib deemed the weather to be perfect. While the girls delighted in skipping through the hills and I enjoyed teaching them to identify flowers and trees I'd known since childhood, Hameera lamented her aching joints and the indignity of hauling picnic baskets up steep paths because the memsahib wanted so. Sometimes we'd go on small trips to the town where Mrs Stager would meet friends visiting from different cantonments.

On one such evening, Mrs Stager decided that Hameera and I would accompany the girls on a small picnic hike while she had tea with a friend. The late afternoon sun bathed the hillside in golden light as we began our descent. I took the lead, carefully scanning for snakes and insects, while Poppy and Lily followed close behind. A grumbling Hameera trailed us, stopping every so often to catch her breath and mutter about her aching legs.

During one of those breaks, Lily, full of energy and mischief, outstretched her arms and began darting through the flower bushes like a bird in flight. The terrain was safe, and her joy was infectious, so I saw no need to reign her in. But just moments later, a cry of panic shattered the tranquillity.

I rushed to her side, calling out to Hameera, who was seated on a rock a short distance away. Sobbing, Lily held out her palms, now red and swollen. I didn't need to look far to identify the culprit. Lily had flown straight into a patch of Bichchhu Ghas, a nettle native to these hills, the sting of which could cause sharp pain and numbness for hours.

Poppy stood frozen, frightened by her sister's distress, while Hameera, equally alarmed, seemed more worried about what Mrs Stager's reaction might be than the immediate problem at hand.

I hugged the child and spoke softly to reassure her as I scanned the surrounding bushes. I was familiar with this nettle, which we hill folk boiled and had as a *saag*. Wherever it grew, its antidote was sure to grow nearby. Sure enough, I spotted a cluster of the soothing plant just a few steps away. I quickly crushed a few healthy leaves into a paste in my fist and gently applied it to Lily's stung palms.

"It's alright," I said, cradling her hands in mine. "This plant takes the sting away. You'll feel better soon." Though her sobs persisted for a while, I explained what had happened, describing the nettle and its antidote in a way I hoped might ease her mind. Gradually, her tears subsided, and after a short break, we resumed our walk back uphill. Poppy skipped ahead, holding Hameera's hand, her earlier fright forgotten. As Lily and I trudged along in the rear, I felt a small, tentative hand slip into mine for the first time.

Charlotte too slowly became invested in my learning, though she seldom showed it openly. I began to notice her subtle pleasure when she saw me grasping the language quickly, a hint of pride disguised under casual indifference. She started including me in the lessons she designed for the girls, often encouraging me to participate. First, she handed me Poppy's books, and as my confidence grew, Lily's more advanced ones followed.

Through these lessons, Charlotte uncovered my knack for arithmetic, a discovery that surprised me and impressed her. She began tasking me to double-check the calculations for her household expenses and savings each month. This small yet significant gesture felt like a quiet acknowledgement of my abilities, and I treasured it deeply. It wasn't just a task—it was a validation, a sign that she saw me as more than just an ayah.

I often watched Charlotte as she worked on her small paintings in the schoolroom, her delicate brushstrokes bringing to life landscapes, portraits, flowers, insects. We would talk about the subjects of her art, and she would share the kind of trivial details, all of which seemed endless to me.

I can't recall the exact moment when my spoken English began to match that of the Britons, but thanks to my time spent in the schoolroom, my command of the language grew.

Whenever we had an occasional visitor at Mrs Stager's, they'd inevitably appreciate how 'perfect' I was, how lucky Mrs Stager was to get an English-speaking ayah with British etiquettes. Their praise never failed to unsettle me. Mrs

Stager, always perceptive of my discomfort, would shift the conversation. When I heard these guests talk about England, I would try piece together snippets from their conversations and build an image of their homeland in my head. It sounded like a beautiful but cold place. They rarely spoke of the mundane, such as shops, streets, parks, so I filled in the gaps with what I imagined: grey skies, cobbled streets, and buildings stretching endlessly towards the horizon. Occasionally, they would mention war and the political unrest within the Empire. But these were just words to me with little meaning.

Despite the formal nature of our relationship, a quiet warmth began to grow between Mrs Stager and me, fuelled in part by my growing devotion to embroidery. Mrs Stager herself would spend hours immersed in her sewing, her hands moving with precision, as though the fabric were an extension of her very being. She was a woman driven by a relentless pursuit of perfection, and in this art, as in few other things, she found it within her grasp.

Every evening when the girls would play with Charlotte, I would sit by the steps and complete my embroidery assignments, with Mrs Stager looking in between her own knitting or sips of tea. As I got better, she stopped checking my work and would instead give me a nod. She taught me crewel and needlepoint embroideries, and many others. She was also passionate about crochet, a skill I was very happy to learn. I thought I was entering a high point on my work front. My employer was happy, and so was I.

Despite all this progress, some nights I would sit outside my house and gaze at the starry sky, and a quiet ache would creep over me. I missed Jitu. Something unspoken had settled between us, a thieving silence that gradually wore away the ease of our once effortless companionship. We saw each other infrequently now; our lives had grown increasingly divergent, our routines and timings no longer aligning. As the Stager household began to demand more of me, Jitu too had begun to recede into the background, as though the space he once occupied in my life was being slowly, imperceptibly filled by others.

I had encountered him a few times on my way back from work, but those fleeting moments were marked by a subtle, yet unmistakable unease. There was something that lingered behind our smiles; a distance had grown that neither of us knew how to bridge. I remember the first time I really felt it. It had been one of those rare days when everything seemed to fall into place. Charlotte had praised me for my improvement in spoken English and Mrs Stager had confirmed that she would be willing to pay me on par with Naeem-bi, my predecessor. I felt as though the world had opened up to me in a way I had never expected. In that moment of triumph, I wanted to share my exuberance with Jitu. But when I saw him, something about the encounter felt heartbreakingly alien. He congratulated me, but his eyes were distant. He soon fumbled an awkward excuse about chores waiting for him and walked away. His smile, though it lingered on his lips, never quite reached his eyes.

A few days later, I tried again. We both happened to step out of our houses early one morning, and I called out to him, hoping for a chance to speak before he left for school.

"Jitu, how have you been?" I asked eagerly.

"I'm doing alright," he replied, offering a smile that seemed more like an obligation than a genuine expression of warmth.

"Is everything alright between us?"

I saw something in his eyes, but it left as soon as it came. "Why won't it be?" he shrugged.

"You tell me. What is it that's gone wrong?" I pressed, my words coming faster now, a mixture of confusion and hope driving them.

"Well, you're busy," he said, his words stiff, like a shield he had placed between us.

"And you're not?"

"I don't know ... we aren't free at the same time, I think," he said, his gaze skirting mine, avoiding direct contact. He lingered for a moment, as though weighing something unspoken, but then, with a quick glance over his shoulder, he turned around and left.

I stood there, with my sinking heart, trying to reconcile his words with the hollow feeling settling in my chest. I wanted to be happy for him, but it wasn't possible. He had the simple joy of going to school, of still having his boyhood to claim. A sharp bitterness, one I couldn't quite suppress, crept in. I wondered how I had been allowed to fall off the map of my own childhood and my friend didn't seem to want to come and find me? Unkindly, I wondered whether it was because I was a servant? That thought made me angry. I could speak better English than that fool or any of the other idiots who whiled away the days at school. I could probably speak better than the teacher. And could Jitu do calculations like I could? Why did I feel so miserable looking at his life from a distance, like a stranger?

It never occurred to me then that perhaps Jitu too was struggling, that perhaps those days were the hardest of his life as well. I had been spending more and more nights in the servant's room at the Stagers', and fewer and fewer at the house. His friend had vanished. Perhaps his refusal to share in my small victories, in the progress I'd made with my spoken English, the approval I'd earned from Mrs Stager, was his way of rejecting the reality that I would never return to school, never live the life he had once imagined I would. Was it a silent protest against the life I had chosen for myself, a life that didn't include him? We both had lost something—I my childhood, and he, his vision of a life we could have shared.

Acceptance crept in, quiet and almost unnoticed, and slowly, I began to store him away in my memories like a favourite old toy, something precious that I couldn't bring myself to let go of. I kept him there, tucked away where nothing could tarnish the sweetness of our shared past. It was the only way I could preserve him, for old times' sake.

Life had forced me to grow up in other ways as well. One evening, when Poppy avoided a mango pit with a wrinkled nose and a quick, "It gets stuck 'tween ma teeth, Ashey", I was momentarily caught in the flash of memory. It reminded me of the times when I myself used to pass the pit to my father's plate. Father would end up with a small pile of discarded pits, a silent ritual between us, one I hadn't thought about in ages. He was so far away now. I was wracked by a searing guilt when my duties distracted me from the ache of his absence.

I truly enjoyed the feeling of having money for the first time in my life. My frugal ways allowed me to save a considerable sum, and though I didn't indulge much, I spent what I had wisely—on a presentable wardrobe and knitting materials that kept me busy and satisfied. Whatever I saved, I kept with Mrs Stager, where it would be safer than in my cottage. I met Amanullah Khan frequently for Mrs Stager's tailored dresses, and I could see the pride in his eyes as he watched my progress. Soon, I started helping the memsahib with design ideas, which he would later stitch for her. One of my creations, a crochet collar, made her so happy that she quite grinned at the design. In that simple moment, I experienced a rare and quiet joy, a sense of pride in my own work that I hadn't known I was capable of.

The Stager household had slowly become my own. I began to store some of my personal belongings in the servant's bathroom and the small storage cupboard. I barely returned home any more, the girls having grown so attached to me. Even baby Louis, now a toddler of just over two, insisted on being in my arms whenever he could. They began to ask me to sleep in their nursery rather than the servant's room, and gradually, I found myself spending almost every night with them. Mrs Stager, once so distant and guarded, had begun to relax around me, and as time passed, her defences lowered and eventually vanished altogether. I had settled into a rhythm with the family, finding a strange sense of belonging within the walls of their home.

But all of this, all that had become so comfortable and familiar, was about to change. After nearly two years of quiet contentment, a letter arrived one day. It was a letter that would shatter the fragile peace I had built and plunge my life into a turmoil I could never have foreseen.

4

20 June 2000
Marlow, Buckinghamshire

A lingering silence hung between them. Rashmi's gaze fixed on Asha, who, in turn, was lost in the past, her eyes tracing the fading light outside the window.

"What happened next?" Rashmi asked, breaking the quiet.

Asha's gaze shifted, her eyes flicking back to her guest with a soft twinkle. "Oh, don't push an old woman too hard, dear! You've had me chatting for hours already."

Rashmi chuckled at the playful accusation and glanced at the clock. The evening was drawing to a close, and if she didn't leave soon, she would miss the wedding festivities. "Well, it seems I'm left with little time and much left to hear."

"Well, I could tell you briefly, dear, because your time is up," Asha said, gesturing outside at the darkening sky.

"I have a dinner to attend ... but if you can spare some time tomorrow, I'd love to hear what happened next."

"Well, you could," Asha replied with a smile. "The door is always open, Ms Rao. You've been a patient audience."

As Rashmi made her way to the taxi, a laugh escaped her, realising she'd been subtly outwitted. She had come to the interview hoping to explore and build upon the angle of Asha's post-independence life outside India, but they hadn't addressed that aspect of her life at length; she had been drawn into a deeper, more personal tale with no idea of the direction of the story—and she'd been left at a cliffhanger!

Damn, she's good. That wily old thing.

Back at the wedding, Rashmi felt strangely out of place. The earlier conversation with Asha lingered in her mind, pulling her to a place from where she didn't know how to leave. The vibrant celebration around her seemed distant, like a scene from someone else's life. Kuki and her friends were on stage, enthusiastically recreating her love story through a parody of Bollywood songs. Rashmi caught snippets of the performance—something about a water dispenser, so it had probably been an office romance.

The next morning, Rashmi was up early to catch the 9 a.m. train to Marlow, and before long, she found herself standing at Asha's door once again. Her host was in the garden, tending to the flowers with a careful hand, each tulip bulb planted one by one with an almost meditative precision.

"Hello, good morning!" Rashmi greeted, folding her arms as she stood just outside the garden gate. "Shall we pick up from the letter?"

Asha paused, glanced up with a knowing smile, and chuckled. "So business-like! Where are your manners, young lady?"

Rashmi laughed and cried out in mock indignation. "You left me at a cliffhanger, Asha!"

"But I offer to wrap it up neatly for you," Asha teased.

"Ah, yes, I'm sure I could have taken up that offer—and been labelled as another one of those journalists," Rashmi shot back, a grin creeping on to her face.

They both laughed and made their way into the kitchen. Once settled at the table, the warmth of the morning sun filled the room, yet Rashmi's thoughts lingered on the story she had come for.

"So, which letter were we talking about, dear?" Asha's voice turned more serious, her eyes narrowing slightly as she looked up from the cup of tea she was preparing.

"The letter that changed everything for you at the Stager household?" Rashmi prompted gently.

Asha's eyes softened at the mention of it. "Ah, yes."

5

When letters arrived, I usually left Mrs Stager alone. But this letter was different—she was visibly happy. Radiant and beaming, she ran to the nursery and hugged her children, scooping up Poppy and showering her with kisses. She announced loudly to the kids and to a curious Charlotte: 'Edward has been promoted and transferred from Secunderabad to Cawnpore Cantonment! We're finally going to live together!'"

Charlotte was pleased. I was amused at this sight—Mrs Stager seemed younger in all her animation, fluttering with joy, a small parchment clutched tight in her hand. From the look of it, I could tell it was a telegram. I couldn't help smiling back, for I'd never seen the memsahib so happy.

Hameera stood at the foot of the staircase and stared at the goings-on without a smile. The radiant Mrs Stager had infected Lily and Poppy with her joy and the trio was marching around, baby Louis in his mother's arms. Mrs Stager ordered Hameera to prepare for a chicken-and-lamb-roast dinner, and ran to her desk to begin writing letters, which I guessed would be addressed to her family in England. In an hour, she sent for a bunch of letters to be dispatched.

As dinner preparations were underway, Hameera, ever observant, had pieced together everything she had overheard from Charlotte and Mrs Stager's excited chatter. She quietly fed me the details and also bade me to bear the pragmatic impact of these events on our own lives, which I hadn't thought about at all in my joy.

Our jobs at the Stagers were now to last just a few more months. What would happen after that? The thought of going through the long, dreary job hunt all over again was enough to make my stomach twist. I glanced at Hameera, looking for some kind of answer, some reassurance that things would work out. But she simply shrugged, a grim look on her face that only deepened my unease. Suddenly, I couldn't focus on anything else. I wanted to rush out of the house, to find help and escape this feeling of sudden panic. But where could I go? Who could I turn to? I had no answer.

I asked Mrs Stager for leave, but she insisted I stay for dinner, mentioning that she had set aside some vegetarian food for me. I thanked her politely, trying to mask the panic rising in my chest, and told her I was planning to eat at home. My voice faltered despite my best efforts, a clear sign of the turmoil I was struggling to contain. Her expression shifted, a flash of concern passing over her face, before she beckoned me to follow her into her room. The door clicked shut behind us, and the world outside seemed to recede.

"What is the matter, Asha?" she asked, her voice unexpectedly gentle.

"It's Ashley, memsahib," I corrected, my throat tight.

Her gaze softened, her features losing their usual sharpness. "It should have always been Asha," she said quietly.

I gave her a half-hearted smile, thinking inwardly with a trace of bitterness that it must be easier for Mrs Stager to adopt this attitude towards my name in her present effervescent mood. I took a seat where she gestured, my mind scattered, my thoughts drifting far from the present. She opened a thick ledger after adjusting her spectacles, the pages crackling in the quiet room.

"Now look here, Asha," she began, her voice steady, "I've been keeping an account of all your savings with me. You've accumulated a decent sum." She pointed to the figures written in neat black ink.

A tear rolled down my cheek as I took in the figure. It was far more than my savings should have been, and I was sure neither of us had made an arithmetic mistake.

She squeezed my hand, her touch warm and reassuring. "Listen, Asha," she said softly, her eyes meeting mine with understanding. "I know the thought of unemployment must be troubling you. You've worked so hard, exceeded every expectation I had. You've taken on the toughest tasks and delivered each time. I'm paying you only what you've earned. You've also earned the recommendation I'm going to write for you before I have to leave."

I smiled at her, a mix of gratitude and sorrow in my chest. I tried to keep my tears in check, but they threatened to spill over. Embarrassed, Mrs Stager busied herself with the ledger, and I took the opportunity to slip quietly out of the room.

That evening, as the family gathered around the table, the barriers between servants and masters seemed to fade. There was no hierarchy, no distance, just the shared joy of a moment, a rare evening of camaraderie. Hameera packed some leftovers for her children. As I made my way home later that night, I tried to feel content about my savings, even if the future still felt uncertain.

We breezed through the next month, packing up the Stager household's belongings, sorting through clothes to donate, and making the luggage lighter for the long journey ahead. Hameera, already looking ahead, was optimistic about finding a job quickly. She reassured me that I would too, once the time came.

And just like that, the Stagers—Mrs Stager, Louis, Lily, and Poppy—were gone, leaving me with not only decent savings but also a surprisingly heavy heart. I couldn't bear to look towards the house, empty of its inhabitants, amongst whom I had started to count myself too. I wondered if the girls would miss me. Poppy had cried herself to sleep in my lap the night before, her small sobs breaking the silence in the room. I knew they would soon find another ayah to replace me. I couldn't help but wonder what kind of woman she would be, and if she would love them as I had.

I decided to take a few days off before diving into the dreaded job hunt again. Amanullah Khan had helped me once before, and I was sure he would again. I spent the next three days walking freely along Thandi Sadak, treating myself to sweets and indulging in storybooks that I devoured with great delight. The days of leisure felt like a long-overdue respite. One of the books told the story of a merchant who travelled to faraway lands by ship in search of fortune, and as I read, I fantasised that I too might one day cross the seven seas, become rich, meet new people, and earn their respect.

Among my purchases were thin booklets with fragile, yellowed pages, filled with diagrams of sewing techniques. They were clearly the discarded remnants of a memsahib's hobby, now tossed into the marketplace.

These books became my escape, shielding me from the harsh reality of my present. The looming necessity of finding a job and the painful effort of forcibly pushing thoughts of Lily and Poppy out of my heart felt less suffocating when I was lost in the pages of a story. For those precious hours, I wasn't just Asha the ayah searching for her next livelihood, I was the hero who slayed demons, the merchant's son who braved pirates.

However, a fortnight into my leave, the novelty of leisure began to wear off and was replaced by a gnawing restlessness and a sense of loneliness. Each morning, as I stirred awake, I felt the instinctive urge to dress for work. But then, reality would sink in. I had no work to go to any more. The days stretched long and empty, lacking the structure that had once kept my mind busy and my heart distracted. Slowly, sorrow began to creep in as an uninvited guest.

So I set out to Thandi Sadak, wearing my bright blue stole again. It had brought me to the Stagers back then, perhaps it would bring me good fortune again.

This time, though, I knew exactly what I didn't want. I no longer wished to care for children. The emotional toll of attachment, only to be left behind, was too much to bear again. With the Stagers, I had been exceptionally fortunate; the experience had given me more than just employment. It had brought growth, companionship, and even a sense of belonging—but I couldn't count on being so lucky again.

My mind a clean slate, I passed by shops, considering what each offered and imagined myself selling jewellery at Ganeshi Lall & Son of Agra or maybe working at Punjab Bible & Book Depot. I considered selling clothes, sewing and embroidering at durzee shops, working at one of the boarding schools, and even considered starting my own little business with my little fortune.

Seeking guidance, I went to Amanullah Khan to discuss these prospects. Patiently, he listened to my thoughts, his face betraying very little. When I finished, he scratched his beard and offered a quiet sigh.

"These are interesting ideas, Asha, but none that I know how to help with. You've gained skills that make you extremely valuable to English households. You know the way they live, their customs, you'd be hard to replace."

I shook my head. "But I don't want to be an ayah again."

"We must take what we get, Asha," is all he said in the end. I was left no closer to a solution than before. I encountered Hameera on Cart Road one chilly evening, as the light faded.

"I've been meaning to talk to you, Asha!" she exclaimed, grabbing my arm and pulling me aside conspiratorially. "I told you you'll be employed in no time. I have a job for you! And you'll earn more than me!" She waved her palms theatrically, as if conjuring my future from a crystal ball.

Puzzled, I queried her, "What job, Hameera-bi?"

"There's this Jones family," she said, leaning closer. "The head of the family is a doctor-sahib and he just got transferred to Barrackpore. Memsahib Jones is finally going back to England with her youngest girl, a four-year-old, so that the girl may join her three older siblings who were sent home last year for their education."

"I don't understand," I replied, my brows furrowing. "How am I supposed to work for them if they're about to leave?"

"Well? You go with them, of course, *bewakoof!* And on arrival in England, they'll give you your payment and your ticket back home, that's how!" Hameera's voice rose, triumphant, as if she'd just solved all my life's problems in one breath. She waited a few moments, her expectant gaze fixed on me, ready for my joy to spill over.

But I just stood there, trying to grasp the idea that had been sprung upon me.

Hameera clicked her tongue impatiently, her hands flying to her hips. "Tch! Don't you get it? Anyone would be glad of this assignment! The memsahib needs an ayah onboard the ship. An English-speaking one. You!" She pointed a firm finger at me, as if that settled the matter.

I didn't want to displease her, but I couldn't summon the enthusiasm she clearly expected. Travel to England? Work on a ship? What kind of a preposterous arrangement was this?

"How long does it take? To go to England?" I asked hesitantly.

"Three weeks, bachche! Not too long. You must consider this," Hameera replied, her tone urgent, encouraged by my question. "They are relying on me to find them a strong young ayah!"

"But how would I know if I'll get my payment for sure?"

Hameera flinched. "What sort of question is that? They are *gora sahibs* ... *pukka sahibs* ... they will give you your money. This is common practice. A lot of ayahs travel and the money is unbelievable. Your luck is changing, Asha!"

I was puzzled, and looked searchingly into Hameera's eyes. The money she mentioned was exceptionally high.

Despite my doubts, I nodded slowly. "Alright," I said, my voice steadier now. "I'll at least meet the family."

Hameera beamed, clasping my arm as if she'd just secured me the opportunity of a lifetime. But even as I agreed, a sliver of unease coiled in my chest.

The next day, I left my blue stole hanging on its peg. I hadn't slept or eaten well. I kept thinking of all the things to ask this family and fully understand the nature of this unusual assignment. I considered visiting Amanullah Khan for advice but I remembered his words, "We must take what we get".

Hameera appeared early at my door, her face eager and resolute. I couldn't help but wonder how much she stood to gain from this arrangement. As we arrived, I took in the large, stately building, its pale stone facade gleaming in the morning light. The name painted on a wooden board outside caught my eye: Dr E.R. Jones. The quarters were bigger than the Stagers'.

"Why did sahib get transferred? Is the sahib a doctor with the British army?"

Hameera looked confused but said, "Sahib left for Barrackpore. Memsahib needs to leave within ten days, from Bombay. Okay? Now don't ask silly questions inside."

I followed her silently, walking through the pedestrian side entrance into the verandah, wondering how well she knew the Joneses. The orderly certainly seemed to know Hameera and darted inside wordlessly to inform the memsahib of our arrival. As we sat on the verandah, I remembered the day when I had waited at the Stagers' verandah with Amanullah Khan. I didn't feel very different this time, except that now I had experience in taking care of children.

After what felt like an eternity, the door creaked open, and a tall, heavily built memsahib stepped on to the verandah. She carried herself with an air of authority, her dark gown emphasising her rigid posture. Her dark hair was pulled tightly into a formidable bun, not a strand out of place. Her sharp, pale eyes swept over me, taking in every detail. Her face was expressionless, but there was something in her eyes that hinted at cruelty.

Before I could offer so much as a greeting, Hameera sprang into action and obsequiously told her that I was the ayah she had mentioned. She relayed my qualities, such as being well behaved and being good with children; she also extolled the fact that I "ate exceedingly little".

As Hameera prattled on about my spoken English skills, I kept my eyes on the memsahib's face, searching for any hint of approval or disdain. It was hard to gauge her thoughts.

Suddenly, the sharp sound of porcelain shattering echoed from inside the house. Without a word, the memsahib stormed off with heavy footsteps. Moments later, we heard her voice rise in fury, bellowing reprimands that made me flinch despite the distance.

Unable to contain my curiosity, I leaned forward, craning my neck to catch a glimpse of the scene inside. The memsahib was pacing furiously, her dress swirling around her ankles, while a little girl stood in the corner, her head bowed in guilt. Her small hands were clasped tightly in front of her, trembling as if bracing for the next wave of rage.

Before I could take in more, I felt a firm tug on my arm. "Don't," Hameera hissed, yanking me back into my seat. "She'll catch you prying."

Hameera and I seated ourselves on the stairs of the verandah and waited. I whispered to her, "The memsahib isn't sweet to her own child, Hameera. How am I to work for her?"

Hameera shrugged, unconcerned. "Asha, the memsahib doesn't need to be kind to the child. You'll be the one in charge, you'll care for her, keep her entertained. That's all she needs from you. It's a good job with a good pay, and once it is over, you will never have to see or hear from the memsahib again."

I hesitated. Her words were persuasive, and the thought of travelling beyond this town, of not having to worry about finding another job for a long time, appealed to something deep inside me. But the nagging doubt about the memsahib lingered. The image of the child standing there, trembling, was still vivid in my mind.

"You said this is common practice?" I asked again, seeking reassurance.

Hameera nodded. "It's common, yes. I've heard of it from others who've served wealthy memsahibs." She surveyed me for a moment, before adding craftily, "Just think of the child, Asha. You'll be the one to make sure she's happy and safe."

I almost smiled at the attempted manipulation.

The memsahib appeared shortly after, flanked by a servant. "The ayah is fine," she declared brusquely, her finger pointing in my direction with a dismissive air. I couldn't help but feel a flash of irritation as her gaze swept over me.

"You know the terms," she continued, her voice cutting through the air. "I'll pay one-fifth of the agreed sum now, and the rest upon our arrival in England. The ayah's duties are simple: she keeps Joanna entertained, fed, and gets her to sleep as you've seen here. There will be other minor tasks, at my discretion, such as assisting me with my dressing in the mornings after Joanna's breakfast, and fetching a hot water pad for me at bedtime. The ayah will reside in the servant quarters throughout the journey and will receive a third-class ticket back home once we disembark in England."

Her tone was cold, methodical, as though she were outlining the terms of a business transaction rather than a personal arrangement. "If all of this is agreeable," she added, towering over us both, "we can begin." It was clear from her expression that she expected no pushback, and that the terms had been set and would be accepted without question.

Before Hameera could intervene, I inhaled deeply, gathering my resolve, and spoke steadily. "Memsahib," I began, my voice calm yet firm. "My name is Asha. You and your daughter may address me as Asha, or Ashley, as my previous employer preferred. I have read and heard from many English people that the weather in England and along the journey could be extreme." I met the memsahib's gaze directly, resisting the urge to glance at Hameera, who seemed to want to interrupt. "Having been unemployed for so long, I've exhausted most of my savings, and even a quarter of the fees would hardly cover a decent balaclava from the second-hand shop."

The memsahib's eyes narrowed. "I would have arranged clothing in your size," she replied coolly, "but I don't have the time with the journey so close. Take a third of the fees and get your provisions in order."

I took the money before Hameera could.

As we exited the gate, Hameera, her voice tinged with disbelief, turned to me. "How could you negotiate like that?"

I gave her a wry smile. "Aren't you happy I did?"

"Yes, but how did you do it? These aren't people who are used to hearing anything from a native beyond a 'Yes, memsahib,' Asha."

"She doesn't seem nice at all, Hameera-bi. My requests wouldn't mean anything to her. But I know she needs me, and that gives me leverage. I just have to be careful with her. Besides, as you said, I'll be out of her way for the most part, and once this is over, I'll never have to see her again."

Hameera nodded in quiet acknowledgement, as we continued walking down the familiar streets. "You seem to have learned a thing or two about this world, little one."

6

I spent the week preparing for the journey. To get appropriate clothing for the cold weather, I turned to Amanullah Khan. Resourceful as ever, he made special requests to a Mrs Barnes, a memsahib whose husband stocked clothes and fabric for ladies of upper-class families. The rejects from Mr Barnes's collection, which were damaged items or items discarded by memsahibs who found them outmoded or unnecessary in the Indian climate, were far better than anything I could afford with my meagre fortune. Luckily for me, Mr Barnes seemed like a kind man, and his assistant took whatever I could pay. I found quite a collection that I could fix up and make serviceable.

Having thanked the Barnes profusely, to their amusement and embarrassment, I took my horde back home and set to work. The garments, though torn and oversized, held potential. One careful stitch after another, I mended the frayed hems and patched the holes, my fingers moving steadily through the night. The fabrics smelled faintly of camphor, mingled with the dampness of disuse—nothing a good sunning wouldn't fix. Wherever possible, I refitted the dresses to suit my smaller frame. When I finally laid out the finished collection of a modest array of coats, scarves, and dresses, it looked unexpectedly dignified. It was not opulence, but it would do. I was quite pleased with my collection.

After that, I began packing my belongings, howsoever few they were. As I was getting done, I noticed Jitu standing outside his house,shifting his weight from one foot to the other. I knew he wanted to talk, so I opened the door and lingered, waiting.

He turned towards me, his voice tentative. "How have you been, Munni?"

It had been so long since anyone asked me that, so long since I heard that name said aloud. Something in the way he said it made me feel warm and unguarded. I'd like to believe that life had toughened me, but that simple question undid me. I felt the irresistible urge to tell him everything, to be honest, to tell him how much I had endured, how much I missed the simplicity of the days when Munni was just a name, not a memory. I wanted somebody to be honest to, and if only it could be Jitu.

But all I chose to say was "I'm well, Jitu", trying to reciprocate the warmth when uttering his name. Isn't there something special about saying somebody's name?

With his hands by his back, he seemed to be speaking to the ground under my feet, "I heard you're leaving … on a voyage."

I nodded, my heart too heavy for anything else.

"How come you didn't tell me?"

I was caught off guard. "I didn't know I had to."

He finally looked at my face. "Aren't we friends?"

Were we? I had never stopped missing him. But did he miss me too?

"I don't know, Jitu. We weren't really talking."

"I'm sorry about that. A lot has changed over the year."

"It has," I replied, a surprising steadiness creeping into my voice. Did he mean my position and societal standing?

"No ..." he said quickly, stepping closer, his gaze locking with mine. "I mean, a lot has changed ... and I don't want things to change between us. You were my best friend, and I shouldn't have left you alone. I'm sorry. I didn't know what to do."

His words stirred something deep within me, emotions I had buried under layers of resilience and forward momentum. A tide of sorrow and regret threatened to sweep me under. But I couldn't afford to drown now. The ship sailing to the future was waiting just over the horizon. I had to keep moving forward.

"I was never upset with you, Jitu," I said, my voice softer. "We all need time to figure things out sometimes. You needed space, perhaps so did I. Maybe it would have been tougher otherwise."

"It didn't feel right, Munni," his voice wavered, but his eyes stayed steady. "I need my friend back. Unless ... unless you don't want that. And if that's true, I'll understand."

I felt a helpless pang in my chest. What was I to do with this now, at this juncture? A friendship mended, just as I was about to leave. An entire year lost to silence. The frustration was sharp, but Jitu was special, and I didn't want him to walk away without knowing that. If nothing else, I could hold on to the hope that my closest friend would still be there when I returned.

"I'm leaving in two days," I said finally, the words heavier than I'd anticipated.

He smiled then—his easy, familiar smile, the one that always made things seem simpler than they were. "Then we'll pick it up from here when you come back." His warmth was disarming, and for a moment, the weight of everything lifted.

"And if you don't mind," he added, his tone light, "come and have dinner with us this evening."

I was gashed by a longing for the past. "But I haven't come in so long. It would feel ... awkward."

"I won't insist if you truly feel that way. Nobody's going to ask about your work or the journey. We'll just eat together, like old times. Would that make it easier?"

"Maybe," I said, biting my lip. After all this time, Jitu still knew me better than anyone else.

Later that afternoon, I busied myself, preparing for my departure. I had my worn-out shoes repaired, stocked up on dry snacks and scarves, bought fresh thread to mend my bedding, and picked up a few old magazines and books to keep me company on the journey. When I returned home, I hesitated for a moment before pulling out my nicest salwar-kurta. The fabric felt crisp and clean as I smoothed it down, readying myself for an evening that felt strangely momentous.

It wasn't like before. Jitu's mother gave me a polite smile as she fried pooris all alone, his father served me generous helpings of *jhangora kheer*, and there were no jokes about gaining weight. Jitu would smile between morsels and we made small talk about the village affairs. After we had eaten, Jitu and I served his parents and watched them eat.

When the plates were cleared and the kitchen tidied, Jitu and I stepped outside. We settled on to the khatiya, its ropes creaking gently beneath us. Jitu reached into his pocket and pulled out a handful of sweet tamarind pods. He had a grin on his face as he offered them to me. I couldn't help but laugh, accepting a few.

"Some things won't change," he said, his grin widening. As if the thought had tugged at something deeper, his expression turned solemn. He looked up at the stars, their cold, distant light catching in his eyes. I drank in the sight of his face in the blue glow of the night. "I wish I hadn't been such an idiot. I let so much time slip away. And now you're leaving."

"No more whining! It's not the end of the world."

"But you're leaving," he said softly.

"I'm not about to die! I'll come back."

"Chhi! Who says things like that!" he exclaimed, horrified. "We don't joke about death that way!"

I shrugged, and returned to studying the stars. Soon enough, he spoke again.

"I just keep thinking, Munni. What if something happens?"

"You mean ... what if I die?" I teased, laughing.

He groaned, covering his ears and shouting nonsense to drown out my words. I laughed harder, swatting his arm in mock outrage. The night was taking me back to how I used to feel—I hadn't laughed so freely since very long.

"My absence from your life has poisoned your tongue," he retorted, laughing.

The stars above felt closer as our laughter faded into warm, comfortable smiles. We spoke about my journey and I told him everything I had got to know about England through my reading.

Jitu listened intently, his fascination flickering beneath a layer of unease. "Crossing the seven seas," he murmured, shaking his head. "It sounds terrifying."

I knew what he meant, but I thought it was adventurous. I didn't have any family to answer to and I could do whatever I wanted.

"You always were braver than me, Munni."

I smiled, looking at the horizon where the stars met the hills. "Maybe. Or maybe I just have less to lose."

I spent the next day stitching my bedding and Jitu came over to help. All he did was sit beside me quiet as a mouse. We took my luggage to the Joneses' bungalow in the evening. I was to leave the next day with Mrs Jones and her daughter.

I had decided to stay the night at their quarters, as our journey would begin early next morning. Jitu and I bid goodbye at the gate of the quarters. It was far too late for him to be there—I knew he would face the wrath of his parents for being out so late. But how could we not prolong our moments together? At that age, a couple of months apart felt like an eternity, especially given how far away I was going. I drank in his face under the moonlight, memorising every feature of my only friend, my oldest friend, the last piece of my childhood. I wanted to store as much of him in my mind as I could, for the journey. He squeezed my hands, his touch tender, before pressing a quick kiss to my forehead. I tried not to feel anything, but the tears welling in his eyes were impossible to ignore. I think I broke down, though it's hard to recall the exact moment. The memory is now a blur—it has faded into a knot of emotion. The details I wanted to remember are gone.

We set out for Bombay before the first light of dawn. Mrs Jones and her daughter settled comfortably in a tonga without a word to me, and that was all that I saw of them for a large part of the journey. I followed in a *theka gari*, an uncomfortable wooden box that seemed to accentuate every jolt and bump along the way. I dozed uneasily through the familiar portion of the descent.

On the descent, our procession was joined by various travellers, including servants on their way back to their native villages in different parts of the country, after having travelled with their masters to serve them on their summer sojourns or medical leaves in the mountains. Halts were infrequent and I grew very thirsty. The wooden box creaked and groaned and I spent much of the ride trying to brace myself against the jolts of the vehicle. That misery finally ended after what felt like an eternity, when we arrived in a town much lower on the mountains from where we were to take a train to Delhi.

The place was overwhelming. Crowded and frantic, the air thick with noise, the heat almost stifling. People surged in every direction, shouting loudly over the crowds in an unfamiliar language. The marketplace buzzed with shouts, the clatter of carts, and the shrill calls of vendors. I felt a pang of panic as I was swallowed by the dense crowd. The platform was a sea of unfamiliar faces, and the thought of getting lost in the mass of people terrified me. I clutched my belongings and kept close to my new mistress, my heart racing, trying to steady my breath amidst the sensory overload.

When we finally boarded the train to Delhi, it was just as uncomfortable as the earlier parts of the journey. The cramped servant's carriage felt isolating, the air thick with the smells of sweat, dust, and the harsh metallic scent of the train itself. The unfamiliar, flat land stretching before me seemed endless and alien. It was a stark contrast to the mountains I had known, and the shift was disorienting. My senses were assaulted with new sounds, new sights, new smells—everything felt magnified and jarring.

I sat there, surrounded by strangers, the distance from the Joneses feeling more pronounced than ever. The further we travelled, the more disconnected I felt from everything familiar. I was too afraid to look back, too far from home to even know what the next steps would be.

When we reached our destination the next day, I was far too drained to take in the significance of being in Delhi, recently made the capital, and a place that was so frequently mentioned on the radio and in the papers. All I could do, when we finally debarked, was cling to the Joneses, the only familiar faces in this foreign place, and stay close to them, seeking comfort in their presence. I don't recall much of the officer's accommodation where Mrs Jones was welcomed warmly for the night. The only memory that stayed with me was the numb exhaustion in my limbs, and how I sank into the bed in the female servant's dormitory. Sleep came swiftly, as if my body knew it could not rest any longer. I slept like a corpse, disconnected from everything around me.

Things finally changed the next day when we boarded the Frontier Mail, which Mrs Jones told me, with an air of great importance, was one of the finest trains in the British Raj. Its grandeur did feel like a different world altogether. The smells of leather, paraffin, spices, and sweat that had surrounded me now gave way to the fresh scent of clean sheets, perfumed cabins, and the rich aroma of freshly cooked meat. The luxurious surroundings, the soft rustle of the linen, the clinking of fine china, made everything feel surreal.

Lieutenant Murray, a young and strong-looking sahib assigned to guide us, escorted us through the bustling station and to our coach.

"Dr Jones is a magician," he gushed to Mrs Jones, manoeuvring through the crowd with practised ease and frowning at the attendants who were struggling with our luggage. "Is this your first trip on an Indian train?" he asked as we stepped on to the train. Mrs Jones mumbled a response, but it hardly seemed to matter to Murray, who continued enthusiastically, "Civilisation has been hard won in these lands, but these trains, madam, are something the Raj can be proud of. Electrification of stations has already begun."

"It's awfully hot, the whole country is, but the train makes travelling through it as comfortable as one can hope for," he declared, as we took in the spacious, air-conditioned compartment that would be our home for the night.

Then, with a slightly more condescending tone, he gestured towards me. "No separate rooms for the servants or the natives, madam. People usually send their coloured servants to travel on the coloured trains," he said with a dismissive wave, as if it was a matter of course.

Mrs Jones finally broke her silence. "That wouldn't do for me. I couldn't have her lag behind and hold up my journey at sea."

My face flushed with resentment, but I quickly turned away, unwilling to let it show. I wasn't used to this, to being so openly dismissed. But Amanullah Khan's warning echoed in my mind, steady and clear: the gora sahibs and memsahibs outside the hills would be different, and my status as an ayah would carry no weight among them. I had to be cautious and avoid mistakes, for a mistake with them could cost me more than my life.

I swallowed my bitterness, forcing my gaze downward.

Our compartment stood at the centre of the train. Two young coolies in red shirts and white turbans arranged Mrs

Jones's *sandook*s and bundles wrapped tightly in dhurries secured by ropes. Two *sipahi*s followed, carrying tin boxes and bedding rolls with practised ease. I stepped inside with my small trunk, unsure of where to put it. The memsahib's suitcases already occupied most of the available space, leaving no room for my belongings among her neatly organised possessions. I glanced around, noting the compartment's thoughtful design, a separate lavatory, a wash basin, and just enough room for three travellers.

After Murray departed with a courteous bow to Mrs Jones, she summoned me to serve her refreshments from her thermos flask and assist her in dressing for dinner. I complied dutifully. Mrs Jones said little throughout, her silence heavy and unyielding. I tried to comfort myself with the thought that Mrs Stager had been similarly distant in our early days, but there was a sullen edge to Mrs Jones that unsettled me.

Even her child, Joanna, remained quiet in her company, her small figure a shadow in the compartment. I realised, with a twinge of guilt, that I hadn't yet spoken to or properly regarded my new charge since we began the journey. Now, however, with the long hours stretching ahead of us, I would have plenty of time to change that.

Once Mrs Jones was ready, she adjusted her hat, and addressed us sharply. "Joanna is to have dinner and be in bed by six o'clock. I'll be in the restaurant car, and it might take me some time to return. I'd like not to be disturbed. Is that clear, Joanna?" she punctuated her words by wagging a finger at the girl.

Joanna's head dipped meekly. Without waiting for further response, Mrs Jones stepped briskly out of the compartment just as the train slowed for the next station. She joined two other memsahibs, who greeted her with the familiarity of old acquaintances. Together, they disappeared towards the restaurant car, leaving the compartment heavy with an uncomfortable silence.

I glanced at Joanna. Hoping to ease her discomfort, I crouched slightly to meet her eye and offered a soft smile. "Hello, Joanna …"

Joanna shrank back, her small frame curling in on itself as she looked up at me, wide-eyed and wary.

"Are you scared of me?" I asked softly.

She nodded, her tiny chin quivering.

The gesture caught me off guard. "You don't have to be," I said gently. "I'm here to be your friend."

Her gaze didn't waver, but a flicker of doubt clouded her expression, as though she wasn't quite sure what to make of me.

"I'm your ayah," I added, hesitating for a moment over the word. It wasn't one I liked using for myself, but I figured it was what she'd understand. "I'm here to take care of you until we get home."

"I don't know if we're ever going home," she croaked, her voice so soft I almost missed it as I turned away.

I paused, glancing back at her. "Why do you say that?"

"We just left it behind," she replied flatly. As the train lurched into motion, I felt a pang of sadness for her.

"Well, that's my home too, you know," I said gently. "But you're going to the country you belong to. You'll have a lot of friends and family there who'll speak your language and eat the same things as you do." I tried to warm her with a smile.

"But I like it here. I don't want new friends. Saru is my friend," she said, her voice firm despite its frailty.

"Who is Saru?"

"She's my friend. She lives in the servant quarters and plays with me in the evenings."

I looked at her freckled, pale face, her sunken eyes, wispy brown hair, and fragile frame. She looked English, but she was as Indian as I was. There wasn't much I could say to reassure her. It was true that she was never going back to Saru or her old house.

"I'm sorry, Joanna. I know you're going to miss home and friends. I miss my home and friends too. But I'm going to return once your mother and you reach your country, so that I can meet Saru and tell her you missed her. Is that something you'd like me to do?"

Joanna's pale face flickered with hope and she nodded with a weak smile.

After that, Joanna quietly followed my lead with her evening routine. Her dinner consisted of chicken soup and bread. I had bread and tea after helping Joanna with her meal. She didn't mind when I changed her into her pyjamas. She was the same size as Lily. Holding the clothes that could have fit Lily too made me miss her sharply. For a moment, I wondered if they missed me too, or was I replaceable?

Joanna's presence was different from Lily's or Poppy's. It was subdued, apologetic, as if she didn't want to take up any space at all. As I massaged her legs, I noticed old scars that looked like they came from *barsati* sores, a skin affliction common amongst the Anglos. What was her life like, I wondered? Some English children just didn't fare well in the harsh conditions of India. Disease was a constant enemy, draining their strength and health. She smiled faintly with her eyes closed as I tucked her in, my fingers gently tracing her forehead. Within moments, she fell asleep, her breathing slowing to a soft rhythm.

I unpacked the memsahib's supplies and set up her bed before lying down on mine. I reached for a book but quickly drifted off to sleep, only to be stirred when Mrs Jones returned.

Once she settled in, I lay awake in the moonlight, the rhythmic movement of the train lulling me into a calmness. This was my first proper train ride, if one could forget the pitiful experience from the day before. Here I was, making my maiden journey in my very own berth. I smiled to myself. Mrs Jones lay motionless in her bed, as inscrutable in repose as she was in motion. She was a stranger, and here I was, trusting her on this vast journey. Looking back, I wondered how I did it so fearlessly, how I stuck to it. Was it simply because I had been conditioned to accept the structures and servitude set up for us by those who ruled the country? In all honesty, the most plausible explanation seems to be that I felt a sense of belonging with Joanna throughout the journey. I wasn't lonely any more.

The next day began with me waking before the first light of dawn. I had slept soundly, and I didn't want to squander any opportunity to make a good impression on my new employer. These small advantages were crucial when starting a new job. I bathed and dressed quietly, careful not to disturb anyone. Afterwards, I laid out Joanna's clothes and made my way to the kitchen car to fetch tea for them at the next station.

The kitchen staff that morning consisted of Nooruddin Ansari, a khansama from Lucknow, and his two helpers, young Peshawari boys no older than sixteen.

"So you can read my name on the badge, dear girl?" Ansari asked, with a broad smile devoid of most teeth.

"Of course I can, chacha," I grinned back.

He handed me a biscuit. "Here's a little something for you. It'll be a while until breakfast is ready for the others. I'll try to sneak some extra food on to your baby memsahib's plate for you," he said with a grandfatherly smile.

"No, thank you, chacha. I'll have breakfast when it's time," I said, holding out my hand for the biscuit.

He smirked, eyes twinkling. "We don't eat leftovers, do we? First job, eh?"

"I can wait, it's something I don't want to do unless I'm starving," I replied politely.

"So where to?" he asked, his hands working quickly over a massive, steaming pot.

"To England," I replied between sips.

His eyes widened, and he let out a soft chuckle, his face creasing in amusement. "England? Your parents agreed to that?"

"I have no parents," I replied with a mouth full of biscuit.

He looked momentarily startled before nodding thoughtfully. "I'm sorry to hear that, beti. No parents would let a girl like you go all the way across the sea, not without good reason." He passed me another biscuit, a quiet sympathy in his gaze.

"How long have you worked on the train, chacha?" I asked, shifting the conversation.

"Ever since it started last year. I was on the Punjab Mail earlier."

"Do you get to meet your family?"

"I do, I do, beti! Just how frequently it should be—once every three or four days. I think that's the right way once you grow older, heh?"

"I think one should see one's family more when they're older."

"That's because you're a nice little girl!" he riposted with raucous laughter, as the boys chuckled and filled little kettles with tea.

I didn't know what to make of that or of this strange khansama, so I just sipped the rest of the tea looking at the fields and houses as we left them behind at great speed. Quiet moments at the beginning of one's day must be cherished, especially when you're in service. It was the only time one could fill one's own cup.

By the time I returned to the compartment at the next station, the landscape had grown clearer, the scenery shifting beneath the train's relentless speed. Joanna was still asleep, her small form curled up in the dim light. I sat beside her, gently brushing my fingers across her forehead, the motion tender and automatic.

She stirred, her eyes fluttering open, her voice soft and groggy. "Were you with me all night?"

I nodded, offering her a small smile. Soon she was dressed for the day and I offered her milk and biscuits. Nooruddin had in fact slipped in some extra breakfast for me on a different plate, and I was surprised to feel a lump in my throat at the unexpected kindness from a stranger.

At Mrs Jones's instruction, I took Joanna for a brief walk along the platform at Baroda station. I suspected she wanted the compartment to herself, free to entertain the other memsahib who had stopped by. As we left, their conversation had already drifted into the mind-numbing details of domestic inconveniences, such as an old manservant whose frequent bouts of ill health had become an unbearable burden on their journey.

When Joanna and I returned, stepping quietly into the compartment, I caught the sound of Mrs Jones's voice. She was quoting from a book with much gravitas to an attentive audience. Intrigued, I glanced at the title of the volume before retreating outside to wait: *A Handbook for Travellers in India, Burma and Ceylon* by John Murray. The book was vaguely familiar, and later I would learn it was regarded as an essential guide for navigating this part of the world, its faded spine seen often in the hands of English travellers.

Their conversation carried through the slightly ajar door.

"Mr Murray advises travellers not to grudge spending on clothes and medical expenses for their servants, as a servant's illness or discomfort would inevitably render the employer doubly uncomfortable. He also recommends settling expenses weekly and allowing a rake-off for little comforts."

"Ugh ... I cannot stand bickering with the grasping sorts among the natives. It's much better to just give the greedy folk what they want and get on with it!" Mrs Ferguson declared irritably.

Mrs Jones laughed lightly. "It's certainly less effort, dear Mrs Ferguson."

I felt an immediate dislike for Ferguson.

"The book says the services of an ayah are more difficult to secure than a bearer servant. How did you find that girl?"

"Pure luck," Mrs Jones replied. "I hadn't heard of English-speaking ayahs up north, but this one just landed on my doorstep."

"Paying for her journey all the way back? That must have cost you quite a bit. When they know they're needed, they'll even start enough to negotiate, if you can believe it. I've seen it before."

There was a brief silence before Mrs Jones said, "Excuse me, Mrs Ferguson. I've just remembered a telegram I must send to my brother about reaching Bombay."

I quickly slipped away from the door as Mrs Jones emerged, striding purposefully towards the Station Master's office.

Joanna tugged at my hand, pulling me towards the restaurant car. Her wide eyes, brimming with curiosity, fixed at the entry door. I smiled and decided to indulge her and take a little tour together. Putting a finger to my lips as a signal for staying quiet, I gently helped her inside.

The restaurant car was unlike anything I had ever seen. Rows of tables lined each side of the aisle, each illuminated by a small wall lamp. The tables were impeccably set with bone china plates, polished cutlery, and crisp white napkins, just as Mrs Stager had always preferred at her table. The manager, a stout man in a well-fitted Western coat, attended to the sparse number of guests seated at this hour. Around him, attendants dressed in pristine white chapkans and matching turbans hovered at the tables, their movements purposeful and synchronised. The colour of their turbans matched the delicate border of the tablecloths and the soft folds of the curtains. It felt like a grand chessboard where every piece, from the smallest pawn to the imposing rook, had its role and place.

Before the sharp-eyed manager could notice us, I ushered Joanna out, and we clambered into the kitchen car. Nooruddin was now a whirlwind of activity, orchestrating lunch preparations with not a moment to spare. The aroma of spices wafted through the air as he stirred a massive pot with a ladle almost his size.

"Not now, dear!" he called out with barely a look towards them. "It's a war zone in here! No place for nice girls and their strange dolls!"

I laughed at his unkind description of poor Joanna. "Just wanted to thank you for breakfast, chacha!"

Nooruddin grinned and nodded an acknowledgement before returning to stir the thick gravy in the drum with rhythmic movements, like an oarsman rowing a boat. Joanna stood frozen in awe at the sheer scale of the kitchen and gasped at the mounds of ingredients and bubbling pots. I trailed behind her as she wandered around, taking in the bustling scene. Nooruddin's watchful eyes observed us from time to time, though his hands never faltered in their task.

Eventually, he handed the ladle to one of his young assistants and approached us. When he was close enough, he fixed me with an expression I couldn't quite place—it was serious, yet warm. He addressed me in an unusually measured and deliberate voice.

"Beti," he began, "if you ever find yourself in need in that faraway land, ask for the India House in London."

"Who lives there?" I asked, tilting my head in confusion at this unexpected remark.

"People who will help you … if you need it."

The sincerity in his words should have been reassuring, but instead, they unsettled me. Why would I need help?

"I think it's time to go back," I said abruptly, also sensing the ticking of the clock. Mrs Jones would return any moment, and I didn't want her to find us here.

As we walked back to our compartment, a strange unease settled in my gut. Nooruddin's words echoed in my mind, each repetition stirring an anxious undercurrent I couldn't shake. Perhaps, he was just being cautious, I reasoned. But the shadow cast by his warning lingered.

I distracted myself by having an early lunch after Mrs Jones and Joanna finished theirs. Before long, the train pulled into the bustling chaos of Bombay, and the clamour of the station drowned out these concerns.

A group of turbaned sipahis marched into our compartment, swiftly taking all the luggage, mine included. When we stepped outside, it felt as though we had entered another world altogether. The platform was a cacophony of sights and sounds. Luggage barrows clattered noisily, dhoti-clad coolies shouted commands to clear the way, and children shrieked with laughter as they leaped over bundles of bedding, their antics drawing disapproving glances from English onlookers who rolled their eyes up to their hats.

Unlike the station at Simla, this one swarmed with more people than a whole village could hold. Rested as I was after the journey, my eyes were drawn to everything—the endless shed of the platform heaving with movement, the clamour of voices, and the whirling activity around me. But there was no time to linger. I tightened my grip on Joanna's hand and kept my focus on Mrs Jones, scurrying to keep pace with the turbans of the sipahis leading the way.

The station was an overwhelming blend of scents—sweat mingled with the sharp tang of pickle, the rich aroma of fresh pakodas and ginger tea, the stale smell of leftover food, and the diesel fumes of the trains. We dodged spilled food that could have spoiled our hems, the pointed ends of umbrellas jabbing dangerously close, and the swinging handbags that came uncomfortably near to faces. Even a stray dog or two had to be shooed off our path.

At last, the shed gave way to the open sky, and the platform transitioned abruptly into a dock.

That was when I saw it for the first time. The *Ranchi*.

It stood there, a giant among giants, a colossal marvel so immense it seemed more a work of divine power than human ingenuity. The black hull loomed imposingly, crowned by two towering funnels, while a clean white band encircled the midsection, stark against the gleaming red of the submerged bottom. The word 'RANCHI' was emblazoned boldly along the side, its letters a proclamation of the ship's might.

I stopped for a moment, staring in awe at the immense vessel. It towered above us, an almost living presence. For a moment, I forgot where I was, caught in the enormity of it. But Mrs Jones's brisk pace jolted me back to reality, and I hurried to keep up, Joanna's small hand still clasped tightly in mine.

Until now, I had spared little thought to the vessel itself that would carry us across an endless, unfathomable sea. Standing before its towering bulk, the physical reality of it all struck me. The thought of surrendering myself to this immense machine, trusting it to hold its course and keep us safe in the vast and indifferent ocean, filled me with a strange mixture of awe and apprehension.

My gaze wandered to the countless tiny windows dotting the hull. I assumed they marked the quarters where people such as me would live during the voyage, tucked away in small, dim spaces far below the grandeur of the ship's upper decks.

There wasn't much time for reflection. Our turbaned helpers, having set our luggage down just a few steps from the long ramp leading into the ship, melted into the throng without a word. We stood there in a circle, our belongings heaped at our feet. Joanna slunk between us, settling herself quietly on a bedding roll. None of us spoke. For a fleeting moment, it seemed as though all three of us were struck dumb by the sheer scale of the behemoth before us.

I continued to study the ship, unable to tear my eyes away. The deck stretched on forever, bordered by rails that gleamed in the sunlight. Suspended along the sides of the upper levels were smaller boats, stacked neatly in readiness, their white hulls shining against the black bulk of the ship. The noise of activity aboard the vessel, a lively, discordant symphony of voices, footsteps, and the clang of metal on metal gave the impression of a city in motion.

Turning briefly, I craned my neck to catch a last glimpse of the train. But the throng of passengers and porters, coolies and children, obscured it entirely. Above the chaos, the letters on the station's shed loomed large: BALLARD PIER.

"Memsahib?"

Mrs Jones turned towards me.

"Memsahib, I thought we were to board the ship from Bombay. This says Bal-lard Pi-er."

She sighed, her impatience barely concealed, and gestured toward the towering *Ranchi*. "This is Bombay. That's just what the station is called. And yes, this is the ship we're boarding."

Her gaze lingered on me, her expression faintly surprised. "I'm impressed you can read English. Quite an asset to have!"

I managed a polite smile and looked away, letting my attention drift to the crowd surrounding us—a colourful tapestry of travellers. Indian men in crisp grey suits, their oiled hair combed back with precision, stood out as likely merchants or professionals. Large European families bustled about, encircled by children darting between gleaming metal trunks while bearer servants struggled to keep pace. Memsahibs in frilly white gowns fanned themselves with lace hand fans, sitting under ornate parasols, their chatter rising above the din.

In the midst of this bustling scene, a peculiar stillness settled over me. I glanced up at the sky—vast, infinite, and untouched. Even the colossal *Ranchi* seemed dwarfed by its boundless expanse. As I gazed into its depths, I found my thoughts turning inward, to the divine. Quietly, I consigned my fate to forces far greater than myself, finding solace in the act of surrender.

Even though I was an untethered kite, I was sure the winds sent by the gods would never blow me astray.

7

"Hullo!"

Jolted out of my thoughts, I turned to see a man approaching—a tall, broad figure in khaki, his genial smile softening an otherwise commanding presence. His badge read "Col. Scott, Linley". Behind him trailed another line of turbaned coolies.

"Oh, Linley dear! It is wonderful to see you," Mrs Jones exclaimed, clasping her hands in delight.

He bowed slightly, his thick moustache twitching with his smile. "The pleasure is mine, madam. I trust you had a pleasant journey? The Frontier Mail is one of the best trains we've got, and the SS *Ranchi* is an equally fine ship."

He crouched down to Joanna's level, his smile growing even warmer. Joanna, evidently charmed, extended her hand, which he took solemnly, shaking it with deliberate care. For a moment, I couldn't help thinking that he seemed like a genuinely kind man.

Straightening up, Mr Scott addressed Mrs Jones again. "We're right on schedule, madam. It's half past twelve, and the ship departs at one twenty. I assume this is all your luggage?"

"Yes, that's everything," Mrs Jones confirmed. "There are separate accommodations for staff and ayahs, I believe?"

He hesitated, glancing briefly in my direction. "Of course. I thought you'd prefer your help to stay nearby, but by all means, she can have a women's cabin in one of the economy rooms. The accommodations are quite up to standard—she'll be comfortable wherever she is."

I tried to decipher what that meant, my gaze darting towards the massive ship looming ahead. The thought of being separated from Mrs Jones and Joanna—the only two people I knew—was unsettling. How would I navigate that colossal labyrinth without losing my way?

Interrupting my mounting unease, Mr Scott cleared his throat. "Mr Jones sent me your tickets ahead of time, but I only received word yesterday about your help accompanying you. Fortunately, we managed to secure a last-minute ticket in economy class, as the servant cabins were already full."

On his orders, the coolies hoisted our luggage and began ascending the ramp leading into the ship. My heartbeat quickened. I was about to set foot on the *Ranchi*, embarking on my first-ever sea journey. I glanced at my ticket, recording the date in my memory: 1 February 1931. Taking a steadying breath, I followed the Joneses up the ramp and into the ship's opulent interiors.

The maze of passageways was overwhelming. I tried to commit the lefts and rights we took to memory, but there were too many turns. My senses were awash with impressions—the dazzling glow of chandeliers, walls lined with polished wood panels, intricate carpets muffling our footsteps, and tapestries that spoke of unimaginable wealth. Upholstered armchairs and sturdy furniture anchored the ship's luxurious spaces. The mingling scents of disinfectants, cigarettes, and fresh linens tickled my nose.

Maids scurried to lay crisp white sheets in cabins, and British children roamed the corridors in sailor suits, squealing with delight at their new-found playgrounds. Behind them trailed their ayahs in colourful sarees, visibly tired yet dutiful. Memsahibs strutted past in broad-brimmed hats, fluttering lace fans against their flushed cheeks. British men, more plainly dressed in their predictable topis and beige suits, kept to themselves, but their polished shoes betrayed their affluence.

I found myself subconsciously categorising the passengers by social rank, a skill I was beginning to hone. Women's outfits, with their intricate trimmings and embellishments, spoke volumes about their status. The men, less imaginative in their attire, required closer inspection; the cut of their clothes and, especially, the quality of their footwear were more telling. This crowd, so poised and privileged, was a world apart from the bustling throngs we had left behind at the railway station.

The elite cabins were situated higher up than the economy quarters. I listened intently as Mr Scott shared fascinating details about the ship with Mrs Jones. The SS *Ranchi*, he explained, was named after the Indian town of Ranchi and initially designed to carry mail. It was built alongside three sister ships: *Ranpura*, *Rajputana*, and *Rawalpindi*. The names meant nothing to me, but Mr Scott spoke of them with pride.

Mrs Jones's cabin was stateroom #74 on Deck A, a first-class suite on the starboard side that, according to Mr Scott, made the oppressive Indian heat more tolerable on the voyage to England. I wouldn't have realised the disparity between first and third class if I hadn't stepped into her suite. It was an opulent 'house' within the ship, complete with a spacious sitting room, furnished with upholstered chairs and sofas, matching curtains draped over doors and windows, and walls adorned with an ivory sheen. A large painting of a ship hung prominently on the wall above the bed, adding to the room's grandeur. Sunlight poured in through three long windows, their lace curtains fluttering slightly.

The sitting room opened into a lavishly carpeted bedroom, its handwoven rugs soft underfoot. At the far end of the suite was an enormous bathroom with a gleaming white tub on golden legs, a full-length mirror with an ornate golden frame, and other fixtures that seemed more fitting for royalty than travel. But the crowning jewel of the suite was the view. Each room, including the bathroom, had windows offering an unobstructed view of the ocean. I wished they could open to let the salty breeze in, but even with them closed, the sight was breathtaking.

Leaving the Joneses to settle in, I was escorted by a kind staff member to my cabin in the economy section. Below the second-class deck, economy cabins were simpler, compact spaces often shared by four or five passengers with stacked berths. The lucky ones, like mine, had a small porthole providing a glimpse of the outside world. Despite its modesty, the cabin was tidy and comfortable.

The walls were bare, with neither panels nor curtains, and the floor was uncarpeted, but everything was spotlessly clean. My L-shaped cabin had two berths at the entrance and two along the far wall facing a large mirror. I had been assigned a lower berth on the longer side. The beds were neatly made, each with a thick blanket folded at the foot. Modest ventilation came through small vents from the upper decks, and the porthole brought in a sliver of light.

I stored my belongings under the berth and took a moment to explore the space. A sense of excitement bubbled within me. This cabin, simple as it was, marked the start of my adventure. I glanced at the passport Mrs Jones had arranged for me. The photograph inside was far from flattering, but the document itself was reassuring. It declared, in bold letters, that I was to be allowed to pass without hindrance and receive assistance wherever necessary. I resolved to keep it on me at all times, tucked safely away in an inner pocket I had sewn into my skirt. I skimmed through the details printed inside: the colour of my eyes and hair, and there it was, my name: Ms Asha Ayah.

I grimaced. That wasn't the name I had been given at birth. Yet, was it a complete description of me? Folding the passport shut, I tucked it away and looked around the cabin again.

A small card was propped up against the mirror. It read:

INSTRUCTIONS FOR ECONOMY CLASS PASSENGERS: SS RANCHI

A) All economy class passengers shall dine only at Dining Saloon B (near the bow).

B) Meal timings shall be as follows:

Breakfast: 8.30 a.m.

Coffee: 10 a.m.

Lunch: 12.30 p.m.

Teatime: 4 p.m.

Dinner: 7 p.m.

Late Snacks: 10 p.m.

C) Any complaints regarding the accommodation or incivility should be at once reported to the Purser or Chief Steward. For purposes of identification, each steward wears an unnumbered badge on the arm.

Inquiries regarding special meals and requests may be directed to the Chief of Kitchen Staff.

As I read through the card, I heard someone clearing his throat behind me.

"Hullo, miss."

I turned and straightened up. "Mr Scott! Is there something you need me for?"

"Nothing that Madam Jones has asked. I was just about to leave the ship, but thought I should offer you a word of advice," he said, stepping into the cabin. He cleared his throat again, looking a little uncomfortable but determined in his address to me.

"It's not easy being on a voyage this long. My advice is to be cautious as you would be in unfamiliar surroundings, but also try to make friends with the other ayahs and those you deal with daily. They'll offer you the support you need. Do be careful."

The ship's horn blew, a deep, powerful sound.

"They've blown the horn. Five minutes to departure. I'll take my leave now. Good luck to you," he concluded in a cheerier tone.

"Thank you, sir. You've been very kind," I said, feeling a small pang of sadness as he left.

Soon, I heard a series of loud horns. Our ship was leaving the Indian coast! I rushed to the porthole for a better view. Over the next several minutes, the coast slowly retreated, increasing the distance between the land and our ship. After an hour, Ballard Pier would be nothing more than a distant memory on the horizon, but I didn't linger for long—there was too much to discover. Curious about my fellow travellers in our all-women cabin, I scanned through the passenger chart. I was expecting two other occupants—Mrs Anthony Pareira and Mr Paanchkodi Sarkar. I reread the last name. That wasn't a woman!

Puzzled by the mystery of the oddly named male co-traveller, I freshened up and changed into a long pleated skirt and a puff-sleeved blouse. I looked at myself in the mirror. *That looks sophisticated and formal*, I thought. I added a belt, like I'd seen in the English magazines back home. I debated whether to wear the peacock-blue waistcoat I had secured through Mrs Barnes, but decided to reserve it for the colder days.

The first few times I navigated the corridors between our cabins, I had to be very careful following the signboards to Deck A, then searching for the right room. It was late afternoon by the time I reached. I knocked and entered, and Mrs Jones spun around, exclaiming, "Where on earth were you! I need to bathe and get dressed! Go get Joanna changed."

I hurried to Joanna's trunk, laid out her clothes, did her hair, and helped her with some tomato soup. I darkened the room and tucked Joanna into bed while Mrs Jones was in the bath. Afterwards, I helped her get dressed.

"You are well trained, I must say," she remarked as I braided her hair into a side plait.

"I've kept it loose. It's best to keep the braid loose if you're sleeping."

She nodded, applying cream to her arms and legs. The strong scent of oranges filled the air, and I held my breath to avoid a headache.

She narrowed her eyes and forced a smile.

"You can wait on the sofa outside until Joanna wakes up. The meal times for children are separate, so make sure you read the card by the mirror and memorise everything. Every evening, I'll have dinner and be out until half past eleven. You are to be with Joanna until then. Every morning, your duty begins at seven, when Joanna wakes. I expect you to fill the tub with warm water after you bathe Joanna, then help me get ready by half past eight after her breakfast. You can take her to the deck and the children's room before meals. But do not let Joanna out of your sight for a second. Ever." She fixed me with a strict look, ensuring the warning in her voice landed.

"You don't have to worry about Joanna. I'll stay by her side until you return after dinner."

"The trunks are outside. Set up the wardrobes quietly and instruct the cabin steward to bring tea and biscuits at 4.30 p.m. for me."

While unpacking Mrs Jones's trunk, I came across a framed picture of the family. In it, Mrs Jones stood beside a man who I assumed was Dr Jones, along with three boys, each appearing two or three years apart in age. I guessed Joanna, the fourth child, was born after this photograph was taken.

Dr Jones stood with his arms folded behind his back, positioned about a foot away from his wife, who looked younger and somewhat more innocent. The children were buck-toothed and gleeful, except for the eldest, who looked at the camera sullenly. I propped the picture on the study table before turning my attention to setting up the vanity.

As I worked, I committed the Children's Schedule to memory:

Children's Breakfast: 7.30 a.m.

Snacks and Milk: 10. a.m.

Children's Lunch: 12. p.m.

Soup: 3: PM to 4. p.m.

Children's Dinner: 6.30 p.m.

Snacks and milk for children shall be available all day with the cabin steward on request.

Satisfied that I had memorised the schedule, I moved on to arranging the perfume and cosmetic bottles neatly into the vanity drawer. When I was done, I made myself comfortable on the sofa outside the bedroom and waited for Joanna to wake up.

A light tapping at the door roused me at 4.30 p.m. I received a tray with tea and cookies for Mrs Jones and gently woke her and Joanna up by drawing back the curtains, a method commended to me by Charlotte as the most polite way for waking up someone. Joanna's eyes lit up when I proposed a stroll on the deck before dinner.

The front deck was bustling that evening, packed with passengers eager to witness the ship's first sunset. The sea breeze was refreshing. I clutched Joanna's hand tightly, steering her through the throng. She could glimpse only the sky above, which held little interest for her.

"Ash, can we sit somewhere?" she asked, tugging at my hand.

"Let's go somewhere quieter," I replied, leading her away from the crowded deck.

We found a more secluded spot along one of the ship's outer corridors. Though we couldn't see the sunset directly, it gave us a view of the ship's enormous breadth and the expanse of water trailing behind us. Standing at the midpoint of the ship, we marvelled at the vastness of the ocean and Joanna excitedly pointed out gulls and tiny boats in the distance.

"This is so beautiful, Ash! I'm going to tell Saru all about it," she exclaimed.

"Oh, you should! And you can call me Ashley. That's what my previous charge used to call me."

"Don't you like being called Ash?"

"Well, I don't fancy that it means burnt stuff in English!"

She snorted with laughter. "You're so funny."

"You let me know if you feel cold, okay?"

She nodded. In the golden light, her hair looked closer to blonde than brown. Her tiny teeth, with small gaps between them, reminded me she was still so young. She had no ear piercings, unlike most Indian girls her age.

"It's nice with you, Ashley," she said with a smile.

"Thank you," I replied, squeezing her hand gently. "I like you very much too, Joanna."

She glanced out at the horizon and asked, "Do you know where we're going?"

"I have an idea, yes."

"My mother says we're going to meet my brothers and get a proper education. Father may visit us sometimes. I only remember seeing him once."

I nodded, wondering how she was going to adapt to a life totally foreign to everything she had known so far.

"What about you? Did your father live with you, Ashley?"

"Yes, he did. I loved him very much."

Joanna waited a second before voicing her thought.

"I don't know if my brothers would like me."

"Why should you think that? I'm sure they love you."

"How can they love me when they don't even know me?"

"That's just how it is with family. They love you no matter what."

Joanna fell silent, contemplating the shimmering gold of the horizon.

"Well, Mother says I'm slow. I have to be sharp like my brothers, or no one will care for me."

I swallowed hard, searching for the right words. "Joanna, you must love yourself no matter what. And I'm sure everyone will be thrilled to see you."

"I don't know." she murmured, swinging back and forth and clutching the railing. "I've bothered Mum a lot. She says I've made her upset and unwell."

"Joanna," I said, my voice firm but kind, "for what it's worth, I think you're wonderful. Parents may get frustrated, but deep down, they never truly think their children are bad. Trust me."

She looked up at me, her expression caught between doubt and hope.

As we stood together in the fading light, I glanced at the horizon again. *Slow?* I thought incredulously. This child expressed her emotions better than my dumb friend Jitu ever could.

Too soon, it was time for Joanna's dinner. I read the signboards and asked uniformed personnel for directions to the first-class dining saloon. The dining area had several small tables, complete with white tablecloth and napkins, silverware and china. I spotted several nannies and saree-clad ayahs with their wards. They were quiet and looked slightly tense in these challenging environs, but each seemed to be in absolute control of their charge. The women moved with precision, their every action reflecting the expectations of the children's absent parents. They wiped sauce-stained mouths, encouraged reluctant bites of vegetables, and maintained a serene authority. I tried making eye contact with some of them, but most responded with wary, suspicious glances.

Joanna ate her dinner without fuss, her appetite undeterred by the stiff atmosphere. Afterwards, I escorted her back to the cabin, where the warm, enclosed space felt a poor substitute for the windy deck, now cloaked in a dazzling, starry night.

Mrs Jones was busy getting dressed as we entered. She greeted me with a sharp, curt remark: "Did I not instruct you to leave hot water in the tub for me?"

"I'm sorry, madam," I replied quickly, trying to stay composed. "I thought that was for mornings only. I'll keep it in mind."

"Well, it's for mornings *and* evenings. Now please, do my hair."

"Yes, madam."

As I reached for the brush, she glanced at me in the mirror. "Have you had dinner?"

"No, madam. Joanna was with me, and I didn't think it proper to take her to the lower-class dining area."

"Hmm ... Well, go now. But be quick. I expect you back in twenty minutes. We can't spare more time for your dinner tonight."

I was starving, hence any time was welcome. Feeling resentful, I scurried through the decks, barely noticing the now resplendent night skies. Even in a rush, I couldn't help but notice the design and aesthetics of the economy dining room. Whoever designed the place had been careful to make it presentable, but deliberately inferior to the upper-class dining hall. The walls had nothing but a single layer of fresh whitewash, the floors were neat but uncarpeted, the tables were set in long endless rows, more like a mess hall than anything. There was no buffet but a self-service counter. I was thankful that I got there early, before the halls were filled.

It was quite a sight to see so much food laid out so professionally. I had never been to restaurants—perhaps this is what they were like? I took some plain rice, dal and yogurt with potato fries. The other items were not vegetarian, so I didn't have to waste time browsing through choices.

Mindful of the time allotted to me, I put my head down and busily chewed my food as fast as I could, having yogurt to wash down each bite.

"What is life good for, if you can't eat in peace?" crowed a voice unexpectedly, shrill and mocking.

Startled and mildly annoyed, I looked up to see an odd old man sporting a boxy hat and an enormous grin. He settled across from me at the table comfortably, with a plate laden with generous helpings from the self-service counter. His smile stretched wide, reaching his glinting, spectacled eyes.

Oh, no. Here's a passenger expecting leisurely conversation, I thought to myself.

I avoided eye contact and kept chewing hurriedly. "I don't know you, sir."

"Does that matter? We're all stuck together for three weeks! Fellow jailbirds, my dear girl. Why not be sociable?"

"I'm afraid today I don't have the luxury of time to be sociable. Please excuse me," I said, shoving fries into my mouth as fast as I could, my mind racing with thoughts of Mrs Jones pacing her cabin in a temper.

"Paanchkodi Sarkar," he declared, ignoring my remarks entirely and raising a cheerful salaam. His toothy grin didn't waver.

The name rung a bell—a picture of the passenger chart flashed before my eyes. Could it be?

"You're ... Paanch ... kodi ...?" My voice stumbled over the name, half-muffled by food.

"That's my God-given name, yes! *Paanch*, five—not less, not more!" he replied enthusiastically, with a twinkle behind his glasses.

"Wh ...? Oh ... No, I'm sorry. I just read your name ... We share the same cabin, I believe," I said, swallowing the last morsel, my tone softening with amusement now rather than annoyance at his peculiar energy.

"Aha madam! Well met, well met! You're truly a fellow traveller in all ways then, madam!" he exclaimed, standing up with a respectful bow and a warm namaskar. "So pleased to meet you."

"Please don't get up, carry on," I said, returning the gesture with a hasty namaste. "I need to be on my way."

I rushed off, acutely aware of the few minutes I had left. I consigned the odd Mr Sarkar to a corner of my mind. This hurried, rushed dinner was not the way I had been raised. My father always insisted that meals were to be eaten consciously, with gratitude and peace. He would never let me gulp down my food and rush off to play with Jitu, yet here I was, running on a full stomach, barely acknowledging a polite attempt at a conversation—all at my employer's whim.

I barely made it back on time. Mrs Jones gave me a haughty look.

"Tomorrow onwards, take Joanna along. I don't mind her going to the economy canteen. Just do my hair before you leave for Joanna's dinner every day," she remarked before striding out without another word.

That would give me enough time to eat my meals properly, I thought with relief.

"Ash! I want to see the second-class canteen! We'll eat together!" Joanna squealed excitedly.

"Tomorrow we will!" I promised, winking at her. "We'll eat together and make friends!"

After a bit of lively chatter, I tucked Joanna into bed, promising her that I'd stay until her mother returned. Once she was settled, I perched on a chair beside her and browsed the small shelf of books in the cabin. My fingers paused on a title. It was *Black Beauty: The Autobiography of a Horse*.

Intrigued, I checked to see whether Joanna was fast asleep and then opened the book. It was a shortened, abridged version adorned with beautiful illustrations. As the story unfolded, I found myself growing sad for the horse. She was an animal with no choice or voice, striving to make the best of her life with each new master, forming and losing friendships as fate dictated. My mind began drawing uncomfortable parallels with my own life—a thought that only deepened my unease. Perhaps it was because I'd eaten in a rush, or because Mrs Jones grated on me, or maybe because I was simply homesick, burdened by the knowledge that there was no way to leave this assignment mid-voyage.

I set the book down and closed my eyes, letting the rhythmic sounds of the ship wash over me. Soon, I heard the door open and Mrs Jones walked in, a little unsteady. I could have stayed to help her, perhaps with undressing for bed or preparing her things for the night, but I couldn't summon the will. Without a word, I bowed and slipped out of the cabin.

Back in my shared cabin, everyone was asleep. Paanchkodi snored gently in the berth above mine. I quietly changed into my nightdress in the bathroom, then lied on my bunk. Unlike the lurching sway of a train, the ship's movements were almost imperceptible, a steady stillness that should have been reassuring. Through the small porthole, the stars glittered faintly, but from this angle, the world beyond was utterly dark.

Pulling the blanket over myself, I tried to will warmth into my chilled feet and hands. The soft strip of light seeping in through the cracks of the cabin door was comforting, as were the muffled footsteps and fleeting shadows of passing figures outside. Yet, beneath it all, a hollow feeling settled in my chest. I was floating on a vast, unknowable ocean, surrounded by strangers, and far from anyone who truly knew me. I felt like a speck of dust adrift in an endless void. A longing filled me—to be back home already, to my hills, to my house, to Jitu and the places my father had lived in.

Before self-pity could take over me, I shut my eyes firmly and thought about my father until I drifted to sleep.

8

I woke up earlier than anyone else in the cabin. The cabin was still dark and filled with the soft symphony of breathing. The porthole offered a stunning view of the horizon, now etched with a thin line of orange against the inky blackness of the sea. Careful not to disturb anyone, I tiptoed to the cabin's common bathroom.

After getting ready, I realised I had time to kill before waking up Joanna. As I stepped outside, the sea breeze greeted me, crisp and cool, rushing over my face and into my lungs, lifting my spirits.

The canteen drew me in with the possibility of an early breakfast. To my delight, the buffet was already set up with tea and biscuits. I decided I could linger over breakfast, savour the simple act of eating in peace, and steal a few moments to myself, unclaimed by anyone.

Settling into a corner table, I sipped tea and nibbled a biscuit. For the first time since leaving Simla, I felt genuinely at peace. Last night's reading still loomed in my thoughts. Was my life really like Black Beauty's? A series of masters, no real choices, just making do with whatever came my way? It wasn't a cheerful comparison. I never thought I'd be rethinking my choices like this, three days into a new job. The reality was stark: I couldn't walk away. The part payment for this job already bound me, and we were on a ship in the middle of nowhere. Joanna, sweet and lively, was the only bright side to this assignment. But even her charm couldn't entirely erase my longing for the easy camaraderie of Amanullah Khan or Hameera. My thoughts drifted naturally to memories of Lily, Poppy, and my old days with the Stagers—and then, inevitably, back to Joanna.

"Namaskar, namaskar! There you are!"

The sudden bellowing nearly made me upset my tea. I turned exasperatedly, half-dreading what I'd see, and there he was: Mr Paanchkodi Sarkar. His wide eyes sparkled through thick glasses, his eyebrows arched high above them, and a full grin stretched across his face.

"I hope, madam, I'm not disturbing you?" he said as he fumbled with his dhoti, attempting to untangle his legs while settling into the chair opposite me.

I sighed. "Good morning to you. I'm Asha."

"Lovely morning it is, Asha-ji! Just lovely! I was wondering," he began, his shrill voice taking on a note of diffidence, "if you'd want to exchange your berth with me? You see, my arthritis kills me climbing to that upper berth. Ordinarily, I'd sit cross-legged on this chair, but the arthritis—oh, the arthritis!"

He carried on, his hands gesturing animatedly, his tone a curious mix of complaint and cheer. It was as if a meddlesome spirit had descended upon my peaceful morning, determined to drag me out of my gloomy reverie. Despite myself, I couldn't help be buoyed by this strange companion and let myself be drawn into the conversation.

At least, I thought with a wry smile, *I'm not thinking about the horse any more!*

"I'm sorry, are you alright? Is the tea stale?" Paanchkodi Sarkar asked, hesitantly sniffing his cup.

"No, sir," I sighed, resigned to the inevitability of a conversation with this sociable and eccentric entity. "And I'm sorry about leaving in a hurry yesterday. As far as your berth is concerned, I don't mind."

"That's very, very kind of you. Thank you, Asha-ji," he said, manoeuvring prodigious amounts of food into his mouth with a practised ease.

"But until I return tonight, please don't move my things without asking me first!" I cautioned.

"I would never!" He touched both his ears, feigning a wounded expression.

For a moment, silence hung between us, and I could almost hear his brain churning out the next topic of conversation.

"Asha-ji? Do you know that I have travelled on this ship several times?"

"Why? I mean … how could I possibly know that?"

"I travel to England often. I am helping my nephew with his business. Electric fans."

"Is your nephew in England?"

"Of course not! He's in Calcutta, but he needs professional help and my diverse contacts," he replied, slurping tea from his saucer with relish.

I wasn't sure why I was asking, but the question came anyway. "And you have contacts with the goras?"

"We're an Indian company. We won't need the goras, except in the distribution networks!" he declared proudly. "My nephew's company will succeed. Consider it my crusade."

No doubt this adamant man could convince people to work with his nephew, perhaps some would give in just to be rid of him!

"But you do know—this ship itself is run by the goras," I ventured, posing a challenge.

"Hai? So what?" he grunted, continuing with renewed vigour. "The coal is ours, the metal is ours, and this food," he tapped the table, "is ours too. I would have preferred to travel via a Scindia ship if I could. There is a need for swadeshi options, Asha-ji," he said resolutely.

I didn't know what to make of that. Opting for silence, I ate the rest of my breakfast in peace. Every now and then, I glanced at Mr Sarkar, careful to avoid eye contact lest I invite more conversation.

When the clock struck 6.30 a.m.; I stood up. "I will have to take your leave, Sarkar sahib. I have work to do," I said, joining my hands in a polite namaste.

He stood as well, mirroring the gesture. "Please carry on, Asha-ji. You seem to be a very dedicated person."

Somehow, by the time I walked towards Mrs Jones's suite, I was in better spirits. I was no Black Beauty. Mrs Jones had hired me because I was the best for the role, not because I was powerless. I had chosen to be here. This wasn't just a job—it was an adventure too. Who from my village could claim the experience of being aboard a giant ship, travelling the world, and meeting people who had never even seen a mountain? I wouldn't let the peculiarities of my employer define this journey or weigh me down.

I got Joanna ready for breakfast and left hot water in the tub for the still-sleeping Mrs Jones. At the first-class entrance, I read out the menu board for Joanna. She settled on white bread with marmalade, grilled bacon, and cocoa. The dining room buzzed with activity, much like the previous day. Ayahs accompanied their exuberant young charges with an air of quiet diligence.

I again offered polite smiles to some of the ayahs, and this time, a few smiled back. Others, however, continued to eye my clothing with suspicion. I was dressed well but very unusually for an Indian ayah. No doubt they were unsure what to make of me. The sarees were clearly sooti, an airier and lighter fabric than the clothes women wore in our village. Didn't they feel cold in their sarees, I wondered? Even amongst these ayahs, the sarees varied significantly in drape, blouse design and sleeves lengths.

After breakfast, Joanna and I returned to help Mrs Jones dress. From behind the folding screen, she called out, "What took you so long?"

"Breakfast with Joanna, madam. But I won't let memsahib get late," I answered genially.

"I expected you to help me undress last night. Have you any idea how hard it was to change clothes in the dark, not knowing where all my belongings were?" she said rather softly.

I felt guilty. "I am sorry, madam. I did not realise. I'll begin today."

Helping her into her corset and a lilac gown, I suggested a more youthful hairstyle. Mrs Jones seemed surprisingly pleased when I finished, her reflection met with an approving nod. Joanna immediately demanded a similar style, and we spent the rest of the morning braiding her hair and mine.

Together, Joanna and I played with her dolls, snacked on fresh fruits, and walked the deck under the warm sun. She shared anecdotes from her time in Simla and narrated stories from Hindu mythology she'd learned from Saru. Her depth of knowledge impressed me, and also showed me why Mrs Jones must be keen on removing her to England. I wondered whether Saru had loved her just as I had loved Poppy and Lilly.

After Joanna's uneventful lunch in the first-class dining room, we went to the economy-class dining area for my meal. As I picked at my plate, I realised—with some surprise—that I was actually hoping to bump into Paanchkodi Sarkar again. His queer, infectious energy had started to become a source of unexpected amusement.

Almost as if conjured by my thoughts, he appeared, his entrance as abrupt as ever. "There is nothing in the world that can compete with *achaar*! Take my word and taste this, madam!" he exclaimed, placing a flaming orange jar on the table with a theatrical thud.

Joanna, who had been languidly picking vegetables from my plate, was startled and clutched at my arm tightly, her eyes wide with alarm. I couldn't help but laugh as I reached for the jar.

I overate like never before. Paanchkodi and Joanna seemed to bond effortlessly after a brief hesitation on her part. He had a knack for breaking through the reserve of others, and Joanna couldn't help but find him amusing. If there was one thing I craved after that heavy meal, it was the freedom to sleep. Thankfully, Mrs Jones was so pleased with her hairstyle that she didn't ask for a new one before lunch. Joanna and I slept through the afternoon, and at some point during the nap, she snuggled into my arms. That's how I found her when I woke up.

I felt content with the present. Things seemed to be falling into place, just as they had at the Stagers' house. Joanna was scheduled for a play date in the evening, and I would not be required. Mrs Jones, I gathered, treated these play dates as opportunities to socialise with passengers of influence.

Granted these rare unencumbered hours, I returned to my cabin. As I approached, I noticed a woman in a white skirt entering the compartment. Curious, I followed her inside. She nodded politely as she folded clothes.

"Mrs Pareira?" I ventured.

"You must be Asha?" she asked with a faint smile.

"Nice to meet you," I said, offering a smile of my own.

She nodded again. "You're an ayah too, aren't you?"

"Yes, ma'am," I replied.

She continued to work at tidying her berth, her eyes briefly scanning me. "Is this a free evening for you?" she asked, as though wondering how I had the luxury of small talk.

"It is."

"Well, then go and watch the evening games outside. The ship is huge, and there's so much to see. Who knows how many other free evenings you will have, if any? Make the most of it," she said, her tone encouraging.

She was correct, of course. "I'll do that," I replied, moving my belongings to the upper berth. "I am just helping the man who exchanged berths with me."

"Oh yes, the man from Calcutta. He asked me, but I couldn't accept. I can't climb berths," she said with quiet dignity.

"I think he understands."

"Where do you come from?" she asked, fastening the belts on her bag.

"Simla."

She nodded, quietly absorbing the information, before venturing some on herself.

"I hail from Kerala. I work as a travelling ayah," she said matter-of-factly.

"What is that?" I asked, intrigued.

"I accompany families travelling between India and England. It's a very sought-after job, you know." She smiled kindly, looking at me with tired eyes. "I've already been engaged for the next two journeys."

"That's brilliant," I said, surprised at this mode of work that I had never even imagined.

"So, how come you're travelling economy, as an ayah?" she asked, her tone tinged with curiosity.

"I'm told the servant cabins were full. My engagement was last-minute, so they managed economy tickets for me," I explained.

"I see. I always travel economy—a condition of my engagement."

What an odd way to work, I thought to myself, as I scurried away a few minutes later. Following Mrs Parceira's advice, I made my way to the deck where a badminton match was underway. The excited commotion drew me in, and I quickly saw why—it wasn't just the game captivating the crowd but the players themselves. Two lovely Englishwomen, dressed impeccably in sports attire, played a skilful game. Their spectacular hits and occasional misses earned loud cheers from the audience of sahibs. They were a little embarrassed by the attention they were gathering, and would lapse into bouts of red-eared laughter in between knocks when the cheering was particularly loud.

The game's energy was infectious, but as the noise grew, I decided to leave. Wandering further along the deck, I found a quiet spot to watch the sunset. The game eventually gave way to a song-and-dance party, but I stayed rooted, the distant sounds of merriment a backdrop to the deepening hues of the sky.

The sunset felt soothing, almost intimate, as though it was meant just for me. I closed my eyes, letting the balmy wind caress my face like the comforting touch of a loved one. Thoughts of Bombay, of Simla, drifted through my mind. Everything I had left behind seemed impossibly distant, not just in space but also in time. I was already looking forward to my return.

In the days that followed, I found myself making friends among the other ayahs. The European nannies, engaged by affluent families, were impressed by my spoken English and the ease with which Joanna connected with me. The Indian ayahs, initially wary, warmed to me over time. This transformation was undoubtedly helped by the credibility lent to me by the subtle endorsement of Mrs Anthony Pareira, who commanded an authority over the Indian ayahs as a mission-educated and preferred "Madrasi ayah". The Indian ayahs aboard the SS *Ranchi* hailed mostly from southern and eastern India, none from the mountains of the north.

However, my work hours in the coming week left little time for conversation with fellow ayahs or Paanchkodi. Mrs Jones's schedule grew increasingly demanding, especially with the ship's dance nights. These evenings meant I had to gulp down my dinner and rush to help her get ready for the festivities. After she left for the party, I would indulge in my nightly ritual of reading Joanna to sleep.

We set aside *Black Beauty* and delved into lighter stories I discovered in the ship's reading and writing rooms. These opulent spaces, adorned with heavy wood panelling, ornate curtains, ornamental lamps, and the occasional stag mount, were rarely crowded and provided a haven for us. I carried my passport and Joanna along to avoid being stopped at the entrance. The library's collection was modest but charming. Joanna particularly loved *The Milly-Molly-Mandy Storybook*. She would study the map of Milly-Molly-Mandy's village after every story and even try drawing her own map to navigate the ship's corridors.

Our walks on the deck became more pleasant as the weather grew colder, driving most passengers indoors. Joanna and I, however, made it a point to catch the sun whenever it appeared on the horizon, savouring the brisk air and the quieter decks.

Among the interesting people we came across was Abdulla Attari, the ship's serang. He was a man with a towering build, a stony face, and a habit of speaking in a few and well-chosen words. His weather-worn face betrayed no age easily, but by his immense strength and the fact that he mentioned grown children, I placed him in his forties. He donned an intricately embroidered knee-length cotton tunic or *"lalchi"*, which along with the golden boatswain's call that hung around his neck, set him apart. Abdulla was a figure of authority, leading a crew of about sixty men who worked the machinations of the ship, many of whom he had personally recruited from his village.

But he cared the most about his cook or *bhandary*, the man in charge of cooking for the crew. The bhandary as master of kitchen was a person of special importance. "Your bhandary must know you and care for you, bachche. Otherwise, how can he prepare these incredible feasts? Could he command his vast team to deliver flawless meals every day, on time and without imperfection, if he did not care?" he mused, tightening the knot of the *rumal* around his waist. "Armies cannot march on empty stomachs. Parties cannot happen on empty stomachs. Never forget that."

A little taken aback by this unexpected fount of passion, I scrambled for a response and managed an insipid, "Well, yes, bhaisaab, the food on the ship is great. Do your men eat the same food as everyone else?" Joanna, bouncing on her toes behind me, delighted herself by repeating random words from our conversation.

Abdulla shuddered dramatically, shaking his head with an exaggerated flourish. "No, bachche! Not in a thousand years! We're village men. We cannot eat what the Goans cook!" He gestured towards the ship's towering funnel, as if it carried the proof of his disdain. "Pork! Beef! Cooked in the same room! My *khalasi*s would revolt this very moment. We need the Goans in the crew to handle those meats," he declared solemnly, pausing for effect. Then, with a glint of mischief, he added, "If you want to taste real food, you're welcome to join us."

Real food. His words sparked a wave of longing in me—memories of jhangora kheer, its creamy sweetness lingering on my tongue, and the pooris and raitas I used to share with my father. That evening, the food seemed particularly unappetizing. I stared at my plate of white rice and curd, its sharp, sour smell doing nothing to entice me. As a vegetarian, my options on board were limited to these meagre choices at lunch and dinner. I usually filled up on fruits and bread at breakfast and tea, but it was far from satisfying.

Mrs Anthony Pareira, who was sharing the table, quickly noticed my disenchantment and leaned in kindly. "If you decide to try non-vegetarian food, you'd be happier on a ship. As the days go by, the supply of fresh fruits and vegetables will dwindle, and you'll be left with grains and meat as your only options. The faster you adapt, the better."

Her advice made sense, but my mind resisted the idea of eating meat. It wasn't something I could reconcile with easily. Mrs Wilson, an elderly English nanny, was the only other person on board whom I noticed avoiding meat, but I could hardly hope for counsel from her as she steadfastly refused to take any notice of me.

Days began to blend together. If I hadn't been checking the date at breakfast every morning, I might have completely lost track of time. Yet, amidst this monotony, I found a sense of belonging. I had formed a loosely knit group of friends—not close ones but enough to stave off isolation. Each morning, as I gazed at the endless ocean through the porthole, gratitude filled my heart—for companionship, for the quiet mercy Mrs Jones was showing by allowing me more time for dinner.

Mrs Jones had recently announced that she no longer needed me to braid her hair every evening. Instead, she tasked me with embroidering the hems of eight of her day gowns with tulips and gladiolas from a pattern book titled *Needlework for All*. I didn't mind. In fact, I felt a quiet joy and the needlework became a form of meditation.

I would sometimes overhear passengers speaking of the infamous seasickness awaiting us at the Bay of Biscay or recounting the many attempts to construct the Suez Canal.

These stories came from varied sources—perhaps the charming first officer warning an eager circle of ladies, or Abdulla Attari, or the lascars sharing their wisdom in low, authoritative tones. The thought of being violently tossed about on turbulent waves was unsettling. I silently hoped our ship would remain a lucky one.

My conversations with Abdulla Attari grew more frequent as the days passed. He would wave at me from a distance whenever I appeared on deck, his stony face breaking into a rare grin. There was a mutual respect in our exchanges, a comfortable equality. He spoke to me openly, free of expectations, and I found myself looking forward to our interactions. Despite his packed schedule, I managed to coax him into revealing some of the ship's hidden workings and stories of the route we were traversing.

We had sailed from Bombay towards the Gulf of Aden, passing the mysterious Socotra Islands. One evening, as the sun dipped below the horizon, Attari gestured towards a faint, flickering light in the distance. "That's the lighthouse on Socotra," he said, his voice tinged with reverence. He launched into the story of the ill-fated SS *Aden*, a P&O ship that had been lost on these treacherous waters during a voyage from Yokohama to London. The ship had struck against the rocks near Socotra's coast, claiming seventy-eight lives. Thanks to the heroic efforts of the Indian marine steamer *Mayo*, forty-six survivors were rescued. "An oil painting of the SS *Aden* now hangs in the officer's wardroom," he added, his tone proud and warm.

But it was his description of Socotra itself that captivated me the most. "That island," he said with the air of a storyteller, "is unlike any other place on Earth. For years, it was cut off from the world. The plants and animals there—bizarre! Trees with fleshy trunks that bleed like humans, and long, curly hair-like leaves swaying in the wind!" I didn't believe a word but it made for a lovely tale nevertheless.

Using a worn and weathered map, Attari traced the route we were taking across Perim Harbour, a gateway to the bustling port of Aden, a fuelling point for ships. We were crossing the Red Sea and advancing towards the iconic Suez Canal. His voice grew animated as he spoke of its global significance. "This canal changed everything—global trade, the fortunes of nations. The Egyptians may own it on paper, but it's the English and French gora sahibs who run the show," he added. This is where, he told me, it would start getting cooler as we would be moving towards England.

Of everything I had heard about the voyage, the part I eagerly anticipated most was the stop at Cairo. The pamphlets in the reading room promised a world of wonders—pyramids rising like ancient sentinels from the sands, monuments to a civilisation so distant that it almost felt mythical. The idea of seeing these marvels in person enchanted me endlessly.

I wasn't sure if I'd have the chance to explore Cairo as the other passengers, but the mere possibility was enough to spark my imagination. Every time I spoke with Attari, I would press him for details about what lay ahead. He would chuckle at my wide-eyed curiosity, his stony demeanour softening ever so slightly. "Patience, bachche," he'd say, amused by my relentless questions.

Attari rarely spoke about anything personal, except that he missed his children. His company was warm and he was a popular leader amongst his ragtag crew of lascars. If I caught him during a quiet moment of rest in the evening, he would hurriedly remove the beedi and invite me to sit beside him.

"We live this life, because it's the only one we know. The sea, bachche, is equally hard on the merry and on the miserable. So we live this life with cheer and joy," he admitted one evening, his eyes fixed on the horizon. "But we aren't fooled. We know that these gora sahibs hire us because we're cheap. They pay us a pittance to do the hardest work."

I listened intently. Back in Simla, I had never given much thought to the lives of men like him. These men stayed away from their loved ones at sea for months together working at a job that was sometimes risky and always immensely physically taxing. They strained and toiled to keep things running, and formed a kinship amongst them that I don't think could be matched, except perhaps amongst the outstation sipahis I sometimes saw in my village. They were their own family on the ship.

I felt a sense of solidarity with them, as I too had no family and was quite literally and figuratively at sea in my own life. I cherished my evenings with all these people. Had it not been for this assignment, I might never have experienced this kaleidoscope of different perspectives and untold stories of life. For all its uncertainties, the sea had brought me a strange kind of belonging

9

The ship buzzed with excitement the morning we were set to steer into the Suez Canal. The breakfast hall brimmed with early risers eager for the day's spectacle. Joanna and I positioned ourselves towards the stern to avoid the crush of passengers at the bow. Mrs Jones and her circle had managed prime spots there, craning their necks for the best view. Though I couldn't see the entrance of the canal as clearly, I had no complaints. The surreal beauty we beheld from where we stood was more than enough.

The vast Red Sea seemed to narrow into a pathway, as if guiding us into another world. After days of endless water, sandy earth stretched along both sides of the canal, a stark and mesmerising contrast. A small crowd had gathered ashore, waving enthusiastically. We waved back with equal vigour. It felt unreal—the sight of land after so many days no matter how other-worldly the unending sea had then looked.

"That's Egypt!" Mrs Pareira exclaimed beside me, enjoying our excitement. "A place of great history, unlike anything you've seen." My mind was already inflamed with images cultivated in the ship's reading room—settlements rising amid barren deserts, cities blooming unexpectedly from the sands, the pharaohs, and the Sphinx!

As we neared the bustling Port Said, the scene transformed. Buildings loomed ahead, some adorned with giant commercial signs that declared their presence boldly. A red cursive sign reading "Bata" caught my eye. Smaller structures with flat and sloping roofs clustered nearby, likely to be homes or shops. Gasps and chatter rippled through the passengers as they drank in the sight.

We were about to dock at Port Said. To my disappointment, I was informed that while Mrs Jones had planned a day excursion to the pyramids in Cairo followed by a lunch at the popular Shepherd's Hotel, she did not plan to take Joanna along. I was crestfallen that we would both be confined to the ship, but thankfully Joanna had other plans. She pleaded with Mrs Jones until, at last, permission was granted for her to join a group of kindly elderly passengers on a simpler excursion. Among them was the affable Mrs Anderson, an old acquaintance of Mrs Jones. Naturally, as Joanna's ayah, I was expected to accompany her—under the strict instructions to stay with the group and never leave the taxi behind. Since the deal sounded too good to be true, we were only too happy to accept these boundaries.

As we waited for our companions at the jetty, Joanna skipped on the firm ground, laughing gleefully. "This feels so solid!" she declared, and I grinned back at her, taken aback by the sensation of being on land once again after days of being at sea. Other children, along with their nannies and parents, roamed nearby. The sun blazed overhead, but unlike others who fretted over the heat, I felt invigorated. The warmth of the sun seemed to seep into my very being, and Joanna and I ran across the jetty, laughing and carefree.

I saw some of the natives and locals at a distance beyond the jetty gate, and drank in their appearances and attire of light-coloured gowns and turbans. Why, they could pass as Indians from warmer climes! I was quite relieved to see them smiling at the passengers.

We stumbled upon a small crowd of children from the ship gathered around a performer. Pushing through, we found the man at the centre—stout and theatrically dressed, with a flat-topped red fez on his head. "Look! The Gully Gully Man!" someone exclaimed. Before I could puzzle over the strange name, the man burst into theatrical laughter, and the balls he was juggling suddenly turned into live chicks. Joanna squealed with delight.

The show ended quickly, and his assistants passed through the crowd collecting coins. I smiled ruefully, having none to offer. As the crowd dispersed, Mrs Anderson emerged, her tall figure striding confidently towards us. She clasped Joanna's hand.

"Come along, little one! Your mother has entrusted you to me. Be a good girl and do as I say, alright?" she said, guiding Joanna towards the waiting taxis.

I followed dutifully, but as we reached the taxi, Mrs Anderson paused and turned to me.

"We won't be needing you, dear. Run along and wait here for us in the evening."

Her words stunned me.

"I'm sorry, madam?"

"Amelia didn't mention anyone but her daughter. She'll be perfectly fine with us."

I took a deep breath, steadying myself. No, this could not stand. It wasn't about seeing Cairo, it was about Joanna. She was my charge, and she needed me. Moreover, I didn't trust this woman. I caught the flicker of panic in Joanna's eyes, and at that moment, it became clear that brown and Indian as I was, I was more family to her than any of these people who looked like her could be.

"Madam," I said firmly, "my assignment in clear words is to never leave Joanna out of sight except in the company of her mother. These are my instructions, and they cannot be broken. If she goes, I'll go too." I added another "madam" to soften the defiance.

She studied me for a moment, her gaze sharp but not unkind. Then her face softened into a smile. "Very well then, come along."

Joanna beamed, her relief as palpable as mine, and I followed them to the taxi. Mrs Anderson seemed to relish the adventure of being out and about in Cairo, and after the initial friction she didn't take any special notice of me and chatted away genially as if I was just another child in the group.

The taxi bounced and swerved through Cairo's narrow lanes, and I couldn't help grinning as the city unfolded before me—a dizzying array of colours, sounds, and scents. When Mrs Anderson instructed the driver to stop at a bustling bazaar, I hesitated and timidly repeated Mrs Jones's strict instructions to remain in the taxi. Mrs Anderson laughed, dismissing my concerns with a wave of her hand. "Oh, don't be such a worryguts! Girls, you're in Egypt—the oldest civilisation in the world! Don't tell me you're not going to see it for yourselves!"

Joanna looked at me with pleading eyes. I weighed Mrs Anderson's words, quickly calculating the hierarchy of instructions. Gleefully, I concluded—surely this was a permissible breach!

The bazaar was a riot of life and activity. Shopkeepers shouted over one another to advertise their wares—vibrant fabrics, gleaming trinkets, fragrant spices, and sweets. Groups of burqa-clad women moved through the lanes, their chatter mingling with the cacophony of street vendors. The heat blazed against the back of my neck. After the monotonous schedule on the ship, this chaos was intoxicating.

Mrs Anderson stopped us in front of a shop with a large sign that read "Kodak Cameras & Films: Films Developed in Two Hours!" She ushered us inside with an air of excitement.

"We must get a picture!" she declared.

"Why would we get a picture? My mother isn't around," said Joanna.

Mrs Anderson chuckled. "It's for my memory, dear, not everyone has to be in it. When I'm bedridden someday, I'll flip through my albums and remember this little trip—and you!"

I smiled. She had grown on me. "I hope you're never confined to bed, madam, and that you keep travelling like this."

Her laughter was hearty. "Thank you, my dear! If it weren't for this wretched knee, we would have taken pictures at the pyramids. Never mind, though. Mr Photographer here can bring the pyramids to us!"

The young photographer unfurled a massive backdrop depicting the pyramids of Giza and the Great Sphinx. It looked magnificent, though a little absurd. We stood together—Mrs Anderson in the centre, Joanna on her right, and me on her left. The flash momentarily blinded us, and the memory was immortalised.

Afterward, she treated us to creamy kunafas and bought a carton of cigarettes in various makes for herself. "No trip to Egypt is complete without a ferry ride across the Nile!" she announced, her enthusiasm contagious.

The taxi took us to the docks. Our journey from Port Said across the city had brought us close now to Port Fouad, where Mrs Anderson purchased ticket for a ferry excursion from Port Fouad back to Port said. The ferry was nothing like I'd imagined. It was more of a floating platform with railings on all sides, carrying people, goods, and even vehicles. The distance between the ports was only a few kilometres and made for a soothing ride, the Nile's gentle breeze invigorating our spirits. The city unfolded in layers—a mix of towering mosques, bustling markets, and quiet corners where grumpy camels chewed cud. Children waved energetically at passing ferries, their laughter echoing across the water.

Mrs Anderson seemed utterly content, her sharp gaze softening as she took in the sights. We could soon see Port Said in the offing.

"Do you know what Kipling said about Port Said?" she asked suddenly.

"Who's Kipling?" Joanna asked, curious.

"He's a popular English writer," I answered instinctively.

Mrs Anderson raised an eyebrow in approval. "Indeed. Kipling said, 'If you truly wish to find someone you have known and who travels, there are two points on the globe you have but to sit and wait, sooner or later your man will come there: the docks of London and Port Said.'

Joanna frowned. "But *you* haven't found anybody yet."

I elbowed her gently, embarrassed, but Mrs Anderson crouched to Joanna's level, her expression mock-serious. "Perhaps then this Kipling fellow is an idiot!" she said, breaking into a delighted cackle.

As the dusk approached, and after our ferry ride, we wandered a while longer through the streets near Port Said, unwilling to let the day end. We passed by a perfume shop, where a sturdy-faced artisan was crafting perfume bottles, creating delicate wonders. Joanna was transfixed by a set of Nubian dolls and lingered with her nose pressed against the shop window. Mrs Anderson indulged her fascination, purchasing a couple of dolls along with perfumes and a box of syrupy baklava. As the sun dipped lower, our driver led us to a small, local eatery for an early dinner.

The other elderly passengers from our group were already there, gathered at a long table the shopkeeper had fashioned by joining several smaller ones. They animatedly shared tales of their own adventures, and I noticed they were all married couples, except for Mrs Anderson.

Dinner was a grand affair, unlike anything I had experienced since leaving Simla. The restaurant buzzed with energy, the clinking of cutlery and the murmur of conversation blending with the soft strains of music playing in the bazaar. Cheerful and brisk waiters weaved expertly through the large, open-air eatery, their trays laden with steaming dishes. I watched, wide-eyed, as an array of unfamiliar foods was laid before me, and tried to follow the names of the dishes which Mrs Anderson narrated cheerfully.

A rich, earthy aroma arose from the spiced fava beans in a bowl of *"ful medames"*, its deep brown surface glistening with olive oil. Beside it sat a platter of fragrant rice drenched in a sauce and topped with some sort of meat. Golden pyramids of crisp falafel, and soft rounds of freshly baked flatbread—*"aish baladi"*—were piled high in baskets. The sight of all this unknown food was overwhelming. Sensing my hesitation, Mrs Anderson leaned over with a knowing smile. "Only vegetarian for the young lady," she instructed the waiters, who nodded and swiftly adjusted their service. I exhaled in quiet relief.

The waiters placed a simple plate of plain rice and fava beans, falafel and aish baladi bread before me, and I hesitated before taking a bite of the steaming rice mixed with the silky, spiced fava beans. To my surprise, it was utterly delicious— and dare I say, not too different from the rajma chawal that had been a staple for me back home! Encouraged, I tried the falafel, which reminded me of pakodas from Thandi Sadak vendors. I was indifferent to the aish baladi, which reminded me of rotis. The warmth of the dishes spread through me, and I found myself savouring the food slowly, letting the flavours settle on my tongue.

The evening unfolded like a dream, one I will never forget. The golden light of dusk bathed the bustling streets outside. In a while, local entertainers from the bazaar took to the centre of the restaurant, spinning and dancing to hypnotic, lilting music. Crowds from outside thronged to watch, their cheers mingling with ours. The warmth of shared food and laughter blurred the lines segregating our group and for a while, there were no whites or browns, no hierarchies or unspoken rules.

For the first time, I realised the peculiar magic of travel, of mutual and shared displacement. Around that table, the 'superior whites' were simply fellow travellers, as far from home as I was. Ladies who had avoided my gaze earlier now smiled warmly, and a gentleman even passed me a plate with a quiet nod. Joanna and I were as much a part of the table and conversation as Mrs Anderson was. I hugged Joanna, pulling her closer to myself, and we tried to sing along to rhythms, making up gibberish words and laughing at our own efforts.

My mouth full of fava beans and pita, I looked around and found a pair of spectacled eyes and a toothy smile directed at me—of course it was my old friend Paanchkodi Sarkar waving at me! Joanna waved back at him enthusiastically before I could. He gestured for us to carry on, already deep in conversation with a group of locals. Seeing him reminded me of home, but it was more than that—it was a reminder of the strength that resilience and adaptability could lend to people like us. Sarkar, with his frayed dhoti and boundless curiosity, seemed as much at ease in Cairo as he had been back on the ship. I grinned at him fondly, realising that the irritating old man embodied a kind of self-assuredness that I aspired to, a confidence that transcended geography, culture, and even status. Perhaps the world was not as intimidating as it appeared to be, and with enough of Paanchkodi's bizarre ease and confidence, even the most foreign of places could become a kind of home.

When we finally left, the night in Cairo was still alive—lanterns casting warm, flickering light over the marketplace. We retrieved our photographs from the shop and returned to the ship, loath to leave behind the bustling marketplace where the night was still young.

After returning from her own excursion, Mrs Jones had gone straight to bed, and Joanna, exhausted but content, soon followed suit. There was no need for words between us—we both knew we'd shared a day that would remain etched in memory. As I sank into bed, I silently thanked the many forces that had conspired to make it possible.

All of us rose late the next day, the hum of the ship softer as it glided through the Suez Canal. The crew had swapped their crisp white uniforms for sturdy blue ones, a subtle signal of our journey's progress. Mrs Pareira, unusually chirpy, greeted me as I shuffled groggily to the deck.

"We're mostly through now, Asha. This voyage didn't feel so long, did it?" she said, her smile bright against the morning haze. "But I should warn you about the Bay of Biscay. It gets rough here, so best not to eat too much over the next couple of days."

"How bad is it, Mrs Pareira? Is it today?" I asked, my voice betraying my nervousness.

"Not today, but some start feeling queasy early. The turbulence can make the ship's movements very perceptible. A few hours of that can unsettle even the sturdiest stomachs. Some passengers deboard at Marseilles and travel by land to London to avoid it entirely."

As our destination loomed closer, Mrs Jones's spirits seemed to sink. She no longer fussed over dressing up in the evenings or asked me to style her hair. One evening, as she watched me embroider in the fading light, she remarked almost wistfully, "You're a deft hand, Asha. If I'd known earlier, I'd have given you my finer gowns to mend. You'd do well in England, you know—an English-speaking servant for the price of an Indian ayah, who's also a seamstress? They'd be lining up for you!"

"Madam," I said carefully, steering the conversation away, "I hear the sea will be rough in the coming days. I've been advised to eat less, and I think it would be wise to do the same with Joanna."

She pursed her lips at my deliberate evasion, her eyes narrowing slightly, but all she said was a low, non-committal "Hmm". I went back to my cabin after Joanna and Mrs Jones fell asleep. I noticed Mrs Anthony Pareira sipping a beverage in the canteen and stopped by to say hello. It was unusual to catch her resting.

"Taking it slow today, Asha," she said in between sips.

"Yes. Are you going to be leaving soon?"

She smiled back and replied, "Soon, at Southampton. Today was a leave day for me."

We both looked around not knowing what to say. With the cold breeze sweeping the canteen from the deck, wistfulness gripped the air. We weren't close, but then again, doesn't travel bond strangers in unique ways? It was probably the inevitable feeling of nostalgia that comes when things come to an end.

"Mrs Pareira, if you don't mind ... How do you do what you do?"

"Work for the whites?"

"No ... I meant, how do you keep travelling all the time? Finish one journey, start another—doesn't it get to you at some point?"

She smiled. "You've spent a few days here, haven't you? Are you the same person who left Simla a month ago?"

I pondered her question and looked at the shimmering, silver sea.

"Your horizons have broadened in ways you don't even know. I began this work to earn money. But I now do this out of choice. These ships feel like home to me. I can go as far as to say that I find it exciting when there's a new ship, a new family, new children ... There is very little scope for monotony. Even if I go back to Kochi, I'll be quite the outcast.

A woman who has travelled overseas, spent so much time without a chaperone, unsupervised, alone on these vessels full of lascars and foreigners … Why pain myself and my family? I send them some money when I can and they seem to be happy. And … no household chores!" she concluded, laughing.

I laughed too. I would have felt sad for her, but I couldn't. Here was a woman living the life she had chosen. If anything, it was inspiring. I would never know all the stories she would live.

Joanna and I spent much of the last few days in bed, reading, as the ship's motion grew increasingly erratic. The day before our voyage was to end, Joanna succumbed to a nap in the afternoon while I began unpacking some of Mrs Jones's warmer clothes. She was nowhere to be found, and I assumed she was socialising, making the most of the final days on the ship. The thought of stepping foot in a new country filled me with growing excitement. Perhaps I'd even have a couple of days to explore before heading back to Bombay.

Mrs Jones returned early, looking drained. The Bay of Biscay had taken its toll; the constant rocking of the ship left her vomiting through the evening. I did whatever little I could to help. She was irritable and I didn't want to bother her but a curiosity about the following day gnawed at me. I knew so little of our schedule.

"Erm … memsahib?"

"Hmmm?" she murmured from her bed, her voice distant.

"What's the schedule like tomorrow?"

She replied tersely, clearly not in the mood for questions. "As usual. Come at seven. I'll tell you then."

I hesitated before pressing on, "Er … What time do we get there?"

Her eyes didn't meet mine as she replied snappily, sounding little irritable. "I'm not the tourist information office! Ask someone else for all that. I'll see you tomorrow at seven."

I bit my lip and forced a polite smile. "Goodnight, memsahib. Hope you feel better soon."

I returned to my cabin just in time to find Mrs Pareira and Paanchkodi sitting together, speaking in low tones.

"Asha-ji! Come, join us for our goodbyes," called Paanchkodi, rising from his seat with a grin. Mrs Pareira smiled warmly. "We're both deboarding at Southampton tomorrow morning,"

"Ah, I see," I replied, my heart suddenly heavy. "I'll say my goodbyes then. This feels too happy a moment to be saying farewell now."

"It will be too early for you," Mrs Pareira remarked. "You're headed to Tilbury, aren't you?"

"I suppose … my instructions are not to disturb them before seven in the morning," I said, unsure.

"That means you will all deboard at Tilbury later," Paanchkodi mused thoughtfully.

"I hope you find the right people for your nephew's company," I said to him. It was hard to pack my sentiments into words. "It was a pleasure knowing you, Sarkar-ji."

Paanchkodi looked at me, his smile warm. "You're a remarkable young woman. At such a tender age, you've become so independent."

I joined my hands and bowed.

"How long will you stay in England?" asked Mrs Pareira.

"I'm not sure yet—my return ticket hasn't been booked. I suppose I shouldn't make any plans until then," I answered. "What about you, Mrs Pareira? What are your plans?"

"I'll stay in Southampton for a few days to help the children adjust to their new nanny. After that, I've got a return ticket booked for about a month from now."

"I can't imagine setting foot on another ship just yet, meeting entirely new people all over again," I said. "Though I've been busy throughout this journey, I'll remember all of you fondly."

Paanchkodi took off his glasses, gazing at them thoughtfully. After a long moment, he looked up, his voice carrying the weight of many years of travel. "I've journeyed far and wide, but this last night on each voyage always brings a sense of dread. Strangers become dear, like family. You both have been remarkable companions, and I'm glad to have met you."

The words we exchanged finally brought it to me. We were parting, us strangers who had shared a few moments were now about to return to our separate paths, with no expectation of seeing one another again. The heaviness of the moment lingered until Mrs Pareira, with a quiet grace, bowed her head, folded her hands, and began to pray. "Let us thank God for showing us this path, and pray that we may carry out His work in our lives."

We all followed her lead, hands clasped in silent prayer. As we lay in our beds, I could almost feel the unspoken thoughts of my companions. I dozed off and was woken up at around half past three at night by the sound of luggage being dragged out to the door. I couldn't resist exchanging brief goodbyes, my heart sinking. I went back to bed feeling terribly lonely, thinking of their faces and felt tears wet my pillow. I had to let go of everything familiar again. As I lay on my berth, feeling the ship's movement, an uneasy feeling crept in the pit of my stomach that I just couldn't dispel.

I tried to pray, but peace evaded me, and I felt feverish, bothered. Nothing seemed to feel right, and I tossed and turned restlessly.

Soon, it was 5 a.m. and I woke up, preparing myself to face the final few hours of this voyage. I needed to see the world from the deck one last time. With the empty cabin at my disposal, I dressed up freely and took time to do my hair. As soon as I stepped out, I was glad of the fur coat. Shivering, I walked across the now nearly empty ship. With the crowds decimated, it felt like an altogether different place, quite empty and alien. I felt ill at ease, suddenly forlorn and anxious. The serang's men had just completed scrubbing the upper deck. With clenched jaws, I walked against the gusts, determined to take in these last sights. The water of the English Channel shimmered in shades of blue and green, framed by the blinding white cliffs that glowed in the early sunlight.

I sought refuge in the canteen, grabbing a few cookies and tea, and sat down alone on the deck to eat. The solitude felt heavier than it should have. *Thankfully, the voyage back home is not too far into the future*, I thought. I was hopeful of making new friends on the way back, though I was sure I would not meet anybody quite like Paanchkodi Sarkar and that I'd miss little Joanna, with whom I felt so attached.

I spotted our cabin steward at a distance and walked up to him to inquire about the time of arrival. He seemed to be carrying a bag of bed linen to the laundry.

He spotted me and stopped short, a puzzled look on his face. "You're the ayah for cabin 74, aren't you?"

"Yes, Amelia Jones and Joanna Jones," I smiled.

"But they've left."

Something turned in my stomach. "What do you mean, left? You must be mistaken. I am to report to the cabin at 7 a.m., they deboard at Tilbury."

"No, you're mistaken. I was the one who took their luggage out at Southampton. Wasn't it the lady with the sleeping child? She even gave me a tip." He showed me some currency.

All of a sudden, a blind panic surged inside my heart. I tried to push it down, but I had no sensation in my limbs. It was a surprise to see my own hands clutching hard at the freezing railing. I couldn't breathe.

"Are you alright, girl? I don't know what to say ..." His voice barely reached me through the ringing in my ears.

I didn't hear him. I ran, stumbling towards cabin 74, my heart pounding, my vision blurry. The purser followed, calling my name, but it was as if I were submerged in a dream, disconnected from the world around me. I threw open the cabin door. Inside, the sitting room was clean, the bed a disarray of sheets, the books I had read to Joanna scattered across the floor. The dressing table was empty, the white towels used and tossed carelessly. My mind refused to process it. This couldn't be real. This couldn't be happening.

The purser was saying something to calm me down. I rushed inside the bathroom, as if I would find Joanna there. But there was nothing. I dropped to the floor, gasping for breath, my chest heaving. Despair overtook me, and I dropped to the floor, trying to find my breath. I turned to the purser, trying to focus on his face through the rush of hot tears, trying to gasp out my agony to him between panicked sobs.

"But I'm from India ... they had my return ticket ... they had my payment ... I don't know anyone ... What do I do!"

The purser looked at me, distressed at my hysterics.

I sobbed, feeling darkness dance around the corner of my sight. What do I do? What do I do?

10

21 June 2000
Marlow, Buckinghamshire

The clock ticked loudly, each tick marking seconds of silence between us.

"I do not remember much of the next few hours," said Asha.

Rashmi gulped.

Asha stared out of the window. It was dusk. She continued in a quiet voice, "It's a bit of a blur. But I remember I collapsed on the ground and couldn't get up for a while. I couldn't wrap my head around what had happened and what was to come. The enormity of that moment was too much for me, and certainly shattered any illusions I had harboured in the past few weeks of having become a seasoned woman of the world."

"I was abandoned in a faraway land with no money or a return ticket. With Attari away at the Southampton port, I knew absolutely nobody on the ship and was made to deboard when we arrived at Tilbury. The purser offered me a cup of hot tea and held my hand until we reached Tilbury. Kindness, dear, from strangers."

Rashmi shook off the impact of the story and brought herself to speak. "That's awful. I cannot imagine how hard it must have been for you, just a sixteen-year-old girl."

Asha said nothing. She got up and switched on the lights. Rashmi poured herself a glass of water on the counter and sipped from it, watching her hostess.

Asha shrugged, and turned back to Rashmi, with half a smile on her face. "It was the worst day of my life, Ms Rao. Not because of what happened. But because that day, I couldn't bring myself to hope that anything good could ever happen to me again. I stood at the docks, watching everything—goods, mail, luggage, food—being unloaded from the SS *Ranchi*. It felt like nothing belonged on that ship any more. It was done with us. It had become a stranger all too sudden. I tried to find some familiarity in the gaunt portholes. I thought, maybe, if I stared hard enough, I could rewind the days and return to the life I knew, to my country, my past.

"But it was cold, and the weather changed as suddenly as my life had. First, a drizzle and then the downpour. I sat on my metal trunk outside the port office, shivering from head to toe. I didn't even know where Tilbury was on a map. I had no family, no one to call for help. We were all strangers there, surrounded by unfamiliar faces."

Rashmi's voice was gentle but insistent. "What did you do?"

"For a while, Ms Rao... I just cried, like a little girl." Asha got up and reached the refrigerator. "Do you mind frozen food, dear?"

The idea of food was entirely foreign and unimaginable at that moment. "Oh, no, thank you. It's got dark, I should probably go. I don't want to impose."

"It's no trouble. But I understand if you want to get home before it gets very late. I must not be so remiss in the future, and feed you better. Shall I call you a cab?"

The ride back felt unusually short to Rashmi, her thoughts swirling and tossing like a storm at sea. She stared out of the window, watching the rain run streaks down the cold glass, her mind replaying Asha's words and the memory of a sobbing girl—cold and rain-soaked at the docks. How could have Asha managed?

At home, Rashmi's cousins had just returned from their evening outing, carrying bags of snacks and souvenirs, their laughter ringing in the air. They gathered in the living room, sharing stories from their outing and complaining about her being held up with work. Rashmi nodded and smiled but her thoughts were miles away, until Karthik, her youngest cousin and a first-year medical student, noticed her silence.

"What's wrong, akka? You've been quiet since you came in."

Rashmi hesitated, then decided to share. She recounted Asha's story in brief, her words halting and heavy. Karthik listened intently but tilted his head when she was done.

"It's sad, akka, no doubt," he said thoughtfully, "but wasn't it a long time ago? The woman seems to have done well for herself. Why does the story shock you so much now?"

Rashmi opened her mouth to reply but stopped. How could she explain? It was already hard to put into words the starkness of her tale, the quiet despair of a young girl abandoned in a foreign land. Karthik's world was one of textbooks, classrooms, and endless possibilities. Her other cousins, now animatedly debating their favourite snacks, were similarly unfazed.

For the first time, Rashmi felt the powerlessness of words to truly convey her feelings. She managed a small smile and nodded, letting the topic slide away into the hum of their animated conversation. But as her cousins returned to merrier subjects, she leaned back in her chair, still silently turning over Asha's story in her mind. It stayed with her, lodged deep within, like a splinter under her skin.

The next morning, over breakfast, Rashmi's father glanced at her curiously over a cup of coffee. "You've been keeping very busy with that assignment of yours," he remarked. "Barely saw you yesterday. Do you see anything in it?"

Rashmi considered the question for a moment, her fork hovering over her plate. Her mind was cleared of last night's emotions and only a quiet resolve remained, sharp and focused: those voices deserved to be heard.

"I do," she said simply. Her father gazed at her curiously, waiting for more.

"It's a story I have to tell, though it's not going to be easy. But I feel if I really want to be a good journalist, I can't ignore this."

Her father nodded, his tone measured. "Then don't. If it's worth telling, give it your all. I'll wait to read it."

Rashmi didn't say anything more, but smiled at her father as she picked up her cup of tea. She knew she was ready.

On her way to Asha's for her final day of the interview, she stopped at a florist. She handed over the flowers as Asha ushered her in with a warm smile and a plate of freshly baked cookies.

"I thought you'd like some with chocolate today," Asha said cheerfully. Her eyes lit up when she noticed the tulips. "Oh! Flowers! Thank you, dear. But why the white ones?"

"Don't you like them?" Rashmi asked, hesitating.

"Of course, I do. But I know they weren't the first thing you saw at the florist's," Asha teased with a knowing smile.

"It's because I'm sorry for yesterday. You had to relive all of that again for a petty interview."

Asha reached out and squeezed Rashmi's arm gently. "You're very thoughtful, dear. But don't worry yourself about it. Now let's have brunch before we talk again. I made a roast today—didn't want to feed you a freezer meal."

And the meal was exquisite—roast chicken with perfectly caramelised vegetables, followed by a dessert of meringue and fresh berries. They chatted lightly about the weather, the neighbourhood, Rashmi's work, and how much India had changed.

Afterwards, as they sat with cups of tea in hand, Asha settled into her armchair with a measured calm.

"Do you feel you can go on, Asha? I'd love to hear what happened next, if it's okay with you," Rashmi ventured.

"Oh please, Ms Rao. Of course, it's okay with me." Asha's voice had a bit of an edge to it. "Don't make the mistake of taking my life for a sad story. Do you think I wished for things to be different? Why would I?"

"Not even for Jitu? To have stayed back?" Rashmi asked cautiously.

"This isn't a movie, Ms Rao," Asha replied, her tone tender again. "Remember, I had to take that journey to earn my living. And don't forget—I got to see places I'd never dreamt of going to. I was a sixteen-year-old with a head full of stories. I wanted the extraordinary. I wanted that day in Cairo. I didn't want to linger in my old life and become irrelevant for my friend. Is that what you dreamed of at sixteen?"

Rashmi stayed silent, evaluating Asha's words.

"People haven't changed, dear. Whether in my time or yours, some things remain the same. I longed for safety, family, and familiarity, yes—but I also wanted to break free, to live beyond the boundaries set for me. I regret nothing."

Rashmi nodded slowly, and braced herself with a deep breath. "So tell me, Asha. How did you fight back? What happened next?"

11

The weight of my situation sunk in gradually, as I huddled on my trunk, unsure of what to do next. By midday, word had spread to the dock office, and an officer came to check on me. He held his hat to his chest, his green sweater worn and frayed. I stood, leaning against the pillar, one arm wrapped around it, as though its solidity might somehow anchor me.

The officer said something I didn't understand.

"What?" I asked, uncertain.

"Ah, so you do speak English. That's a relief." He let out a short, awkward laugh before continuing, his tone softer. "I'm sorry about what happened. People inside have been talking about it. Sadly, it's not the first time. Have you had anything to eat?"

I couldn't believe how casually he mentioned something so devastating having happened before.

"I'm not hungry."

"I understand," he said, "but you'll need to keep yourself going. Do you know anyone here? Anyone whose address you have?"

"I don't," I admitted. Then I added, "But you work here. Can't you find out where my employer lives? And get my ticket from her?"

He shook his head with a rueful smile. "I'd bet my last shirt that there *is* no ticket. And I'm no king, lass, just a clerk. I can't do much from this desk, but I may not be entirely useless to you either. Think hard—anyone you know, anyone you could contact? Goods and mail go all over England. We could get you on one of the transports."

A sick feeling churned in my stomach. Fear of getting further lost in this vast, unfamiliar land gripped me.

"Can't you put me on a ship back home?"

"Well, I could," he replied. "Do you have money for a ticket?"

"I have no money—just a few rupees for the journey from Bombay to Simla."

He sighed, shaking his head. "Then you'd better think hard, miss," he said before turning and disappearing inside.

A while later, he sent out a plate of food—mashed potatoes, peas, and a slice of some kind of meat. I ate everything but the meat. Never before had I touched anything that had been near meat, but today I didn't know where my next meal would come from. Hunger silenced my hesitations.

The day dragged on as I sat on my metal trunk in the verandah of the dock office. The air was heavy with the clinging humidity of an earlier, unexpected shower. My thoughts drifted. I thought of home—my village, the cool shade beneath the trees where I would lie with father, and of Mrs Stager. How happy I had been in her household. I gazed out at the vast, unbroken expanse of water before me.

No matter how hard I looked, my country lay far beyond its reach. A tear slipped down my cheek.

Bitterness surged inside me as I thought of Mrs Jones. Had Joanna protested? Had anyone at Southampton noticed Mrs Jones leaving without me? My mind ran through the days we had spent together, searching for signs I might have missed.

I thought of the train journey. The English lady's probing questions about servants in India. The train cook, Nooruddin Ansari's hesitation, his cryptic advice ... had he not mentioned an India Office in London?

The thought was electric. I dashed inside, abandoning my trunk in the verandah. My heart pounded as I searched every room, my eyes darting over unfamiliar faces until I spotted the clerk who had shown me kindness. Without hesitation, I hurried to his table, aware of the curious stares from others around.

"May I speak to you?" I asked, my voice trembling. Please, God, let this work.

He looked up, startled by my urgency, then gestured towards a chair.

Perching on its edge, I leaned forward, clutching the table with both hands. "Please," I said, my words tumbling out. "Can you arrange for someone to take me to India House in London?"

The clerk frowned, muttering to himself. "India House? Is there such a place?"

A quick inquiry confirmed its existence—a place at Aldwych, London. As some sense of relief surged through me, I silently offered my humble gratitude to Nooruddin. The clerk in the shabby sweater spoke to someone there and learned that I should be instead sent to a place called the Ayah Home. It was a sanctuary for stranded women like me, they said—a refuge.

"There's really such a place?" I asked, incredulous. "Does this happen so often that they had to create a home for us?" The thought that so many women endured this plight shook me deeply. What kind of world was this, where betrayal was so common it required a shelter for the abandoned?

The clerk arranged for me to travel on an open mail truck, armed with a set of instructions and a letter addressed to someone in charge. Fear surged within me, sharp and unrelenting. The sea was the closest connection I had to home and it would now disappear behind me as I sunk deeper into an alien land. I was at the mercy of foreigners in their own country, with only my halting English and a letter commending me to unknown protectors. Dread clawed at my guts, but I breathed deeply, clutching on to prayers until I steadied myself enough to climb aboard.

As I settled in the back of the truck, the clerk pushed my trunk beside me and said, "I've given the driver clear instructions. He's a decent chap—nothing to worry about. And you've got company for the journey."

He gestured towards a thin, brown-skinned boy about my age. Dressed in a pullover and loose trousers, the boy waved farewell to a group of men who looked like lascars.

"Who is he?" I asked.

"Kasim. A good lad. He's heading to London too—found work there, I think."

"What's your name?"

He chuckled lightly. "You can call me Alfred. I should have asked yours earlier."

"Asha," I said, forcing a smile despite the dry, stretched skin of my tear-worn cheeks protesting against the cold.

Alfred returned my smile warmly, lifting a hand in farewell. I watched him as the truck pulled away. Though I would never see him again, his image lingered. More than a young clerk in a shabby sweater, he was a beacon of kindness to me, a man with a golden heart who extended a hand when I was on the verge of collapse.

The boy called Kasim leaned over the gate of the truck, waving merrily to the crowd of his people, who cheered for him in what sounded like Hindi. I swiftly wrapped my scarf around my head and neck, and draped my fur coat over myself. I caught Kasim eyeing me with quiet curiosity.

"You've ... clothes," he said, his words reaching me faintly over the growl of the engine. I nodded, not trusting my voice above the noise.

He held out some bread to me. "Want some?"

"No, thank you," I called back, clutching my fur coat tighter around me, the ache in my stomach growing.

After a moment, Kasim walked over and squatted near my trunk. His eyes scanned the surroundings before he pointed to a spot against the driver's pod. "The wind doesn't hit too hard here," he said, his voice casual. We both settled there, and he again offered me the loaf of bread. This time, I accepted a small chunk.

"I heard about your day. Tough luck," he said, biting into the bread, his mouth full as he chewed noisily.

I said nothing. His words offered no comfort, and he sounded indifferent. He continued, "I'm heading to London now ... I have a great job waiting for me! Kitchen helper at a fine Indian restaurant. My luck is turning! No more pushing boxes at the miserable old dock for peanuts. I love to cook, and soon, I'll be making good money as a chef. I can feel it," he said with a faraway smile.

I looked at him dully, the distant hope in his eyes doing little to stir any feeling in me. "How did this happen for you?"

"My father's a sailor. I wanted to be one too, but the last few years have changed my opinion about living my life at sea. Same dirty lascars who never take a bath, toiling all day in the sun. The ghastly songs, the vile drinks at the shore, and every day, the same food cooked by the same bhandary. What a life. The dock was no better. At least there I had a place to sleep, and I begged every Hindustani I knew to get me a better job. See where that's got me?"

His voice trailed off for a moment, as though lost in his own thoughts. But then he brightened again, "I've been told it's doubly hard for brown-skinned people here, but I know there are those who survive. If they can, why can't I? Hindustanis don't break easy," he added, a smile creeping back on to his face.

I managed a small smile in return, feeling unexpectedly lighter, and asked, "So, where is this place you're going to work?"

"It's a curry place, as the goras call it," Kasim said with a shrug. "Hindustani food—the Brits are fascinated by it. So, some of us should get richer, right? Though I should tell you, Hindustanis don't run the place."

"Really?" I replied. "I'm from India, but I barely cook Indian food. My work has trained me to cook like the Brits," I said, quickly adopting the expression.

"If you stick around in London long enough, you could visit me. It's a place called Veeraswamy, on Regent Street."

I could never remember that name, no matter how many times he said it. And visit him in London? The thought first frightened me, then made me angry.

"I'm not going to visit you in London," I said sharply. "I'm not going to be in London for long. I'll find someone who can help, and then I'll get on a ship and go back to Simla."

"I hope so too," he smiled.

I turned away, embarrassed at my unkindness. Truth be told, I wasn't even sure I'd make it back to Simla if I reached Bombay. I shoved the thought away, desperate to keep panic at bay.

Kasim cleared his throat, as though hesitant, and asked, "If you don't mind me asking … Where are you headed?"

"Somewhere called Ayah Home," I said, not really knowing what it meant. We rode silently, enduring the cold wind, and listening to the low rumble of the truck's engine. It's not easy to speak when the chill runs through your bones.

The drive wasn't long, but by the time we reached Regent Street, the darkness had settled in. "That's me," Kasim said, pointing to a building complex nearby. He hopped out of the truck, waving to the driver first, then to me.

Alone again, I clutched the sides of the truck, bracing myself as it swerved through narrow alleys. I marvelled at the complexity of the city. An intricate web of streets and passageways, where ornamental buildings stood side by side with shabby slums. Giant chimneys belched out thick smoke, towering bridges arched overhead, and colossal stations rose up like monuments. Everything was new, unfamiliar. The words on the billboards meant nothing to me, the routes were all unknown, and the people seemed like strangers from another world.

The driver dropped me off at The Triangle, giving me instructions that I hurriedly memorised, panic creeping up my spine. Repeating the name over and over to myself so I wouldn't forget, I walked down King Edward's Road, my trunk dragging noisily along the cobbled alley.

After what felt like an eternity, I spotted the right building ahead. The number 4 was clearly marked, and the sign on the door read:

LONDON CITY MISSION
AYAH HOME

I hesitated, my eyes tracing the cold, metal gate, and then knocked my chilled knuckles against the door. No answer. I knocked harder, this time feeling the sting as my knuckles reddened. Then, there was a clank of a latch, and I jumped back instinctively.

A plump, severe-looking woman peered out. "Yes?" she asked, curt and suspicious.

"I need help," I said, hesitatingly.

She craned her neck to glance over my trunk, then gave me a quick, appraising look before opening the door wider to let me in. I followed her through a narrow, dark corridor, handing her the letter from the dock office clerk. She muttered something under her breath as she led me, eventually sitting at a desk. From her gown pocket, she pulled out a pair of glasses, peering through them at the letter.

"Hmm …" she muttered, shaking her head. "Ahema… awful. God knows we need help to stay afloat with what we have…" she trailed off before turning to me. Her expression softened slightly, though still business-like. "Please sit down, dear," she gestured towards a long oval dining table.

"English? How much?" she asked, each word slow and deliberate.

"I can speak enough to talk to you, ma'am," I replied, trying to steady my voice, despite the flutter of nerves.

She heaved a sigh of relief and poured me sort of flavoured warm water.

"You can call me Mrs Upton. I am sorry for what happened to you, child." She paused, regarding me with a kind of gruff sympathy. I was still cold, still shocked, but the warmth of the house, quiet and enclosed, seemed to steady my nerves. It meant a lot to sit there gripping a warm cup, in the presence of the matron of what could be a harbour, just when hours ago, life had seemed without direction.

"Unfortunately, we're running at more than full capacity, so I do not know how we will manage. You are able to understand my English?"

"I have nowhere to go if you turn me away," I said, my voice tight as I fought back the flood of tears threatening to spill over.

She leaned forward slightly, her hand stretching across the table towards me. "There, there, no need for all that. I did not say you'll be turned away. We will find a way. We always do."

I felt bad for her, but in truth, I felt worse for myself.

She gave me what was meant to be a reassuring half-smile before standing up. "Let me consult the others."

I rose, assuming I should follow, but she turned back to me, her voice firm. "Be seated, dear. Finish your tea and get warm. I'll return soon."

I couldn't stand being alone and waiting for this mysterious tribunal to pass a judgement on my fate. I slipped out of the room, quietly trailing her footsteps down the corridor. I reached an open door where I could hear the murmurs of a whispered conversation and, unable to resist, looked in.

Mrs Upton was conferring with another woman, thinner, more worn out, and dressed similarly. The letter lay open between them, and they gestured at it occasionally as they spoke in hushed, urgent voices. They sounded worried.

I could sense their sympathy, but I wasn't sure if they would actually help. I prayed fervently, feeling ashamed for turning to God now, after neglecting Him on the ship when I had been caught up in excitement at the new world around me. That time felt like another person's life, a life I had borrowed, but now I had to leave behind. This moment felt far more real, as I stood hoping for mercy in a strange house in a strange city, with no one who knew me or cared for me. So I prayed, desperately grasping for comfort.

Mrs Upton suddenly turned to me, her decision seemingly made. She had clearly been aware of my presence at the door, but the conversation had been too urgent to address me sooner. "It's alright, girl. We've decided how to accommodate you. It may just have to be a bit of a stretch to make things work, that's all. We can't turn anyone away. In a couple of months, perhaps, beds will open up. Until then, all I can offer is my extra mattress on the floor." I stared at her, incredulous, making sure I hadn't misunderstood. "That's the best I can do for now," she added.

I mouthed a quiet thank you.

"Praise only the Lord, dear. Now, let's get you settled in."

I followed Mrs Upton through the dark, curious house that had suddenly become the most important place in the world to me. I tried to memorise the corridors and details as she explained the basic routines of the home. She told me that dinner time had long passed, so I would have to eat alone in the dining hall. A plate of bread, some soup, and a glass of hot milk were laid out for me. There were no lights, so she gave me a candle and left me to my own devices. No one saw me sob through my dinner in the dark, this time out of relief. I felt too ashamed to even thank God. I was getting a meal, undeservedly, at the mercy of a stranger. And it was also because of a stranger that I landed up in such a state—or perhaps, it was owing to my hunger for novel experiences and better wages, or simply a desire to fill the void of routine after my time at the Stagers'. Had I been arrogant? I forced the meal down, hoping to find a place to hide and cry alone, undisturbed. It seemed the other occupants were already in bed.

Mrs Travers, the concerned-looking matron with whom Mrs Upton had conferred, handed me a register to sign and asked me to deposit my passport. She explained that all residents entered their names when taken into the home as lodgers. Adjusting the candlelight, I scanned the pages. The list seemed endless. I spotted a few distinctly Indian names among many more exotic or indecipherable ones, most written in the same tidy hand, perhaps Mrs Travers's. I wondered how so many women, many of whom perhaps couldn't read or write English, had managed to find their way here after being abandoned. What if some of them never found it at all? What became of them? The thought sent a shiver down my spine.

The shock and exhaustion of the day were beginning to weigh on me. After finishing the meal and signing in, I dragged my heavy trunk up the narrow staircase, following

Mrs Travers through a long corridor lined with rooms. At the far end of the corridor, she led me into a small, bare room dimly lit by two flickering candles.

Inside, Mrs Upton was crouched on the floor, struggling to stretch the corners of a sheet over a thin mattress. The room was stark and unwelcoming, clearly intended for storage rather than living. A single bed was pushed against one wall, while the only other furniture consisted of a small table beside it and an open shelf, its wooden planks bare.

Humble though it was, the mattress felt like a gift. I settled on to it for the night, noticing the pot of coal glowing faintly beneath Mrs Upton's bed, its warmth spreading unevenly through the room. The simple relief of lying down on a mattress overwhelmed me. I don't recall when sleep finally claimed me that first night at the Ayah Home, but I vaguely remember Mrs Upton quietly watching to ensure I wasn't crying.

Morning arrived with the peculiar disorientation of waking up in a strange place. Mrs Upton came for me early, leading me through the shadowed corridors. Despite the daylight outside, the house remained eerily dim.

The dining hall started buzzing soon as women began to filter in, some cheerful and vibrant, and others like me, more subdued, carrying silence as though it were a protective veil. A few Indian women recognised me as a countrywoman, and offered kind, fleeting smiles. Others, neither Indian nor white, were figure of intrigue. Their features belonged to lands I couldn't match to any half-remembered geography lessons. Not one appeared younger than me.

The women found seats around the oval table, some spilling over to a smaller table tucked into a corner. Each table was presided over by one of the matrons. Mrs Upton stood at the head of the main table.

"Good morning, everyone. We have a new resident with us." She gestured towards me. "This is Asha, from Simla city, India. Let us make her feel at home here until she finds a new one."

I looked around, forcing a smile, though a fresh wave of unease rippled through me. The mention of a new home reopened a worry that had gnawed at me since the day before. I didn't need a new home. I had one, far away in my own country. I needed a way back to it.

The matrons began their prayers, the ayahs seated quietly around them. Some joined in, their murmurs blending with the matrons'. I bowed my head, though the words felt distant and foreign. A phrase caught my ear—about God being the father of the fatherless—but my thoughts drifted away almost immediately. I resolved to speak to Mrs Upton after breakfast. It was imperative she understood: I wasn't here to take shelter indefinitely or burden her or this home. I just needed a ticket back.

As soon as the meal ended, I found Mrs Upton in her office, the same small room where I had signed the register.

"Ma'am, may I speak with you?" I asked, standing hesitantly at the doorway.

"Yes, dear," she replied briskly. "Come in, please, and have a seat. I hope the others have been kind to you? I must introduce you to Alice and Rangamma from Kerala. There are a few more from India, though I can't recall all their names just now. Some of them barely speak English or even each other's' languages."

I interrupted her, mid-sentence. "Madam…"

Mrs Upton stopped short, a flicker of surprise crossing her face. "Oh, I'm sorry, dear. Do go on."

"I … I don't intend to stay here for long," I said, my voice firmer than I expected. "I want to return to India at the earliest opportunity. I need your help finding a way to get home, where people are waiting for me. Until that happens, I don't want to make myself comfortable." I hesitated before adding, "Please don't think I don't appreciate the kindness you've shown me … but I don't want to make friends, if you'll pardon me."

She studied me quietly, her focus sharp. I faltered, unsure if I should say more, but something in her expression encouraged me to continue.

"In the meantime," I said carefully, "if there's anything I can do to make myself useful here, I'll gladly do it. I understand how noble the work of this home is."

Her face softened and she sighed. "I should have explained things better to you last night."

I watched as she rearranged a few papers on her desk, sipped from a glass of water, and sighed again before continuing.

"Do you know why this place was established, dear?" she began, her tone measured. "This home exists because there were far too many women like you, women from all corners of the empire, finding themselves stranded in this land with no way to return. They were taken in by unscrupulous employers who discarded them once the contract, to their mind, was discharged. Some were deceived or coerced by agents, or simply never understood the terms of their journeys.

"Each of these women is a deep wound to the collective conscience of the English. It would be immoral, unforgivable, to let them fall into destitution, work as factory labour, or worse. Each of these women is as scared and lost as you are. Each of them is as desperate to get back home, some even more because they lack the ability to even give tongue to their fears and sorrow in a language that any of us will understand. But the truth is …" she hesitated, her voice tightening with restrained emotion, "the home itself operates on limited resources. Donations, while generous, are inconsistent. We cannot offer every woman exactly what she hopes for. This is not a place of luxury, Ms Asha—it is a place of compromise."

I nodded, urging her silently to go on.

"There are two paths we can offer," she continued. "We can send an ayah back to her country with a family travelling there who wishes to employ her. But there are few families who would take on a new nanny for a long ship journey, and fewer still who would be going where the ayah needs them to go. Or we can find work for the ayah here, with a family in need of a nanny. The latter allows her to support herself and the home, and also gives her the chance to save enough to eventually purchase a ticket back. These are the realities we face."

I listened intently, weighing the stark options she presented.

"While deciding whom to send first with a family in need of an ayah, we cannot be arbitrary. We consider who arrived first. Residents cannot stay here indefinitely—we simply don't have the resources. But you, my dear, you're young, you speak English well, and you've already served a couple of families. That makes you employable, whether with a local family or one travelling back to India, whichever opportunity comes first."

I silently processed the unfamiliar future mapped out for me. I could now understand the dilapidated look of the house and the utterly simple attire of the matrons themselves.

Mrs Upton leaned forward, her expression softening. "Listen carefully, my dear girl. You do not have the luxury of specific choices. If a local family expresses interest in hiring you, we'll ensure they have good references before recommending you for the position. Your ability to speak English gives you an advantage, but you must understand—this home cannot support you for months while you wait for the possibility of a family travelling to India. Even if such an opportunity arises, others who have been here longer will be given priority."

Her words carried a gentle but unyielding finality, a reminder of the limits imposed by their strained generosity.

"Shouldn't the others be employed before me too?" I asked quietly.

"They could, if the local family likes them," Mrs Upton responded. "As I said, they must know some English and be accustomed to the demands of an English household. A local family would require a longer commitment, and we usually allow them to choose from among the ayahs. It also depends on how much they're willing to pay. Those who pay more often expect the choice. And this home needs that money to continue supporting more girls and women like you. God forbid another one knocks at our door tonight—I would need the funds to buy more bread and find her a warm place to sleep."

I felt disappointment, sharpened by a faint, inexplicable sense of betrayal rise within me. Tears welled up, blurring the dim room around me into a shapeless haze. "So my life is for sale now ..." I whispered, covering my face with trembling hands.

Mrs Upton shifted uncomfortably, her composure faltering for a moment. She moved to sit beside me, gently patting my back. But the dam within me had already burst.

"I'm done for," I sobbed, my words tumbling out like broken shards.

"There, there—" she started, but I cut her off.

"I could have been free if I'd just slept on the docks …" I wailed, the thought both irrational and painfully raw.

She straightened abruptly, her voice now edged with sternness. "That is enough!" she said, her tone final. "This is where I draw the line. We cannot force you to work if you don't want to. You are free to leave this home and sleep on the streets if you so choose, with no consequence to us. But if you wish to stay here, there is a system in place to ensure respectable living conditions, and you will do well to obey it."

I sniffled, wiping my tears with the back of my hand. "There has to be some way I could go home, Mrs Upton," I said, my voice cracking. "I could help the home make money, I can knit and embroider beautifully. I can cook English food. I … I just don't want to be stranded."

Mrs Upton softened again, sitting beside me once more. "You are only stranded, dear, if you insist on thinking of yourself that way. Both the options I've outlined can lead you to *a* home. And if you end up with a local family, you'll have an even broader set of choices. You'll earn money, and with that, you can decide to do whatever you wish."

Even through the pounding in my head, I had to admit that Mrs Upton made sense. *That's all it is—a change of perspective,* I tried telling myself.

"And as for knitting and embroidery," she added gently, "we do that here every day, child. If you're good at it, you'll be helping us sustain the home and make it stronger. So God bless you."

I thanked her quietly and left the office, her words swirling in my mind.

Outside, I lingered in the corridor, peeking into the hall. The other ayahs were bent over embroidery booklets, their hands deftly guiding needles through fabric. Mrs Travers moved among them, her sharp eyes scanning their work as she circled both tables.

I dashed to my room and rifled through my belongings, gathering all the embroidery magazines I had—some from Simla, others gifted by Mrs Jones. Holding the precious bundle close, I hurried back to the hall.

At the threshold, I paused, acutely aware of all the eyes lifting from their work to study me. My heart fluttered, but I straightened my shoulders and held the magazines aloft.

Mrs Travers turned towards me, her gaze inquisitive. "Yes, dear?"

"I ... I have a collection of embroidery magazines," I said. "If anyone would like to use them ... And may I join a table too?"

The room was silent for a moment. Then, a few of the women smiled. A chair scraped softly against the floor as someone shifted to make room.

They had made space for me.

12

I did not feel like a stranger for long once I immersed myself in needlework. It gave me a sense of achievement and direction, anchoring me on days when idleness would have been a cruel companion. More than that, it became a bridge to the other ayahs, many of whom shared no language with me except the silent rhythm of thread through fabric. Over the weeks, I worked alongside this patchwork of women—the jetsam of the empire—and found their companionship unexpectedly warm and comforting.

Rangamma was initially shy, but grew talkative as the days went by. She insisted on wearing a saree and always had her beautiful golden earrings on. She had been told her ticket would be handed over soon, but never heard from her employers again. Alice spoke little English, and had not understood that her ticket was only one way. Kalyani was an elderly ayah from Kochi whose employers were dissatisfied with her services and never purchased her return ticket. Ah Tai was an elderly *amah-chieh* from Mei Foo in Hong Kong.

She barely spoke and kept mostly to herself, so I couldn't ascertain what brought her to England. Putri from Magalang, Philippines was only a few years older than me. She was quieter than the other younger ayahs, but her kind smile and obvious pleasure at being part of the group endeared her to all of us.

Few were any good at embroidery. I took it upon myself to train them, starting with simple designs to foster confidence. I was surprised by the elderly ayahs, whose eyesight I thought wouldn't leave them with much skill. Ah Tai revealed immense ability with extremely fine and detailed oriental patterns, and seemed pleased at stunning me and the rest of the girls. After an hour or so of exertion, she would slow down the pace and rest, sometimes nodding off over her embroidery. Kalyani could stitch, but seemed to prefer just watching, preoccupied in her own thoughts. She barely ever smiled. All the discarded clothes collected from nearby charities were used for practice. Some women were enthusiastic about needlework, while others opted for kitchen duties and cleaning. I was more than happy to be a part of the embroidery group. I knew that it was a remunerative industry for the home, and held hope that if I were instrumental in earning the home money, they would be reluctant in surrendering me to a local family.

Since the winter months had passed, I was told that it was time to work on designs for summer dresses. The Ayah Home would sell embroidered dresses during summers and knitted sweaters and balaclavas during winters. Together with Mrs Travers, we pored over magazines to understand trends, and prepared elaborate charcoal drawings. She would run the designs by her contacts outside the home and return with suggestions on the colour of threads and materials to be used. Those of us deemed skilled with the needle were tasked with bringing these designs to life. Overnight, we would embroider the approved patterns on to a handful of sample garments. These prototypes were presented to a charity that sold clothes to raise funds, and once they passed inspection, we replicated the designs en masse. The culmination of our efforts was the spring and summer fundraising sale in late April.

It felt important and gave us a mission. It wasn't work just to keep us busy—we were part of an effort, we had targets to meet and goals to achieve together. We felt empowered, after a long period of feeling powerless and lost. I emerged as a bit of a star in the group and it built my confidence greatly to see my designs being pored over, discussed, approved, and replicated. Mrs Upton and Mrs Travers, firm but fair, extended kindness without compromising discipline, and the other ayahs seemed to like me and didn't mind being helped and guided through work. Two of the ayahs were absorbed by local families in the coming few weeks. With some more space available, I was shifted to a bedroom. The matrons assigned rooms by nationality, hoping shared roots might nurture familiarity and ease the pangs of loneliness. I found myself sharing a room with two other ayahs from India, and with Putri, who had attached herself to our group.

Some mornings began on a different note. The matrons would instruct us to "clean ourselves up" particularly well, and would bustle around the house, tidying up and putting their work records in order. These were the days when the supervisors from London City Mission would visit for their inspection. The ayahs were always curious to see the inspectors, mostly solemn, elderly men dressed in suits and ties. We would try to catch glimpses of them as they walked into Mrs Upton's office. At the end of their visit, they would attempt to interact with us, but more often than not, we were too ill at ease or found it too amusing to watch these kindly old men speaking to us in slow, simple English.

The progress of the fund-raiser seemed to be an important topic of discussion during these inspections. One day, I overheard part of a conversation between Mrs Upton and Mr Booth, one of the inspectors.

"... I'm quite pleased with all the girls. One is as good as the other," Mrs Upton said.

"I'm sure they're all a credit to your institution," replied Mr Booth in a baritone voice. "However, Madam, the board needs to know which one of them at present is most deserving of being sent home."

Mrs Upton's voice grew indignant. "Recommendations like that are against the rules, Mr Booth. You know that! The burden of such a decision is not mine to bear."

"I'm aware of the rules, just as you are aware that those rules must be shaped by the very real practical concerns that arise when the subject matter concerns human lives, Mrs Upton. We won't get many offers until November, if any. If you have someone here who is particularly ill-adjusted, someone struggling to adapt, who can't take it here any more, it would be unconscionable not to prioritise sending them back. Please, think of the person, not the rules."

There was a long pause before Mrs Upton sighed deeply. "I never expected to have these questions on my conscience. And this isn't the first time you've put this burden on me, Mr Booth. If this were not a choice of going back to India, I'd have wanted poor little Putri to go back to her family. She's very much alone here."

The unexpected vulnerability in Mrs Upton's voice startled me.

"Hold yourself together, Mrs Upton. Please propose an Indian name. As you know, the family is India-bound."

I held my breath, and then Mrs Upton spoke again, her voice cracking. "Kalyani should go back soon. She isn't keeping well, and she yearns for her family more than anyone here."

My heart sank. I wasn't sure which feeling was worse—the deep disappointment I felt at being passed over, or the sharp twinge of jealousy that arose despite my understanding of why Kalyani had been chosen. I was ashamed to admit that, in my heart, I had hoped it would be me. I decided not to share what I'd overheard.

Things moved quickly. Later that afternoon, Mrs Upton made the necessary announcements. By evening, Kalyani was shifted to the family who would be taking her home. Mrs Upton avoided meeting the eyes of any of the Indian ayahs. To their credit, they all clapped and rejoiced for Kalyani without questioning the reasoning behind the decision. Her documents were handed to Mr Booth, and we wished her well.

Kalyani couldn't contain her happiness. For the first time, I saw her beam. She smiled through dinner and promised to send a postcard through the sahibs once she was safely home. It was the last time I saw her.

Later that night, I heard Alice sobbing into her pillow. I moved to her side and gave her arm a gentle squeeze. She looked up, her face barely visible in the dim light seeping through the cracks in the window.

"I thought I'd be next," she whispered, tears streaming down her face. "But the family wanted an elderly ayah. Why?" Her sobs were uncontrollable.

"I'm sorry, Alice ... I wish it hadn't been like this."

"I don't want to be employed in this country, Asha. I really have to get home soon."

I hugged her tight and spoke to her softly. "I know ... I know. We all need to get home. I've never prayed harder for anything."

She sniffled, her voice breaking. "I ... I have somebody back home. Our families had arranged for us to marry when we were still children. They were strongly against me taking up this job, and we had a row just before I left. He supported me, but I should've returned months ago. I know his father will marry him off if I don't get back soon. I didn't understand that my employers wouldn't send me back ... that it wasn't part of the deal ..."

A thousand thoughts rushed through my mind. I thought of Kalyani's quiet, unsmiling face; how she could never fully join in, how happy she had been that she would see her grandchildren again. Then, Alice and her situation, her fear of receiving a letter one day telling her that her betrothed had been married off. A part of me argued that both Kalyani and Alice had come to England under the same circumstances, and that both had known, or should have known, that a swift return to India was never guaranteed. Perhaps it was fair. The home had favoured Kalyani because of her age and the burden of supporting her declining health. Alice had taken a chance and had her youth on her side, but perhaps hers would be a life full of regret.

I sank into my own bed once Alice had fallen asleep. My head burned with fever, but sleep came and went, like waves crashing restlessly against the shore. The decisions had already been made—Kalyani and Alice's fates sealed. I hadn't realised until then how universal my hope of being chosen was. The next day, I kept wondering whom I would send home in my place, if I could choose. I watched closely every person who came to check on me or brought me a meal. When I really thought about it, each of them had a story that deserved sympathy, just like Kalyani's or Alice's. Unmarried girls had families waiting for them, parents, siblings, lovers. Married women had children or grandchildren. I couldn't help but feel sorry for everyone who longed for their families, but I could offer them nothing more than kindness. The days flew by in a whirlwind of activities and preparations as the fundraiser drew closer. The February which had ended with my abandonment at the docks turned to March, and in no time it was April. Our attentions were focused on the fundraiser scheduled for the end of the month. Unbeknownst to me, a strange catalyst for change was approaching. The matrons were ecstatic, announcing that this year's collection from the Ayah Home was the best they had ever seen. We were tasked with managing the Ayah Home stall at the fund-raiser. Mrs Upton assigned me the responsibility of accounting and maintaining the record books, while Mrs Travers was appointed to guide visitors through our pavilion, explaining the origins of the designs created by the ayahs.

On the day of the fund-raiser, our nerves were at edge. We waited with bated breath for the first visitor, then the next, and then another. Soon, we realised that our pavilion was gaining popularity. Mrs Travers was a vision of efficiency, darting about the pavilion, not only explaining the history behind the designs on display but also sharing the stories of the artisans and where she herself came from. I watched with surprise and amusement as this previously unseen side of Mrs Travers worked its magic. I could see customers being drawn in, enchanted by the pieces and the stories behind them. Every so often, she would shoot us a flushed look of joy, and we would grin back at her.

We were selling faster than we had anticipated. Many customers inquired if we would consider working on custom designs for them. Mrs Upton was thrilled at the prospect, as it promised continued work and a steady income. By lunchtime, the crowd was expected to thin, so Mrs Travers took a break and asked me to attend to any unexpected visitors. Rangamma and I stood there, listless, waiting for nothing in particular. We had very few items left, and the end of the day seemed imminent. We were both looking forward to the quiet and the chance to rest our weary heads.

I was jolted to attention by the arrival of a distinguished-looking visitor, a cheerful young woman who approached our stall with an easy smile, examining our work with a bright curiosity. She spoke slowly, gesturing at the articles with a beautifully gloved hand. "These are beautiful," she said, and Rangamma, slightly dazed, nodded in response.

For a moment, I was puzzled, but then I realised the lady probably assumed we didn't understand her language. It gave me a chance to take in her appearance.

She was a vision, her vivacious face lit by bright, searching eyes. Her face bore an elegance that didn't entirely mask her youthfulness—I wouldn't have placed her at more than thirty years of age. She wore an elegant white dress adorned with bold, red floral patterns, complemented by an impeccably styled handbag and a large matching hat. Every movement exuded grace and charm, and she was very direct in picking up the items, examining them herself instead of waiting for us to present them. When she spoke, she would gaze earnestly at us, her eyes arresting our attention immediately. I couldn't help but smile back, captivated by her lovely voice and the warmth of her refined, courteous manner. She asked about the pieces with genuine interest, her charismatic laughter making her even more endearing. It was clear to me—this was someone important, well loved, and clearly of some means.

We helped this unexpected guest as best we could, showing her cushion covers, handkerchiefs, bonnets, and tablecloths. She made several purchases, which I carefully noted in the register. By the time I had counted the change and looked up, she had already left. I scanned the area, but Rangamma yawned and told me she had already walked away. Without hesitation, I rushed after her.

"Madam ... You forgot your change!" I called out, panting.

She raised her eyebrows and smiled. "Oh, that's all right, dear ... I meant for you two to keep it."

With a polite smile, I replied, "We do not charge anything beyond our quoted price, ma'am. There's a separate donation box over there, if you wish to contribute to our home."

She laughed, cocking her head to the side, giving me an appraising, playful look. "Look at you!"

I wasn't sure what she meant but kept my smile in place, waiting patiently. After a few moments of studying me, she took her money back and left. As she left, she fixed me with a smile that I reciprocated but couldn't quite decipher.

Our materials were sold out within the hour after lunch, and we returned to the Home feeling like winners. We'd made a decent amount of money. On the way back, I mentioned the incident with the lady to Mrs Travers in passing, but by the time we reached the home, I had forgotten about it. The matrons announced plans to increase the prices next year, given the widespread appreciation for our work. Requests for customisations had been noted, along with generous advances. The Ayah Home had fared well in the fund-raiser!

The next day, Mrs Upton announced a day trip across the town on Sunday, perhaps meant as a reward for all our hard work. We were briefed about the places we'd visit, though I was just happy we'd be outdoors. In preparation, I quickly embroidered a few daisies on the collar of my blouse. I got up early Sunday morning and took some time doing my hair. All of us thoroughly enjoyed the warmth of the sunlight on our skin. The matrons led us to attend a prayer service inside Westminster Abbey, and then around the Big Ben and to the banks of the Thames. We drew curious glances and by now were adjusted enough to our odd situation that we could smile back cheekily and giggle at the reactions we were drawing.

That sunlit afternoon was the first time I really saw London for what it was, rather than a threat to seek shelter from. Taking in the sight of the splendid and imposing buildings, I thought of Paanchkodi Sarkar and what he would say about London. They built their houses by plundering ours … what good is that to the world? It was true, but it was hard to invoke those feelings in my young heart.

We took a bus to Hyde Park, where we enjoyed a cheerful picnic lunch amidst families, pets, vendors, and laughing children. We spoke of our native lands, and many of us resonated over how much we missed our food. The matrons suggested that we have a cultural food day each week, and seemed quite pleased to see that the idea had drawn out some of the more shy ayahs who had difficulty communicating and were not very involved in embroidery.

In the evening, we boarded a bus to Hampstead Heath. We chattered and navigated through the grassy walk, excitedly pointing out kingfishers and herons as we crossed a chain of ponds and reached a panoramic view of the city. As the group drank in the view silently, I thought about my father and how things changed after he left me. I wondered how much more growing up was there in store for me. For a moment, I was asking God, "Why me?", but that was no good, and I didn't want to ruin a perfectly good day.

As I lay in bed that night, I wondered what was next, now that the fund-raiser was over. I wanted to pray for a passage home but instead, with all my heart, I prayed for a purpose.

The next morning, I was summoned by Mrs Upton while I was discussing the new custom assignments with Mrs Travers. I found her in her office, in conversation with a female visitor dressed in an enviable hat and dress, seated with her back towards me. I overheard Mrs Upton's voice trailing "… she's bright as a button, you see."

"Yes, dear," she said, gesturing me in. "I believe you have met Mrs Stanley yesterday."

The woman turned to face me, and I was taken aback to see the same person I had returned the change to, smiling broadly. I felt an unexpected warmth in returning her smile.

"I did mention the incident to Mrs Travers," I said, smiling politely. "I hope there's no issue?"

"Oh, no, no problem at all," Mrs Upton quickly reassured me. "In fact, quite the opposite. Mrs Stanley is very impressed with you and would like to know if you'd be interested in working for her."

I stood, confused, looking between Mrs Stanley's gentle smile and Mrs Upton's expectant gaze. What did she mean?

"Well, we don't refuse an order," I began cautiously. "We've already planned next week's work, but I'm sure extra hands could speed things up ..."

"Oh, no," Mrs Upton interrupted. "Mrs Stanley is asking if you'd like to be her children's ayah."

The thought of being employed in a foreign land hit me like a gut punch, and I couldn't hide my dismay. I had been hoping to go back. But how would that work out if I was sent somewhere to work? Mrs Upton immediately sensed my discomfort and quickly tried to salvage the situation.

"Oh, Mrs Stanley ... I completely forgot I have a meeting with the gentlemen at the City Mission just now. Old age, you know," she chuckled nervously. "Would it be all right if I got back to you tomorrow, madam?"

"Certainly, certainly," Mrs Stanley replied with a pleasant smile, picking up her ornate black hat. Before leaving, she turned to me directly. "You're a well-spoken and honest young lady, and talented beyond your years. I do hope you'll consider my offer, won't you, dear?"

I met her gaze for a brief moment, trying to gauge whether she truly meant what she said. She seemed to carry an air of enigma, and while it was difficult to fully understand her personality, it was equally hard to mistrust her.

Once we were alone, Mrs Upton gestured to a seat. "How was it for you yesterday?" she asked.

"Um ... It was a great day. I hadn't felt this good in a while."

"We're glad. We try our best to make things nicer for all of you."

I nodded.

"Did you like being outside?"

"Very much."

She fiddled with some papers, choosing her words before speaking carefully.

"Asha, not long ago, I laid out your options. I'm not saying you must take this job, but life will be better for you outside of the Home. It will give you financial independence—something you won't find here, no matter how hard you work. It was a miracle we could send Kalyani home now. Families don't usually travel until November, and despite our fund-raising efforts, supporting all of you until then will be difficult."

I stared back at her as she paused.

"I'm asking you to consider living independently—outside charity," she continued. "I know better than most that money is power—it's a privilege." She sank back in her seat. "You can take the day to think it over."

I looked out of the window behind her, watching the weak mid-morning shower trickle down the glass, distorting the street outside.

"If I decide not to go ... then what?" I asked softly.

She sighed. "Well, if you don't take it, someone else from the home will, I hope."

I hesitated before asking, "If I go, and a sailing opportunity arises in November, would I be considered?"

Mrs Upton looked at me for a moment before responding.

"We usually don't do that, since it wouldn't be fair to your employer. However, if your employer agrees to let you leave, I don't see why we couldn't make an exception."

There was no way to gauge Mrs Stanley's generosity, and I doubted Mrs Upton would always be this accommodating when it came to future sailing opportunities if another family made demands for my services. I was young, good with children, experienced with British families, skilled in embroidery, and fluent in English. I had travel experience and appeared adaptable. On paper, I was a good fit for many households. What did it matter that I longed to go back home?

I knew the Ayah Home would benefit if I chose to work with Lady Stanley until an opportunity came up to accompany a sailing family to India; but once employed, I'd be bound by obligations that could prevent me from seizing that opportunity to travel home. Would I ever earn enough to afford a ticket home? As someone from a British colony, I couldn't expect to earn as much as a European nanny.

I felt trapped in what was supposed to be my chance at freedom. Worse still, the choice to stay at the Ayah Home or leave was really not mine to make, it was up to the management.

That night, I lay in bed, lost in thought. I glanced around the dark room, looking at the other girls from India, fast asleep. Their stories of resilience felt distant to me. I only knew my own story. Mrs Upton's words echoed in my mind: "outside of charity", "money is power", "privilege". As I drifted off, I couldn't shake my confusion. Was this really my decision to make, or would I be asked to do as the Home deemed fit?

The next morning, I woke up late, not feeling the usual urge to be the first at the table or help with breakfast. I sipped warm water, staring out at the street, trying to clear my thoughts. To my surprise, Mrs Upton came in soon to check on me. She joined me by the window silently, and we gazed out contemplatively.

"I wanted to make one thing quite clear to you, dear," she said, still looking outside. "As long as I'm the matron here, you'll never be forced out of the Home. We've always managed, and the Lord won't test us beyond our abilities. Think carefully about this opportunity. But don't feel that I'll let you out on these streets if you choose otherwise than as I advise."

I had a lump in my throat I couldn't get rid of.

"So, if I dislike it there …"

"If you're not treated well, you can always come back here and continue as before," she said firmly.

I smiled at her.

That evening, the girls at the home threw me a farewell feast. Together we made soft, fluffy pooris and creamy, decadent kheer, and I relished watching everyone savour the flavours of my land.

"We should've done this before!" many of them exclaimed. Putri grinned when I asked if she liked her meal. As they helped me pack, I insisted on leaving some of my embroidery magazines behind. Tight hugs and teary goodbyes followed. I wasn't sure what to expect from the new family, but I knew if things felt wrong, like with Mrs Jones, I'd run away without a second thought. For now, I could only pray and face my destiny.

13

The next morning, I set off to Mrs Stanley's residence, with Mrs Upton accompanying me. To my surprise, the house wasn't in London but in a nearby countryside I'd never heard of. We were slightly uneasy inside the large cab sent by Mrs Stanley, who had apparently insisted it would be too difficult for us to manage public transport. We arrived at our destination after a quiet ride through London and the misty countryside, and pulled up outside the large iron gates of the estate.

It was immediately clear that the Stanley residence was unlike any house I had seen in London. I craned my neck to see through the fog, but all I could make out were expansive fields, a lush garden, and a winding driveway leading into what appeared to be a patch of planned wilderness. 'Bradbourne Manor, Derbyshire,' the sign read. I followed Mrs Upton up the muddy driveway, dodging puddles as she hopped nimbly over them. I couldn't help but giggle at her unexpected adroitness.

We turned the corner and finally glimpsed the house.

"Woah …" I breathed.

"I had no idea either, dear," Mrs Upton whispered.

We stood still for a moment, taking in the imposing Edwardian manor that emerged regally from mists before us.

"They seem to be important people … is this a good thing or a bad thing, Mrs Upton?"

She studied the house thoughtfully. "Asha, dear, I knew the family was influential and well-off, though I didn't expect this mansion. Still, I don't see why that should change anything. She seems like a moral, God-fearing person who will treat you well."

I studied Mrs Upton for traces of doubt. She placed an arm around my shoulder, and we walked the final steps towards the house. The stone lobby felt cold beneath our feet. As we stood in front of the giant door, I could feel a sudden drop in temperature under the stone roof.

Before the door opened, I whispered urgently to Mrs Upton, "How many families live here?"

"Just Mrs Stanley's, of course."

"No, I mean … how many people?"

"Just the Stanleys—husband, wife, and their daughter. And, of course, the staff—cooks, gardeners, security, housekeepers, and possibly scullery maids. You'll get to know them soon enough."

Her answer came with an air of impatience, but before I could ask more, a tall gentleman in a dark suit appeared at the door, regarding us politely and waiting for an explanation.

"Good morning! I am Gloria Upton from the Ayah Home in Hackney. Mrs Stanley is expecting us," Mrs Upton said.

He nodded and led us into the parlour. The wood panelling on the walls seemed ancient, and the gentleman's polished shoes gleamed under the soft light. I followed, my mind racing with a million questions. Gloria, hmm? Mrs Upton didn't seem like a 'Gloria' to me—more of an Ingrid or Jocelyn maybe. My mind rambled on nervously.

The gentleman showed us to a seating area and left, informing us that he would fetch madam. I whispered breathlessly, "I thought that was the husband!"

Mrs Upton gave me an offended look. "Really, dear! Because you speak English, I often forget that you know nothing about the English and their ways of living here in their own country. Wealthy houses have butlers attend to the door, and you never mention the husband. Ever! You're not her friend, do you understand?"

She pursed her lips and sighed in exasperation. Slightly abashed, I glanced around at the heavily carpeted floors and the ample seating area furnished with exquisitely carved chairs and sofas. Clearly, entertaining and hosting was a significant part of the Stanleys' lifestyle. A French window opened to a garden, where two men in flat caps tended to the plants. I looked at a side table at the far end of the hall, and I gasped with joy when I saw it—an ivory tablecloth, the very same I had stitched and we had sold her.

Before I could make a remark, the tall figure returned, and turned around to hold open the door. He then stepped aside deferentially, and there she was—the enigmatic Mrs Stanley herself. She walked in with a cheerful smile, emanating poise and an energy that felt like it could turn the winter to spring. With easy grace, she extended a delicately gloved hand towards me. "I am so glad you decided to join us, Asha! We are delighted to have you. Will Mrs Upton prefer tea with cookies?" she asked, continuing seamlessly as she tilted her head in a charming way to address the matron, before lowering herself gracefully into an armchair.

I sat, slightly taken aback by how casually I was invited into the conversation between these two English ladies. I chose to withdraw into my thoughts, preferring to drink in my surroundings. My gaze lingered on Mrs Stanley's animated gestures, her eloquent hands punctuating her every word. They spoke briefly about the weather and the rains, the quintessential English topics that seemed to make every encounter more *proper*.

My thoughts wandered from their conversation to the stag mount over the fireplace, its antlers all twisted and curved. The mantelpiece held several family photographs. One showed a newly married Mrs Stanley, radiantly smiling with her tall husband. Another was a family photo where Mrs Stanley was absent. There was also a recent one of her in a riding habit, an English foxhound sitting loyally at her feet.

"Do you like the house?" Mrs Stanley's voice brought me back to the moment. I looked away from the pictures and nodded hesitantly, still a little unsure. I could feel her focus on me, like a spotlight had turned in my direction. Her attention was so full and complete, it made me feel both important and like an equal in that moment, though I couldn't fully grasp why.

Mrs Stanley's smile slowly receded into a thoughtful expression as she regarded me with earnest curiosity. "What are your expectations from us?" she asked, her voice gentle yet sincere.

None of the families I had worked for before had ever asked me anything like this. Was I allowed to have expectations?

This new employer was hard to read. I quickly recovered my poise, not wanting to betray any expectations of astuteness she may have of me.

"Ma'am, the family I worked with for two years always treated me fairly and respectfully, and that made it easy for me to remain focused on my work."

She listened attentively, her attention unwavering as if she truly cared about my answer. I pressed on, the next part of my response trickier than the first. "And ... well, I request that my pay be given to me every month, and if for any reason this arrangement is terminated, I wish to be safely returned to the Ayah Home," I finished in a single breath, trying to sound more confident than I felt. I wasn't sure how she'd respond to this. I ignored the surprise on Mrs Upton's face and held Mrs Stanley's gaze, hoping my words had been clear.

Mrs Stanley placed her tea cup on the table with a soft clink, nodding thoughtfully. "Hmm, alright," she said, considering my request. "Anything else? How much do you want to be paid?"

"As much as Mrs Upton deems fit for me," I replied without hesitation.

She nodded thoughtfully, and Mrs Upton smiled, looking slightly flustered.

The rest of the tea was enjoyed in a comfortable silence, and once it ended, Mrs Stanley led us through the French window to the gardens outside. I was struck afresh by the beauty of the estate. The gardens stretched out before us, vibrant and meticulously tended by the gardeners. Mrs Stanley spoke elegantly and fondly of the estate's history, offering bits of trivia at Mrs Upton's behest, clearly proud of the land the family had tended for generations.

She pointed to various additions to the mansion, mentioning the year and the ancestor who had sponsored each one. It was clear that the Stanleys were an old and respectable family. The names she mentioned were often accompanied by military titles. I learned that the mansion was over a century old, and the wing where the Stanleys resided had eight functioning bedrooms. A mirror image of the house stood adjacent, connected by a corridor, though it was staffed minimally and opened only when hosting large parties.

The estate had a vineyard, though such was the astonishing variety of flowers and trees that I would have never realised had I not been told. Flower beds lined the garden, and apple and apricot trees provided cover along the boundary walls. The mansion had withstood the ravages of the Great War, and the previous generation of Stanleys had carefully restored and modernised parts of the estate, especially the lower levels, to make them more comfortable for contemporary living.

"Living here must be a lot of work, Mrs Stanley," Mrs Upton remarked.

"No end of it," Mrs Stanley replied with a rueful smile. "We couldn't possibly manage without Mr Hedley, our estate manager. I only look after the accounts, which Lord Stanley has little time for. Our butler, Nally is quite indispensable too. We've been very fortunate to retain such dedicated staff."

Our tour was drawn to a close by Nally's appearance at the far end of the garden. He bowed and informed Mrs Stanley that her daughter Elizabeth and a Mrs Glasse were ready for her. As we walked to the house, I found myself in a contemplative mood. Previous experiences as an ayah had taught me that integrating into a new family could be a delicate process, especially when the other servants regarded you as either an outsider or an inferior. It seemed the challenge here would be even more formidable. The rigid structure of the estate, its long-established hierarchies, and the stringent rules that probably governed every aspect of life here would doubly underscore me as an intruder.

Once inside, Mrs Stanley left, and I turned to face Mrs Upton, feeling unexpectedly melancholic. The realisation that she and I were about to part ways hit me suddenly. Yet another goodbye.

Mrs Upton seemed to sense my mood. She offered me a kind smile before her expression turned serious. "Be steady in this house, dear. Don't lose your head. Just keep at it, and you'll find your place."

The words felt empty, and I stared back at her with uncertainty.

"Come on now," she continued, softening. "You are by far the smartest sixteen-year-old I've met. You can do this."

I fought back sudden tears that threatened to spill over and managed to respond, "I'm seventeen. If I'm not treated well here, you'll find me at the Home any day."

Mrs Upton rolled her eyes and for the first time—as it turned out to be the only time in all the years I would know her—she pulled me into a brief, tight embrace. I held on, and I've held on to that bitter-sweet memory. Our relationship in the years to come saw a lot, but never again reached that note of tenderness.

After bidding her goodbye, I followed Mr Nally as he escorted me to my room. He carried out the task with a disinterested air, his detached demeanour making it clear he found this duty beneath his station. I remained silent, dragging my metal trunk over several flights of stairs. Each landing offered a brief reprieve to catch my breath, and I tried to process that this was the beginning of a new era for me.

When we reached, I watched Mr Nally push the door open with some apprehension. This was to be my sanctuary in a strange house. The door opened with a creak that echoed in the quiet corridor. I stepped in, the wooden floor squeaking beneath my weight, and paused to take it all in. The room was little more than an attic by any standard. It wasn't exactly cramped, though the geometry was peculiar: it was twenty steps in length and seven in breadth, with an odd, elongated shape and a slanted ceiling that gave the space a stifling feel. The ceiling hovered just a foot above my head.

My eyes were drawn to the far wall. It was dominated by a long, single-pane window stretched across its length, filling the room with dim, dusty light. At the far end lay a makeshift bed that seemed hastily assembled. Crates lined the other walls, wearing a look of neglect.

"Those are the spare belongings of our mistress," Mr Nally said, gesturing towards the crates with a dismissive air. "As you may have gathered, the original purpose of this space was not to serve as an accommodation. However, given the current situation with the staff quarters, I'm instructed that you'll have to make do here."

"What's the matter with the staff quarters, sir?" I ventured, hesitant but curious.

"They are not able to accommodate any further members at present," he replied curtly. His tone made it clear the subject was closed. "If you would prefer to be housed more comfortably in the other wing, there are serviceable quarters there that could be readied for you by tomorrow. However, you may find it challenging to attend to your duties promptly from such a distance."

The thought of staying alone in the adjoining manor sent a shiver through me. I quickly signalled my acceptance of the room by dragging my trunk further inside.

"You must bundle up and draw the curtains after dark, or you'll be cold," he continued, glancing over my modest belongings with detached scrutiny. "I trust you have in your effects appropriate warm garments."

I glanced around the room, unsure if he expected a reply or if one was even warranted. His words lingered uneasily in my mind. *What was he hinting at by saying I would have to make do here because the staff quarters couldn't accommodate me?* With a sinking feeling, I wondered whether I was an unwelcome intrusion, an outsider who would be discussed and shunned. My gaze flicked to the crates, their contents silent witnesses to the life of the mistress whose space I now occupied. Would my origins handicap me here? I wrapped my arms around myself, suddenly aware of the chill in the room.

"Oh, and you must try to not walk around the room or talk aloud after 9 p.m."

"Why?" I asked, my curiosity piqued.

"Lord Stanley makes a habit of retiring to the study room after his dinner and walk, and does not tolerate any disturbance there. His study is right under this attic, and he would be absolutely livid if he heard any goings-on during his time of repose."

I was not at all sure how I felt about that. The idea of having to stifle my existence, to tiptoe through my own room as though I were an intruder, made something in me tighten. Was this to be my life now—an unobservable disappearance for the convenience of a man fate had made my employer?

"Meals will be served to the staff in the kitchen thrice a day, with twenty minutes of time to eat in groups and return to their duties," Nally continued, his tone clipped and efficient. "You will report to either Lady Stanley or Mrs Glasse."

"Who is Mrs Glasse?" I asked, hoping for some insight.

He raised an eyebrow, as though the question were unnecessary. "You will meet her soon," he said curtly. And then he was gone, the door clicking shut behind him.

For the first time in hours, I exhaled deeply and let myself collapse on to the bed. The mattress was lumpy, and the ceiling seemed uncomfortably close, but at least I was alone.

The reprieve however was short-lived. Barely had Mr Nally's footsteps faded into silence when I heard the approach of another—lighter, hesitant, with a pause at the threshold that seemed to weigh the decision to enter. Then, the door creaked open, and a girl backed into the room, balancing a tray of food with both hands, her movements careful and deliberate.

She turned to face me, her eyes widening slightly with curiosity before a tentative smile softened her expression.

"Umm ... I'm Adaline," she said in a voice tentative but tinged with friendliness.

"I'm Asha," I replied simply, mirroring her smile.

She was slender and awkwardly built, perhaps around my own age. Her cheeks and nose were densely marked with freckles, and her maid's uniform, slightly wrinkled and askew, lent her an air of youthful disorder. It was clear she had never encountered someone like me before and her gaze lingered, openly intrigued. For my part, I had never seen so many freckles on one face. We observed each other unabashedly, each struck by the odd novelty of the other.

The silence stretched until Adaline, with a shy but determined air, took the first step to bridge it.

"You'll need help setting this place up. Let me lend you a hand." She peeled the dusty sheet of the bed and set to work arranging a fresh sheet on it. In a flurry of movement, she had the bed made, the wide window ledges dusted, and the room aired out. Meanwhile, I busied myself tidying up odds and ends around the crates, eager to contribute to the transformation of my accommodation.

When the room was finally in order, I perched on the ledge by the window. She joined me without hesitation, and nodded to the plate she had got me.

"If you need anything, you can let me know," she offered.

"That's very kind of you," I said sincerely, and picked up some potato fries and cutlets from the tray.

Adaline rubbed her nails absently against her apron, then overcame her shyness and looked up at me again, studying me like one might a curious artefact.

"You're Indian, aren't you?"

"Yes," I replied, my tone even. "Have you met anyone from India before?"

She shook her head, her red curls bouncing slightly. "No, never. But we all heard we'd have an Indian nanny come in."

I didn't quite know what to say, so I continued eating, wondering what they expected from me.

"So, you really can speak English, then. Quite well, better than some of the others even, I'd say," she remarked, her tone a mix of curiosity and amazement. "We couldn't believe it when we heard. Everyone's going to be mighty surprised, though English words do sound funny coming from your mouth."

Her words weren't malicious—just unfiltered and direct. I remained silent, allowing her to take me in.

"It's really true, then," she mused, half to herself. "Madam chose you to take care of Lizzy, of all people ... it's all so strange."

I couldn't blame her. To them, I suppose, I *was* an oddity. I chose to let it pass, and asked, "How long have you worked here?"

"About a year now," she said, fidgeting with the hem of her apron. "I mostly help in the kitchen and clean the guest rooms."

"Do you like working here?" I asked

"Of course," she replied without hesitation. "We're mighty lucky to have jobs in a house as nice as this one, and Lady Stanley treats us well."

"Do you also stay in an attic like this?"

Adaline laughed, shaking her head. "Oh, no, no. Our hall is in the basement. But I'd take the attic any day," she said, her eyes sweeping over the room. There was a moment's hesitation before she added, "The only downside is ... well, it might get awfully cold during the winters. And, err ... there isn't even a fireplace," she finished with a self-conscious smile, as though trying to soften her words.

I shrugged lightly, trying to appear unaffected. "Then I'm fortunate that winter is far away."

She grinned at my response, and the unease in her expression melted away. After a moment, she probed further, her voice soft and curious.

"What's it like—where you come from, I mean?"

Her question startled me, though it shouldn't have. "It's … very different from here," I began, carefully choosing my words. "It's warmer, for one. The air smells of pine and wildflowers in the hills where I'm from. The people … they live very differently, very simply, but there's a sense of community."

Adaline listened intently, her wide eyes fixed on me. "That sounds nice. Not like here. Here, it's all rules and people minding their own business either too much or not at all."

I gave a faint smile, unsure whether she was lamenting her own life or cautioning me about mine.

"So, do you miss it? Your home?"

The question lingered before me for a moment. I thought of the hills, the warmth of the sun on my face, my father's voice calling out to me. A pang of longing settled in my chest, but I pushed it down. "I do," I admitted softly. "But I can't live in the past. I have to make the best of what's ahead."

Adaline seemed to consider this, her gaze flickering to the sparse room around us. "You're brave," she said unexpectedly, after a pause.

I chuckled dryly. "Or foolish."

"No, brave," she insisted, her voice firm. "I'd never leave home, not unless someone dragged me kicking and screaming. But you—you came all the way here, to a place where everything's strange. That's something."

Her words surprised me, but I didn't reply. Instead, I turned my attention to the window. Perhaps bravery was what you called survival when you had no other choice. I couldn't deny that this unexpected warmth made me feel surprisingly emotional.

After a few moments of silence, Adaline stood up. "Well, I'd best be off before Nally finds me loitering. He's got a knack for sniffing out idleness. I'm supposed to take you to Lady Stanley whenever you're ready. Are you up to it just now?"

I nodded, hoping my smile conveyed some of the gratitude I felt for her kindness. We set off and I followed her, trying once again to memorise each floor and turn as we made our way through the corridors. Unlike the grand parlour, the other rooms I glimpsed were smaller, yet far more inviting. They exuded a quiet warmth, their thick curtains drawing the light just so, and the soft furnishings—upholstered headboards, four-poster beds, plush carpets—gave the impression of a more lived-in comfort.

I saw Mrs Stanley seated near the French window in the parlour, absorbed in a thin book. As Adaline curtsied and announced my arrival, Mrs Stanley looked up and smiled warmly. "There you are, Asha! I hope you're settling in well. I was eager to introduce you to Elizabeth. Are you ready?"

I nodded, and she gracefully rose from her seat, expecting me to follow.

We ascended a different flight of stairs this time and soon reached the nursery on the first floor. It was a cosy room, with a lovely fireplace at one end, flanked by two windows that let in the soft rays of the sun. Peach curtains draped the windows, trailing on to the thick grey carpet below. Against the peach-and-grey striped wall stood a large bed which could easily accommodate even a teenager. Opposite it was a small play area with cushions and a wooden toy horse, along with a little round table set for a tea party.

"We don't have a separate night nursery," Mrs Stanley said as she walked over to the window. "This is it. I've always wanted Elizabeth to be in a brightly lit space, and I think this room works well for her."

It was nicer than any nursery I had previously encountered. "I think it's just right, ma'am," I said, following her into an adjoining room she called the "schooling room". It was considerably smaller than the nursery, and felt colder, the stone walls bare and unadorned, in stark contrast to the warmth of the nursery. A couple of well-worn wooden desks, one for a teacher and one for a student, were cramped together, flanked by a couple of tall bookshelves. An easel stood with the letter 'R' drawn on it.

This room wasn't as attractive as the nursery, but it did have a redeeming feature—a massive window across from the student's desk that offered an enchanting view of a giant tree in the garden. I was immediately captivated by the sight. Had I been in Elizabeth's place, there was no way I could have focused on my lessons with that beautiful scene before me.

"The furniture in here was last used when Lord Stanley was a boy," Mrs Stanley remarked, her voice tinged with affection as she scanned the room. "I couldn't bear to replace it. Not that he's sentimental about such things, but we have so very few pieces from his childhood. It's nice knowing our daughter is surrounded by the same furniture her father once used."

I nodded. "Well, yes, ma'am. The view is gorgeous too."

We moved towards the window together and looked outside. A pair of goldfinches flitted about, chirping from a tiny, cup-like nest. Their bright colour made them stand out against the leaves they were nestled against. Mrs Stanley's face lit up as she exclaimed, "I should have expected goldfinches at this time of the year ... Aren't they delightful to watch?"

"Without a doubt," I smiled.

We stood there, observing the cheerful little birds, when Mrs Stanley continued softly, "My late aunt Sylvia held strong views on finches. She believed that finches signify new beginnings and adventure." She turned to look at me, her eyes twinkling with a mischievous gleam. "If she were here, I'm sure she would make a prophecy about this sighting and somehow tie it to your arrival in the house!"

For a moment, we exchanged glances, and then she laughed. I felt a flush of embarrassment. The conversation felt so different from what I was used to, and I wasn't sure how to respond. Should I remain silent, as I might have with previous employers, or should I engage with Mrs Stanley and embrace the tone she seemed to be inviting me into?

"Where I'm from, ma'am, superstitions are everywhere," I said, deciding to engage. "But our elders always say there's logic behind them."

"Really? What kind of logic?" she asked, intrigued.

"For instance, ma'am, we don't sweep after the sun has set. At first, it seems odd, but the idea is that small, precious things might get swept away and lost in the dark. It makes sense, really."

Mrs Stanley smiled thoughtfully. "Solid reasoning, indeed. I've also heard that people in India don't cook for about a fortnight after a death in the family. What do you think the reasoning behind that is?" I could see she was enjoying drawing me into a conversation.

"Yes, that's true. After my father passed away, my neighbours sent food for a month. I think it's to give the family the time to grieve, without the added burden of cooking. It was a great comfort to me."

I couldn't explain of course that convenience had been the least of my blessings there. Remembering the gift of food from Jitu's parents at that tender moment in my life, and remembering Jitu at all, suddenly tugged at feelings that had been dormant.

She looked outside contemplatively, and I diverted myself with the finches.

"Were you very close to your father?" she asked gently.

"He was the only parent I knew, the only family I had. But it's been a few years now, and I think I've come to terms with it, ma'am."

She paused, her expression softening. "I'm sorry for your loss. I'm also sorry for what happened when you arrived in our country," she said with a sincerity that felt almost maternal. "If there's ever anything that bothers you or makes you uncomfortable, don't hesitate to come to me."

For a moment, it was hard to remember she was my employer. Her concern felt real, as though she truly saw me for the person I was, not just as the hired help.

"Thank you, ma'am. You're very kind."

We quietly left the school room and came back to the nursery, where both of us took seats on Elizabeth's Lilliputian chairs with the dolls. Mrs Stanley cleared her throat and entwined her fingers. I could tell she was moving to an important topic.

"Asha, Lizzy is my only child. She turned four last week. She has a governess, the old Mrs Glasse who takes her work very seriously. We intend to home-school her for a few more years and then we might send her somewhere else for education when she's old enough to be without her mother."

I remained quiet and attentive.

"Lizzy is growing up in a very sheltered world," Mrs Stanley continued, her voice tinged with concern. "Her only companions are those who are paid to serve her. To them, she is simply the mistress's daughter, someone to be pampered and spoiled. I do not want her to grow up in a bubble, friendless and ignorant of the world beyond the confines of Bradbourne Manor, on a pedestal of privilege. That's why, after meeting you, I made the very deliberate decision to ask you here as her companion."

She seemed to weigh her next thoughts carefully before continuing.

"I've heard a lot about the love and care an ayah can give to a child," she said, "but above all, I chose you because I want Lizzy to have a friend, someone she can connect with. I don't have a strict list of duties for you, Asha, other than seeing to Lizzy's general care, such as bathing, dressing for school, and putting her to bed. What matters far more is that Lizzy doesn't see you as someone beneath her, but as an equal."

She paused, taking a breath before adding, "So, I will introduce you to Lizzy as her friend, and nothing else."

A long silence followed. I realised that my eyebrows had lifted in surprise. Mrs Stanley seemed to be waiting for my response.

"Err …" I stammered, unsure of how to respond.

"Is that alright?" she asked.

Between considering whether she was delusional or merely an idealist, and wondering if this wouldn't just complicate my already delicate duties, I wasn't sure how to reply. Did she really overlook the elephant in the room when she chose me as her daughter's friend?

"Ma'am, I've ... never been in such an arrangement," I began cautiously. "Most children know I'm their caretaker. Besides, it might be more complicated than it seems." I paused, unsure about how to broach the subject. "I mean, I don't really *look* like her, Mrs Stanley," I added hesitantly.

She answered me simply and disarmingly. "I don't believe that *looks* ought to matter in friendships, Asha."

I didn't have an answer to that. How could I explain to her that my race might already be an obstacle to my survival within the household surrounded by an army of English servants?

"Can I ask you something, Mrs Stanley?" I ventured.

"Please do."

"Wouldn't it have been easier to hire a young girl from the countryside to play with your daughter and keep her company?"

Mrs Stanley leaned back in her chair, her demeanour suddenly more merry and headstrong. "Well, Asha, I found you! My instinct led me in a particular direction, and I followed it. I'm convinced I'll be proven right in the end. Having you around my little girl will do her good. You've had far more experience than any other girl your age from the countryside, and it hasn't made you bitter. It's made you stronger."

I furrowed my brow. "What if she asks me ... about myself?" I asked cautiously, recalling Mrs Stager's concern about Hindustani influences on her children.

"My dearest Asha, what would be the benefit of all this if she doesn't?" she retorted with a playful, lopsided smile.

Throughout our conversation, I couldn't help but feel puzzled by Mrs Stanley's expectations and what seemed like her naivety. A quiet anger stirred within me. She assumed, without any foundation, that I wasn't bitter. But there was a bitter part of me and it didn't want to be part of what seemed like a misguided experiment for a privileged woman who, despite her affable demeanour, perhaps did see me as a disposable asset, something to be bought and used. Yet, as much as that thought wanted to take root, it faded when I looked at Mrs Stanley, young and poised beyond her years, sitting before me with complete ease, smiling comfortably. She was sincere to her beliefs.

Despite my serious doubts about this arrangement, I reminded myself that not long ago, I had been just a little girl who too didn't distinguish between economic classes or race. I hadn't been brought up to believe that we were inferior, and perhaps that was why I couldn't treat the goras with the reverence others did. There was a bleak possibility that Mrs Stanley's whimsical moves might even do me some good. As far as I was concerned, the assignment did entail just providing company to a little girl, and I could certainly do that and collect my pay.

We sat in silence for what felt like an eternity. I was ill at ease, yet nothing seemed to disturb Mrs Stanley's composure. She sat there, perfectly at ease, smiling warmly, as though we were simply waiting for something pleasant to happen.

"That'll be she."

I heard the loud, clumsy footsteps, followed by the door bursting open. In rushed the child, barrelling towards her mother and enveloping her in an embrace with a joyful shriek.

"Mama!"

Mrs Stanley laughed with delight as she scooped Elizabeth up. "My darling!"

The child quickly wrapped her small arms around her mother's neck, pressing a kiss to her face. Mrs Stanley, beaming, ran her fingers through her daughter's thick blonde hair and gently placed her on the chair beside her.

"Lizzy, dear," Mrs Stanley began, her voice soft yet deliberate. "Mama has found you a friend, and she wants you to meet her."

"A friend! I want a friend, yes!" Elizabeth trilled, clapping her hands with excitement. All the while, I stood by the large window, unnoticed by her. I hadn't been welcomed so enthusiastically by any of my previous wards. Uncertain, I stepped forward and offered her a smile. She turned her gaze towards me, her round innocent eyes locking into mine. Her face lit up with a beaming smile.

"Is she my new friend?"

"She is," Mrs Stanley confirmed, her tone warm. "Would you like to speak to her?"

Elizabeth slid herself down from the chair and, without a moment's hesitation, walked towards me. She stopped right in front of me and declared, "I'm Lizzy. What is your name?"

I knelt down, smiling. "I'm Asha."

She grinned and tried to mimic my name, "Aashha," with a playful smile. "Aashha, will you read to me?"

"I would love to," I replied with a smile of my own. "Which is your favourite book?"

Without missing a beat, she jumped up excitedly and shouted, "*Velveteen Yabbit!*"

I smiled, "*The Velveteen Rabbit* it is then."

As I began to read, I caught a glimpse of a tall figure standing at the door. Mrs Stanley, who had been quietly observing our interaction, now moved towards the door. I couldn't hear the hushed conversation she was having with the figure, but I was too engrossed in narrating the story. Elizabeth sat on her doll chair, her rapt attention focused on me, a small expectant smile tugging at the corner of her lips. It warmed my heart, and I felt lucky at that moment to be where I was, with the promise of safety, food, and perhaps a little rest after this long day.

Just then, the figure at the door cleared her throat, which I took as a signal to stop reading. I stood up, setting the book down. Before me was an elderly woman, surveying me from behind round-rimmed glasses resting on her lined cheeks.

"Asha, this is Mrs Glasse, Elizabeth's governess. She's the one who looks after Lizzy's education," said Mrs Stanley in her introduction. "We had planned to start Lizzy on reading soon, but Mrs Glasse thought it was best to begin even sooner. We are very lucky to have her."

Mrs Glasse bowed her head slightly in acknowledgement of the compliment, then turned her attention to me.

"I'm glad to see you read well," she said, her voice stronger, steelier than I had expected. "To be truthful, I had some concerns. Your diction needs work, but how is it that you read English so well?"

"I had the opportunity to attend a home school in India with my charges during my first assignment, madam. They required me to speak only in English," I explained.

"How long did it take you?" Mrs Glasse asked, studying me with sharp, calculating eyes.

"I spent close to two school years with the children, and before that, I regularly attended my own school," I responded.

Mrs Glasse regarded me coolly for a moment, her expression unreadable. "Your diction still needs improvement.

We can't have Elizabeth picking up poor habits. Please attend my classes with Miss Elizabeth and make sure you work hard at them."

I suppressed a smile trying to fathom everything that was happening. *This just keeps getting better*, I thought. I nodded, trying not to appear too eager. She seemed like a tough, no-nonsense woman, but I was eager for any opportunity to learn.

Elizabeth wasn't pleased with the interruption and began tugging at my skirt, clearly wanting me to sit down again.

Mrs Glasse shook her head disapprovingly at Elizabeth before making her way out, followed by Mrs Stanley. I was left alone with Elizabeth to read, but before long, her energy waned and she dozed off in the chair, her head drooping gently. I carefully tucked her into the cot, smoothing the blankets around her small frame. Mrs Glasse settled into an armchair by the cot with a cup of tea and some embroidery and sent me off for the day.

As I climbed into my own bed in the attic, I finally allowed myself to breathe deeply and relax. The day had been full of strange moments, with so many new people I was to interact with—Nally, Adaline, Mrs Glasse, Elizabeth, and of course, Mrs Stanley. Everything here was so different from what I was used to, and somehow seemed to revolve around the enigmatic Mrs Stanley. Were her ideas truly sincere, or were they just a flight of fancy? Would this arrangement turn out to be just a fleeting obsession, and fade into a regular job as an ayah?

At that moment, though, I couldn't worry about it. I smiled to myself, appreciating the simple fact that I had a paying job. The amount I earned didn't matter. I'd already decided that my first salary would go to the Ayah Home.

What mattered was the thought that, one day, I might have enough to buy a ticket home. Until then, it seemed that life, for all its peculiarities, was being merciful.

14

The pleasant first day proved to be a pattern that held true over the next few months as I integrated happily into the rhythm of life at Bradbourne Manor. In many ways, those days were idyllic.

Elizabeth revealed herself as a precocious child, full of raucous and infectious joy. It was a stark contrast from the defensive Lily, who had emerged from her shell only slowly, or from the immediate gratitude of Joanna, whose warmth had been both disarming and heartbreaking. In some ways, Elizabeth reminded me most of Poppy, whose memory still made my heart swell. Maybe Poppy would grow up to be the kind of happy child that Elizabeth was. Sometimes, during my quiet afternoons, I'd simply watch Mrs Stanley with her daughter. In those moments, I couldn't help dreaming about Elizabeth blossoming into a fine, charming woman, just like her mother. She certainly had the family for it. And almost as if in the same breath, my thoughts would jump to my possibilities and what life had in store for me—what would I be like? Where would I be?

Mrs Stanley remained as enigmatic as ever, her presence at the manor oscillating between two striking extremes. During her frequent periods of absence, she was consumed by her charitable pursuits and society functions. On those occasions, we saw her only fleetingly. Yet whenever she did grace us with her presence, she seemed radiant, her energy almost electric, her passion for her work palpable. Her attire would be immaculate, her movements graceful, as if she thrived best in the world beyond the manor walls. It was clear that her causes, whatever they were, brought out the very best in her, a woman burning with purpose and conviction.

What stood out most to me during these intervals was her ardent love for Elizabeth. Each time she prepared for a spell of busy days, she lavished her daughter with affection, cradling her as though trying to compress a lifetime of love into those brief moments. None of my previous mistresses had shown such demonstrative devotion, and certainly not with the fervour that marked Mrs Stanley's interactions with her child. It wasn't merely motherly tenderness, it felt almost like a race against time, as if she feared losing something irreplaceable.

During her quieter spells at the manor, Mrs Stanley seemed a different person altogether. The fiery energy of her absences was replaced by a placid, almost languorous calm. She would linger in the nursery, reading or simply observing us with a faint, faraway expression. I couldn't help but notice the occasional flicker of listlessness about her, as though she were weighed down by a burden I couldn't name. She was never inattentive to Elizabeth for long, though. At the first tug on her sleeve or the smallest plea for a game, Mrs Stanley would snap out of her reverie, throwing herself into the play with the same unreserved enthusiasm as before.

Adaline, or Ada as she soon became to me, turned out to be an absolute blessing. Her awkward facade soon crumbled to reveal a naive, curious girl who was both eternally hopeful and perpetually preoccupied with worries about her lot in life. I gathered from her oft-mended clothes that she let slip that she came from a poor family.

She never mentioned what her father did, though she did mention that her mother was the hardest working woman she had ever known. Ada had an older sister who, by her account, had achieved the pinnacle of success—a marriage to a 'factory man' who could afford to buy her a new dress every month. This sister, living in her own modest home, managing her own kitchen, and dining at tea shops when the weekly pay arrived, was Ada's beacon of hope. It was her dream to follow in those footsteps and she fretted constantly about her own looks and prospects.

She had taken the job because it paid very well, and let her put some money away towards her marriage and send some back to her mum. She had a younger brother too, who had recently taken to smoking, much to her mother's worry. Ada represented a mundane sense of normality which was fascinating to me. She worried about her appearance, dreamt of domestic bliss, and navigated her days with a heartening optimism. She ignored the obvious differences between us, and for the first time in a long period, I had someone my own age to talk to and laugh with.

The candour of our conversation was startling at first, very different from the formalities and unspoken hierarchies I had expected of the household. "Asha," she'd say with a grin, "do you think men notice when you wear ribbons in your hair? My sister swears it's the reason her Bertie fell for her, but I don't see it."

"I'm not sure," I'd reply, laughing, "but if it worked for your sister, it might be worth a try."

When Elizabeth napped and Mrs Glasse didn't need me, I'd sometimes visit her on her chores. She'd be elbow-deep in suds or bent over a bubbling pot in the kitchen and her face would flush with delight to see me. "Asha!" she'd exclaim. "Have you come to rescue me from this drudgery?"

"I can't stay long," I'd say, though I always lingered longer than I intended.

With Ada's help, I slowly eased into the everyday life at Bradbourne Manor. At first, I was invisible to the staff, little more than an afterthought in the bustling hierarchy of the household. It was likely that they hoped I was some foolish passion project that the mistress had taken up and would cast away in a few weeks when the fervour subsided. But as the weeks passed, my continued presence became harder to ignore, especially with Ada acting as my unspoken advocate and the staff slowly accepting their disbelief that I could indeed converse with them in English.

Mr Nally, the butler, remained an imposing figure, steeped in authority and precision. He rarely addressed me directly, his cool demeanour hinting at quiet disdain. I couldn't help but feel that he disapproved of my existence in this space.

The others, however, softened over time. Dora and Holly, the scullery maid and parlour maid, included me in their chatter when we crossed paths, their initial wariness giving way to curiosity. Even young George, the stable hand, tipped his cap at me now and then, though he hardly spoke more than a word or two.

Mrs Alice Kensley, the head cook, was a figure of quiet authority in the manor's kitchen. She had a demeanour that brooked no nonsense—her sharp eyes missed nothing, and her gruff voice could stop even Patrick Spade, her deputy, mid-joke. She ran the kitchen like clockwork, every movement deliberate and efficient, every instruction clear and firm. Yet beneath her stern exterior was a heart that, while not easily won over, revealed itself in moments of subtle kindness.

I had my first real interaction with her on a morning when I was sent to fetch some biscuits for Elizabeth's tea. The kitchen was a flurry of activity, with trays being loaded, ingredients measured, and the occasional clang of pots echoing through the room. I stood at the door, waiting for a moment to catch Mrs Kensley's attention, but her sharp voice rang out before I could speak.

"Well, girl? Standing there like a statue won't get you what you need," she said without looking up, her hands deftly kneading dough.

"I'm here to collect biscuits for the nursery tea, Mrs Kensley," I replied, keeping my voice steady.

"Biscuits, is it?" she muttered, brushing flour off her hands. "You'd think those of us feeding the household would have time to cater to every whim. Patrick!" she barked, and the deputy chef, who had been loafing near the pantry, straightened immediately. "Fetch a tin for the lady," she ordered, her tone laced with sarcasm but not unkind.

Patrick disappeared with a muttered "Yes, ma'am," leaving me standing awkwardly under Mrs Kensley's watchful eye. After a moment, she spoke again, her tone softer. "For Elizabeth? Sweet child, that one. Takes after her mother."

"She is," I agreed, unsure if I should say more.

Mrs Kensley paused her work and looked at me for the first time. "And you. How're you finding things here?"

I hesitated, then answered honestly. "It's different, ma'am, but I'm learning. Everyone's been … mostly kind."

Her lips twitched in what might have been a smile. "Mostly's the best you'll get in this world. Keep your head down, do your work well, and you'll find your place." Then, with a brisk nod towards the returning Patrick, who handed me a tin of biscuits, she added, "Now off with you before the tea goes cold."

Patrick Spade was impossible to ignore. The deputy chef had a cocksure air about him and a way of needling everyone, his jibes as much a part of the kitchen as the clang of pots and the aroma of fresh bread. Mrs Kensley was the only one who could rein him in with her mere presence when his antics threatened to disrupt the kitchen's rigorous rhythm. Still, he was undeniably talented, and his quick wit and confidence made him a popular figure with the maids and helpers.

One morning, as I lingered near the kitchen door after a message delivery from Mrs Stanley, Patrick caught sight of me. He leaned against the counter, tossing a tea towel over his shoulder with a sly grin. "Well, well, if it isn't our resident lady of leisure," he quipped, loud enough for the room to hear. "Must be nice, sitting about reading stories to the little miss while the rest of us sweat over hot stoves. Cushy job, that."

A few chuckles rippled through the room, but Mrs Kensley shot him a sharp glance, her knife slicing through a carrot with precise authority. "Patrick!" she warned, her tone clipped.

I felt the weight of every gaze in the room, but I didn't flinch. Instead, I looked directly at Patrick and said, my voice calm but firm, "It may seem easy to you, Mr Spade, but I think every job has its own challenges. You know the heat of the kitchen, but have you ever tried earning the trust of a child? It's work too, though it might not leave flour on my hands or burns on my arms."

The room went quiet for a while before Mrs Kensley let out a dry chuckle, her stern face softening for a moment. "My, my. She's got you there, Patrick," she said, slicing through another carrot.

Patrick's grin widened, and he tipped an imaginary hat in my direction. "Fair enough, Asha. Fair enough," he said with a laugh. From that moment, his jibes became friendlier, laced more with camaraderie than teasing malice.

Over many hurried breakfasts taken in the early hours of the kitchen, I began to learn more about the rest of the staff and the kitchen crew. Those mornings were a whirlwind of activity, and it was quite a challenge to navigate the unfamiliar custom of eating while dodging bustling bodies and balancing a plate in my hand. Indians never had meals standing! Back home, meals were a ritual, eaten seated and with care—not snatched in hurried bites amidst chaos. Mr Nally and Mrs Glasse, with their white collars and airs of seniority, dined in their rooms, served neatly and without the bustling interruptions of the kitchen. They represented a tier of staff far removed from the kitchen maids or the footmen. I, however, belonged to neither world. I learned to quietly slip into the kitchen, eat quickly, and make myself useful where I could. Patrick, ever the joker, often made light of my balancing act.

"Careful, Asha," he'd say, his grin half-mocking. "Wouldn't want you getting ideas about joining us *real workers*. You might just burn a finger or two!"

Mrs Glasse was the toughest person to understand in those first few weeks. She maintained a polite distance, interacting with me only when necessary, as if unsure how to navigate my admittedly peculiar presence in her routine. Her words were measured, her tone formal, and her manner often brisk. Yet, there was no mistaking her precision when it came to her lessons. She would patiently explain things to Elizabeth, and every now and then, her sharp eyes would flicker in my direction, gauging whether I was following along.

At first, I thought she was testing me out of mere obligation, perhaps even suspicion. But over time, I began to sense something deeper. Despite the novelty of teaching an Indian ayah—an arrangement I imagined must have struck her as unusual, if not improper—there was a certain satisfaction she took in seeing me grasp her lessons. It was in the faint, almost imperceptible nod of approval when I successfully sounded out a challenging word, or in the way her voice softened, just a little, when I asked a question.

Initially, I wasn't sure whether Mrs Stanley and Mrs Glasse really meant for me to join Elizabeth in her classes. I remember the first day that I joined in. It had been a bright morning. I stood outside Elizabeth's room, waiting for the clock to strike seven, before stepping in to gently wake her.

"Did you sleep well?" I asked softly.

"I did. I dreamt of sailing on a cloud ... What did you dream of?" she asked, her sleepy face lighting up with curiosity.

"I had a dreamless sleep," I said as I picked her up.

Elizabeth bathed peacefully in her little room and sat for breakfast with her dolls, carrying out an animated conversation between them as I served her.

"What are you looking forward to today?" I asked her as we sat down and she put away her dolls.

She thought for a moment, her face brightening with excitement. "I want to ride a pony today! Mummy said she'd take me on Wednesday. What day is it today?"

I smiled at her earnestness. "I believe it *is* Wednesday."

Her delight was contagious. "What are *you* looking forward to?" she asked, mimicking my question with an impish grin. I realised then that she enjoyed turning my inquiries back on me, a habit that charmed me greatly.

"I'm looking forward to reading with you," I replied with a small laugh.

When it was time for her lessons, we moved to the schoolroom. I arranged her table, setting out her slate and pencils, but when Mrs Glasse entered, she disapproved immediately.

"I do not want you to set up her table," she muttered, casting me a sharp glance. "She is to do it herself every day."

I nodded, stepping back.

"Pull a chair, won't you? I thought you wanted to be in my class," she said, her tone brusque but not unkind.

I obeyed and seated myself in a corner. The lesson began with Elizabeth tracing the letter 'S' on her slate, embellishing it with little yellow flowers under Mrs Glasse's guidance. Then, to my surprise, she turned to me.

"Can you write on your own?" she asked, her sharp eyes studying me.

"I can, but not very well," I admitted, careful not to overstate myself. "I can read with ease."

Without a word, she handed me a book: *Tales from Shakespeare: Designed for the Use of Young Persons* by Charles Lamb.

"Let's see where you stand with literature," she said, her tone deliberate. "*The Velveteen Rabbit* is easy. By the end of the day, I want you to recount what you've read and understood."

I nodded, feeling both challenged and grateful, and began to read. The language was dense and unfamiliar, nothing like the stories I'd read before. I struggled to grasp meaning from the context. As I pressed on, the words seemed to unlock themselves gradually. One page gave way to another, and slowly, I began to understand the tales. I was exhausted by the time we finished for the day, but Mrs Glasse seemed quietly pleased with my attempt.

Her discovery of my love for reading brought no change to her demeanour, but she began to assign me books, asking me to report to her. Sometimes they were titles Elizabeth had outgrown; other times, they were heavier works that I knew she had deliberately chosen to challenge me. With time, I realised that beneath her conservative, old-fashioned exterior, she was a teacher to her core—not just a governess fulfilling her duty but a true educator who valued the spark of curiosity wherever she found it.

Years later, I would go on to read Shakespeare's original works and marvel at their brilliance. But it was in that little schoolroom, with little Elizabeth by my side and Mrs Glasse's watchful eyes, that I first discovered them through Charles Lamb's retellings.

It was just before the end of my first month at Bradbourne Manor that Mrs Stanley and I had our first long conversation since my arrival. I was enjoying the sun in the front lawn while Elizabeth was chattering away as Mrs Glasse arranged her books, when Mrs Stanley joined us. She sat with a cup of tea, holding Elizabeth in her lap like a favourite doll, both glowing in the bright morning light.

After a few moments of casual chatter, Mrs Stanley turned to me. "Asha, dear," she said gently. "Would you accompany me on a walk?"

"Of course, ma'am," I replied, setting aside my tea.

Mrs Glasse distracted Elizabeth with the promise of a story, and Mrs Stanley and I slipped away towards the back gardens. The walk was quiet at first, save for the sound of birds trilling in the trees and the occasional crunch of gravel beneath our feet. We wound our way through the perfectly kept paths of the estate, past roses in full bloom and hedgerows buzzing with life.

Finally, as we reached the estate's main gate, Mrs Stanley paused and turned to face me, leaning lightly against the iron bars.

"I am quite pleased with how you and Elizabeth are getting along," she said, her expression kind. "I know this is your job, to be done to the best of your ability, but I want you to know how fortunate I feel knowing Elizabeth has you."

I blinked, caught off guard by the unexpected compliment. She didn't need to acknowledge my work, but it warmed me that she did. I smiled. "Thank you, ma'am."

"You may have noticed my absence in recent days," she said, her tone light but probing for a response.

"Elizabeth didn't mention it," I replied honestly. "She's been quite cheerful, ma'am."

Mrs Stanley laughed softly. "I'm sure she has been. I let her know I'd be away. I've been tending to my social commitments, travelling, attending fund-raisers, and contributing my time to causes I care about. It's been easier knowing she's in such good hands with you."

"I'm happy to have earned your trust, Lady Stanley," I said sincerely.

"And are you comfortable here, Asha? Truly?"

"I have been most comfortable. Thank you," I replied.

She hesitated, then asked, "Have you thought about your future?"

I paused at the question. Of course, my foreseeable future was tied to Bradbourne Manor until I could save enough for a ticket home. But I knew better than to frame it that way. "I haven't given detailed thought to any future plans, Lady Stanley," I said carefully.

She studied me intently. "I'm not asking about your plans to find a way back home, Asha." Her voice softened as she continued. "Your first month here is almost over. Would you like to visit the Ayah Home, to let them know how you're coming along? You have a keen mind. Mrs Upton told me you picked up fluent English in less than two years. I've seen your embroidery. I sense that you can do a lot more with yourself if given a chance."

She continued earnestly, "I want to offer you the chance to learn, and eventually do more with your life. And I'd like the girls there to know you've done well for yourself, and that they also can."

I noticed her perfect smile, kind eyes and rose-tinted cheeks and I thought about what she said. That this accomplished, poised woman believed I could be an example to others felt surreal. I had been meaning to visit Putri, Rangamma, and the others once I received my wages, but her encouragement made the idea all the more pressing.

She looked to the horizon smilingly, and drew in a deep breath, as if to fill herself with the cool air and the fragrance of the garden. "Asha, how wonderful it is—you're so young, with all roads ahead of you. If I were you, I'd want to be the next Ada Lovelace or Florence Nightingale!"

I smiled back, though I had no idea who these people were. Her enthusiasm was infectious. Was she naive, or was I, for letting myself be swept up in her optimism?

"Lady Stanley, if I may ask—what would you tell your seventeen-year-old self today?"

She looked surprised by the question, then dropped her eyes with a smile.

"I'd tell her to be careful what you wish for."

I tilted my head, curious, but before I could ask more, she laughed, a carefree, bell-like sound that echoed her laughter at the fund-raiser weeks ago.

That night, I lay awake pondering her words. Was Mrs Stanley truly happy? She had everything—social standing, charitable achievements, a beautiful estate, a devoted staff, and a happy child. Yet I couldn't shake the feeling that she was somehow burning her candles at both ends. While I admired her kindness deeply, I also knew my possibilities weren't as endless as she imagined. I was a person of colour, and my roads were narrower. Yet her optimism seemed so genuine that I let myself hope.

Soon I had my first earnings in hand. Holding the wages of my first month in my hand, I couldn't help but feel that the crisp, precious notes were a precious treasure to be secreted away. I whispered a quick prayer to the goddess of wealth before hiding the notes inside the curtain rod in my room. When Saturday evening came, I asked Mrs Stanley for permission to visit the Ayah Home the next day. She readily agreed, and it was arranged that Mrs Glasse would drop me halfway, after which I would take a bus. A bus ride in England, to me, felt like my first independent, fearless act in this foreign land.

Before leaving, we made our way to the dining hall to inform Mrs Stanley about our departure. To my surprise, she wasn't alone. Sitting across from her was the forbidding Lord Stanley, glowering over some papers. He looked older than Mrs Stanley, and there was a sternness to his features, a tautness in his jawline, a slight downturn to his lips that hinted at a man accustomed to being obeyed without question.

"Ah, here she is," Mrs Stanley said warmly, standing to address her husband. "Dear, this is the young girl I mentioned."

He looked up, his gaze briefly sweeping over me before settling on his wife. "Right. Of course," he said, nodding absently. Then, turning to us, he asked curtly, "Do you both need something?"

"I had requested a half day off," I said, my voice steady but careful.

"And she is to help me with some errands before she goes," added Mrs Glasse, her tone as measured and polite as her curtsey.

"Alright then," he said, his brow furrowing as he glanced at me once more before turning back to his breakfast. "That is up to you, Claudia."

"It's all in order, dear," Mrs Stanley replied, her smile returning as she resumed her seat.

Once we were out of earshot, Mrs Glasse let out a small, sharp breath. "Asha," she said, her voice low and firm, "when you are in the presence of Lord Stanley, you will speak only if spoken to. And you will always address him as 'my lord'. Do you understand?"

"But he asked me..." I began, confused by her admonishment, but was interrupted.

"Asha," she said firmly, stopping to look me in the eye, "not everyone in this house is like Mrs Stanley." I nodded. The Stanleys might inhabit the same house, but they clearly played by different rules.

Our cab ride up to Bloomsbury was easy. Mrs Glasse gave me instructions on riding the bus to Hackney.

"You're certain you remember the stops?"

"Yes, Mrs Glasse," I said, clutching the little slip of paper she had scribbled on earlier. For the first time since my arrival in England, I was travelling independently. The bus door opened and I climbed aboard, carefully counting out my fare and trying to not notice all the astonished looks and whispers.

For the first time, I saw the Derbyshire landscape without distraction or haste. Vast green fields stretched endlessly, broken only by the silhouettes of ancient trees dotting the gently rolling hills. Small market towns appeared like painted scenes. Soon, we reached the city and the bus barrelled through London's streets. I watched children dart between vendors, men in top hats striding purposefully along cobbled roads, and women hauling bundles through narrow alleyways. The sights stirred something in me, an inkling of possibility that I might carve out a place in this vast, indifferent city. I gripped my bag tightly, ready to step out into the next piece of my journey, ready to see faces that might, even briefly, feel like home.

"Look at you! Only a couple of months ago, you were scared to step out. Now you're taking the omnibus?" Mrs Upton greeted me with a quiet smile, holding the door open as I climbed the steps, beaming. Rangamma sprang out from behind her, pulling me into a tight hug before I'd even entered. Putri and a few other familiar faces crowded around, their eyes bright with excitement.

Laughter and chatter filled the air as I stepped inside, swept up in their joy. Tea was served, and we gathered in the common room, the warmth of their company putting me at ease. They peppered me with questions—about Mrs Stanley, Elizabeth, and the routines of my new life. Some listened intently, their faces alight with curiosity, perhaps imagining what their futures might hold. Others seemed quieter, their gazes turned inward, as if reaffirming their desire to return home.

After tea, when the room was quieter, Rangamma leaned close and whispered, "They sent Ah Tai back … out of turn, you know."

I tried not to react, but I felt a pang of panic. *They sent Ah Tai back?* I was happy for her. She had been so lost here, with no one to speak her language. But why had they sent her ahead of the others? Hadn't they asked me to take the job with Mrs Stanley to save funds for returns? Had something changed? Had there been an unforeseen opportunity—did they even consider informing me? Or was I more valuable to Mrs Upton here—as a success story for the others?

I forced myself to nod and smile at Rangamma. *Ah Tai needed this more than I did,* I reminded myself.

Mrs Upton and Mrs Travers arrived just as the teacups

were being cleared away. Both women greeted me warmly, but I found myself unable to match their enthusiasm. The lingering doubts from Rangamma's whisper dampened my spirits, though I hid it behind a polite smile.

"Asha!" Mrs Upton exclaimed. "It's so wonderful to see you doing so well. You're looking healthier, happier—clearly, Mrs Stanley's household agrees with you." I murmured something agreeable, unsure how to respond. The room was quiet as Mrs Upton turned to address the other ayahs.

"Ladies," she began, clasping her hands together, "Asha is an example of what can happen when you seize opportunities. She was brave enough to step into a new situation, and look where it's brought her. Not every girl has the chance to work for a family like the Stanleys.

"I encourage you all," she continued, her voice growing firmer, "to consider employment rather than simply waiting for us to send you back. You'll gain experience, confidence, and the means to eventually return home under your own steam."

The ayahs listened in silence, their expressions ranging from thoughtful to unreadable. I sat among them, an unease growing with every word. The room was quiet when Mrs Upton finished, and I could feel people's gazes on me. I stood slowly, in the grip of a quiet determination to speak my mind.

"Mrs Upton is correct. I've been fortunate," I began, my words measured. "It is also true that not everyone might find a family as kind as the Stanleys or a situation as comfortable as mine."

The ayahs turned to me.

"What went right for me, could have also gone horribly wrong. I could have been abused and miserable; they could have underfed or underpaid me, or not fed or paid me at all.

I could virtually have been held prisoner and I would never be able to get word out to you. That was the chance I took, and the chance you're being asked to take. So you should be careful."

I glanced at Mrs Upton, whose smile had tightened into something less generous.

"And whatever you decide," I concluded, "I hope you'll never feel ashamed for wanting to go home. You're not here by choice ... you have a right not to take this chance and to go back home."

The silence that followed was heavy. Mrs Upton cleared her throat and changed the subject, chatting with Mrs Travers as the ayahs streamed out of the hall. She turned to me once we were alone.

Her voice was low but forceful, vibrating with an anger barely contained. "What was that all about, young lady?"

The heat of her words fanned a fire in me I hadn't known existed. It was sharp, raw, and unrelenting. For the first time, I wasn't just disagreeing with an adult, I was confronting them. Anger coursed through me as I turned to face her, determined to meet her as an equal.

"I know you want them to take up jobs here," I said, my voice trembling but resolute. "But you're using me to convince them. I will never do that—not for you, not for anyone."

Her eyes flared with indignation, and she abandoned any pretence of composure. "I did not *make* you do anything," she snapped. "You chose to visit them here—for what? You've done well—for what? Shouldn't they learn from you?"

"They have a right," I said, my voice trembling but unwavering.

"Yes, they have a right to go home," she retorted fiercely.

"But who's going to give them that right? And is it more important than their right to be warm, safe, and have a roof over their heads? The Ayah Home gives them that. How can we keep doing that, Asha? For someone to be saved from drowning, someone needs to be brave enough to swim."

Her words poured out, unrelenting. "Is it wrong if I encourage them not to wait for their so-called 'right' here, but to go out, assimilate, and make something of themselves?"

"And on whose conscience would it be," I shot back, my voice quiet but clear. "If they go right back into the dangers from which the Home rescued them? Is it fair to ask this of them, Mrs Upton? These women are weeping for their lost lives. How can you expect them to just forget all of that pain?"

We faced each other, the room electric, silent, sparks flying between us. I held back my tears, refusing to let them betray me, and gazed at the face of the woman who had hugged me goodbye just a month ago. Her hand clutched at the cross at her neck as if drawing strength from it, the silver glinting faintly in the dim light. Her voice, when it came, was low and calm, and she spoke with unquestionable conviction.

"There is nothing—*nothing* wrong in what I'm doing."

I swallowed hard, the heat of my own anger cooling into something heavier—exhaustion perhaps. "You do it your way," I said quietly, my voice hollow. "But I won't be a part of it."

She looked at me with sorrow. "This is not how it was supposed to be, Asha. I had hoped you would work with me, for their good," she said, her tone almost imploring. "Be careful, Asha. Cowardice often hides as neutrality."

"And what about convenience, Mrs Upton? Was it

convenient to send Ah Tai back, because she couldn't take on any employment?"

The colour drained from her face, then came rushing back as her hand flew up. For a second, I wondered whether she would strike me. But she didn't. Her hand faltered, then slowly moved to her chest as she crossed herself. Without a word, she turned and walked away with heavy steps. I stood frozen, the anger that had flared so brightly now receding, leaving only shame in its wake. I had crossed a line, and I knew it. My words had been a weapon, wielded without care for the wound they might leave behind.

Before I left, I counted my earnings carefully and donated nearly all of it to the Ayah Home. Mrs Travers looked startled, her hands pausing over the ledger. "Oh dear ... that's a lot of money. Are you sure you want to part with so much?"

"I'm sure," I replied firmly. "It's not much anyway. Please tell Mrs Upton that this is my way of contributing, and I'm sorry I can't do it her way. I'll send more when I can. And tell her ... tell her I'm grateful."

I didn't ask to see Mrs Upton before I left, nor did she come to see me. Perhaps it was better this way.

I had a lot of time before Mrs Glasse would pick me up from Bloomsbury. As I walked the streets, my mind replayed the confrontation with Mrs Upton. I couldn't tell which one of us was right or wrong, and whether it even mattered. What lingered was a heavy misery. Another home lost. I would always love the Ayah Home, but it no longer fitted me. And then there was another ache. Had I carried a faint, foolish hope for something like a mother's tenderness from Mrs Upton? In reality, she and I were divided, our beliefs pulling us in opposite directions, turning our will to do good into a quiet battlefield.

Could this have happened to my father and me, I wondered, choking back a sob. I remembered his face, panicking when the details took longer to resurface. Do we outgrow our parents? Does home ever remain, or do we all lose it eventually—and I just lost mine a little sooner?

Taking in the sights, I reached Victoria Park and found myself on a bridge over Regent's Canal, drawn into the laughter of a huddle of children pressing against its railings. My steps next carried me east and soon I found myself at the Hackney flea market. Its buzz of activity was intoxicating—stall after stall spilling over with ceramics, fabrics, furniture, and gleaming trinkets. Milliners displayed their wares next to butchers and vendors of ale. The din of bartering voices, the mix of scents from spices and food stalls—it all reminded me of Simla's markets. The ice cream vendor caught my eye, and I treated myself to a cone, savouring the cool sweetness as I found a set of stairs to sit on. As I licked my ice cream, someone approached from my side. I cupped it protectively and turned to face the one approaching. There, grinning wide enough to brighten even the gloomiest day, stood a boy in a barrette cap.

"Kasim!" I shrieked with joy, leaping to my feet.

"I knew it was you!" he said, pointing a playful finger at me over the huge paper bag in his arms. "How have you been, Arti?"

"It's Asha, you chump! But that's alright. I'm so happy to see you!" I laughed, grinning from ear to ear.

"Sorry, yes, Asha," he said, beaming. He looked nothing like the scrawny, soot-covered boy I had met over a month ago. His cheeks had filled out, his complexion was healthier, and his nose—once blackened from soot—was now enviably sharp and clean.

"Are you still at the restaurant?"

"Why, yes, of course! I'm doing well there, if I may say so myself. Came here to buy some new clothes. So ... you decided to stay here?"

"Um ... yes and no. It's a long story. I'm working in Derbyshire until I have enough to travel back home. How come you're not working on a Sunday?"

"I get one Sunday off every month to see this beautiful city and to sleep in," he said, circling his finger in the air with a theatrical flourish.

We found a spot to sit and shared a bowl of cherries while we talked about our work. Kasim spoke with the same easy cheer I remembered, though now it was laced with a quiet pride. He told me he had made a few friends and seemed entirely grateful for his life, never uttering a word of complaint.

When it was time to part, he handed me a slip of paper asking me to take down his name and address, and insisted that I memorise it.

"You see, Asha, I cannot read or write myself, but I'd like to get letters from friends too. Promise to write?"

"I wouldn't have guessed—you speak so well! But if I write to you, how will you read it?"

"One of my friends will read it to me. And I promise to make them write back too!" he said, flashing a warm smile.

I smiled back, marvelling at the serendipity that had brought Kasim into my life. I reached Bloomsbury well in time for Mrs Glasse to pick me up. She showed me "a doll carriage for Elizabeth from Gamages", a bunch of wool for knitting, some lace for the valances in her room and some new books for the library. I was touched. I could tell from her selection that the books were purchased keeping me in mind. We were driven back to Bradbourne Manor. On the way, Mrs Glasse spoke of her rheumatism pills, and I ruminated over my first month and thought about Elizabeth.

15

The first year with the Stanleys was, in many ways, the happiest for me since my father passed away. I spent much of my time alone with a book, except when Ada or Mrs Kensley invited me to the kitchen. I could never complain about those nights in the kitchen, filled with laughter, games, and camaraderie. When all else failed, everyone made Patrick the subject of their teasing. The more time I spent in the kitchen, the more I felt like a part of the group. Mrs Kensley always set aside some chips for me; the kitchen boy Jem was the first to claim me for his team; and Ada would pull me aside for gossip—we had become a formidable duo at charades, much to everyone's delight.

Lord Stanley was a rare and foreboding presence. He was seldom seen around the estate, and I made it a point to steer clear when he was. His expression was perpetually dour and unsmiling. Once, he visited the schoolroom during one of Mrs Glasse's lessons with Elizabeth. Flustered, Mrs Glasse stuck to Elizabeth's favourite topics, revisiting a lesson she had already taught. Lord Stanley appeared satisfied and left without a word. Beyond these occasional appearances, he seemed largely uninvolved in Elizabeth's daily life.

I wrote to Kasim from time to time. His letters brimmed with hope. His supervisors were impressed with his progress and he dreamt of excelling at the restaurant one day. I kept my letters light, sticking to topics he would enjoy, like the books I was reading, and refrained from sharing much about my life at Bradbourne. I did, however, encourage him to learn to read when he had the chance.

We saw plenty of Mrs Stanley in the schoolroom, the garden, and the nursery. When her husband wasn't around, she devoted much of her free time to Elizabeth. There were periods wherein she'd be confined to her room, or would be travelling, but she'd make it up with her warmth to the child when she returned.

She often asked me about my reading. I embroidered the collars of her gowns and occasionally offered suggestions for entertaining the many guests she hosted at Bradbourne Manor. Sometimes, she took Elizabeth out on to the estate to ride the pony or stroll through its wooded paths. Other times, they ventured to London with Mrs Glasse to shop for clothes or toys.

I cherished the days of their outings. Left alone in the house, I retreated to my attic room, curling up with a book and a hot beverage. In those moments, life felt unimaginably good, almost too good to be true. The curtain rod was getting too narrow for my savings. I decided that I'd entrust my savings with Mrs Upton on my next visit, where they would be the safest and handy when I needed to purchase a ticket back.

An event that proved transformative was my first self-assigned book. It had been a busy morning with lessons, and I was pleased when Mrs Glasse told me it was about time I picked a book of my own choosing.

I scanned the shelf and picked up a slim book, *So Big* by Edna Ferber. Mrs Glasse peered at the title and nodded approvingly, hiding a smile. The bright orange cover and Persian blue spine with bold, confident letters seemed to promise adventure.

"This book looks interesting, Mrs Glasse, but it seems too difficult for me," I confessed, flipping through its pages. The sentences felt dense, with many words I didn't recognise. "And it's not even a British author, is it? It's written by someone from … Michigan. Do you think I should try something easier?"

"How could I say?" she replied, her tone light but firm. "If you know the language, don't let any book intimidate you. Even if you don't understand every word, there's meaning in the sentences, and meaning beyond them too. What's the worst that could happen? If you don't understand it all, so what? You might still see a different world. Isn't that why we read?"

I knew she meant to encourage me, but something about her declaration was also a challenge. I was determined to prove myself. Instead of the doll chair, which was beginning to ache against my bottom, I settled on the bench by the window, the sunlight spilling over the pages, and dived in.

The book turned out to be more than a story. It was a mirror, a map, and a quiet reflection on things I had felt myself but never put to words. I was transfixed, drawn deeply into Selina's world. I read of her father, of his quirks, his wisdom, his failures, and his inevitable end, and felt her heartbreak so vividly that it stunned me.

I read and reread his words to her:

"I want you to see all kinds," he would say to her. "I want you to realise that this whole thing is just a grand adventure. A fine show. The trick is to play in it and look at it at the same time."

"What whole thing?" Selina would ask.

"Living. All mixed up. The more kinds of people you see, and the more things you do, and the more things that happen to you, the richer you are. Even if they're not pleasant things. That's living."

I read that two, three, four times, and wondered if I could think of my life like that. Was I living it, and looking at it at the same time? I borrowed the book after dinner and ran to my attic, pulling the curtains closed and lighting candles for an uninterrupted reading session. Hours passed as I devoured Selina's story, savouring its raw beauty. Some lines seemed to leap off the page, reaching a deep place within me:

> Beauty. Yes. All the worthwhile things in life. All mixed up. Rooms in candlelight. Leisure. Colour. Travel. Books. Music. Pictures. People—all kinds of people. Work that you love. And growth—growth and watching people grow. Feeling very strongly about things and then developing that feeling to—to make something fine come of it.

I was mesmerised by the beauty of the story and Selina's capacity to find wonder in the ordinary was a revelation. I read late into the night until sleep overcame me.

That night, I dreamt of a cabbage field. My father was there, sitting across the field, clutching a handful of envelopes. The envelopes were the pale green of the cabbages, and he extended them towards me. "Read one every day," he said. But as I reached for them, they vanished, and I was left alone in the field, calling out to him.

I woke up to the soft knocking of a woodpecker outside the window. The sun hadn't yet risen, and the cloudy sky outside hinted at rain. I stood by the window, breathing in the fresh air and thinking of my father.

"I know that a lot of people do not think this way in our village, Munni, but you must understand that education uplifts us. You must go to school. You must do better, especially because you are a girl," my father had once said. That was the only time he ever told me to do something especially because I was a girl. I was surprised to notice that collars of my nightdress were wet with warm tears, thinking of him at that moment.

The days that followed were richly filled with books and lively conversations with Mrs Glasse. Lord Stanley remained a distant figure, his shadow rarely darkening my path, and my focus remained on Elizabeth and my newfound literary companions. Elizabeth and I grew closer with each passing day. Every morning, she'd eagerly recount her dreams—flying lessons with butterflies (who, she swore, resembled Mrs Glasse) or indulging in a world full of cream tarts. Her appetite for stories soon outgrew simpler books, such as the abridged *Velveteen Rabbit*, and I found myself improvising tales. Some were simplified versions of the Ramayana or folk stories from my village. To my surprise, she adored them. Watching her giggle and gasp at tales of brave monkeys and clever princes, I realised something profound: stories transcend borders.

Books became my sanctuary and my adventure. I journeyed with Allan Quatermain to the heart of Africa, mourned alongside Jay Gatsby, and wished for a love story of my own, like Elizabeth Bennet's. Each book opened new worlds, but some lessons came more easily than others. There were times when all I took from a book was a good laugh, but often, stories taught me truths about life, love, and courage that felt universal.

Certain things that happened that year made me acutely aware of the passage of time. The first related to the Ayah Home, which I visited regularly. Though my relations with Mrs Upton were fraught, I did feel happy seeing some of my old friends. I was happy to help them with various fundraisers and donate a little bit of what I had made. It slowed the progress of my own savings but always made me feel like I was making some difference. Despite my contributions, I had gradually made good savings which I hoped would be enough to take me home.

On one such visit to the Ayah Home Mrs Upton drew me aside, and spoke to me stiffly but directly. Rangamma needed to be sent home—she had received word that her father was desperately unwell.

"The Home recently sent Alice back. We scraped together enough for her ticket and hoped she'd make it in time to pick up the pieces of her life, her marriage." Her lips pressed into a thin line. "But that effort left us completely depleted. We don't have the means to do it again."

There was a pause. Then, directly, she asked, "Could you contribute?"

After Alice had been sent back, Rangamma was the only true friend I had left at the Home. She was the only one remaining from the days we had put up the exhibition, where I had met Mrs Stanley. Now she needed me, so what could I do except support her? It meant letting my last friend from the Home go, but it had to be done. I hugged a sobbing Rangamma goodbye, and at my request Mrs Upton never told her who had facilitated her return.

After Rangamma left, the Ayah Home changed for me. I didn't mingle much with the new inhabitants and spent most of my time with the matrons. It felt sad sometimes to see these ayahs as a bunch of strangers, who glanced at me with curiosity or perhaps mild reverence. I had become something of a figure to them. I suspected some of them found me a betrayal, a prop in a narrative they hadn't chosen to be part of. Gradually, the faces I knew had disappeared entirely, replaced by unfamiliar ones, and I realised I had long since ceased being informed about opportunities to travel back with families.

Mrs Upton was distant but appreciative after our falling out. From time to time, she would let me know, almost as an aside, that my contributions had helped purchase provisions for the winter, or had helped some ayah's medical treatment, or helped towards some ticket home. I had stopped asking for an opportunity to travel home with a family, and soon I realised I had stopped counting my savings to check when I may be able to buy the ticket back. I was happy being with Elizabeth, and I could see no reason to give that up just yet.

One day, a few months into my second year with the Stanleys, I reviewed my savings again. Even after sending Rangamma back, I had made enough for my own ticket. It was the moment to ask myself the difficult question I had brushed away: What was I doing here being an ayah when I could be anything in India?

I lost sleep over the decision, burdened by the freedom to choose what I wanted to be. I imagined my life back in Simla, but the vision felt more like a question than an answer. Would Jitu already be married? All these years, I had avoided writing to him, unwilling to disrupt his life when my return was uncertain. Now that I could go back, I wondered if it was kinder to let him believe I was lost, or better still, not think of me at all. The thought of writing to him and never hearing back was unbearable. Wouldn't he have moved on? Forgotten me entirely?

If I returned, what could I do for work? I knew English well enough to teach, but who would trust an Indian girl as a governess—rather than an ayah? I hadn't forgotten the way they saw us. The villagers back home too would see me as tainted by my time abroad. Teaching my own people seemed an option, but I knew they'd whisper about me besmirching my character in a foreign land. I remembered Jitu's mother's face. Even she wouldn't be able to recommend me to the villagers. Amanullah Khan hadn't employed me at his shop because I'd have to work alongside men of another faith. So what prospects would I have now, after all these unaccounted years away? Marriage was out of the question—perhaps forever. It would be enough if I could simply earn a respectable living. But would it be possible if people didn't respect me for what I had become?

I began to doubt whether sending other ayahs home was doing them any favours. Would they not face the same struggles, the same walls I foresaw for myself?

That night, I thought of Mrs Anthony Pareira, the eternal traveller. She remained adrift on the ocean, cycling through new wards and new faces. There was a reason she stayed on the ship, I realised now. Perhaps no one really wanted her home. They might accept the money she sent, but a lost woman was more convenient than a woman returned, tainted by the intrigue of an independent life amongst foreigners. I saw now how the ship's constant motion allowed her to hold on to the dream of home without ever facing the reality of it. I pitied her for carrying that knowledge, but I also envied her freedom. She lived on her terms. Didn't I want the same? And for what would I leave Elizabeth, Mrs Glasse, Mrs Stanley, Ada, and my life at Bradbourne?

Through my tears, I promised myself I wouldn't let fear or nostalgia steal my peace. I would remember that I made this decision calmly, deliberately, and on my own terms. I tried to forget my address, so that I would never let myself crave for my lost friend and send out a letter. I wept many nights, until one night I didn't.

16

It was during my second year at Bradbourne that things changed.

Outwardly, the flow of life at the estate continued undisturbed. Mrs Glasse took my education seriously, insisting I write my thoughts on the books I read—a daunting task, but one I approached with determination, eager to learn and please her. We read essays, discussed famous personalities, and delved into world history, science, and mathematics. Every Friday, she asked me to prepare a session about a famous personality and present it in a way Elizabeth, now six, could understand. Often, I wondered if girls my age outside Bradbourne were made to work so diligently on their education.

Much to everyone's delight, Elizabeth was blossoming into a perceptive little girl, thriving under Mrs Glasse's unconventional yet effective methods of teaching. At six, Elizabeth read well beyond her years and demonstrated a natural aptitude for numbers, horse riding, even poetry, to Lady Stanley's boundless pride. Her love for stories had matured alongside my own. No longer content with oral tales, she now preferred to read them from books, often curling up in bed just as I did. I couldn't help but smile, realising how much she had grown.

One cloudy afternoon, Mrs Stanley was going over the estate accounts with Mr Hedley, the estate manager. Mrs Glasse and I were passing by with Elizabeth.

"Mrs Glasse? Would you be kind enough to calculate these interests for me please?" requested Mrs Stanley.

Mrs Glasse leaned over. "These calculations here are the sums borrowed by the farmers from us?"

"Yes, at simple interest," said Mr Hedley. "I have calculated the interests and the total amounts. Lady Stanley just needs to check these figures."

"Of course," smiled Mrs Glasse, and busied herself scribbling away with a pencil, focusing on the calculations. I craned over Mrs Glasse's shoulders and said, "That's £8.42 for farmer Pelham."

Everyone turned to me. Mr Hedley looked confused, Mrs Glasse surprised.

"You worked that out? Can you see about farmer Andy?" probed Mrs Stanley.

I used my right thumb to write on my left palm, "That would be … £4.78."

One out of ten calculations in that list were incorrect. Of course, Mr Hedley embarrassedly apologised for the error and promised to redo the records to check for any other errors.

From that day forward, Mrs Glasse incorporated more arithmetic and practical number studies into my lessons. Mrs Stanley herself sponsored the purchase of books on accountancy. I threw myself into these lessons with enthusiasm. Numbers, I realised, carried a comforting logic, the same in Simla as Derbyshire.

"I should have known this was your strength," remarked Mrs Glasse one day, watching me work through problems with ease.

"I didn't realise it myself."

"It's not your job to realise these things," she said softly. "It's mine."

Occasionally, I accompanied her to the doctor, and we'd stop for meals at busy markets on the way back. Once, she insisted on buying me a new pair of shoes. Mortified at the thought of someone else paying for something so personal, I protested, but she silenced me with a firm tap of her umbrella. "I will not have it any other way, and I will not be dictated to! Now come on, we do not have all day."

That evening, as we walked up the Bradbourne driveway, the shoebox tucked tightly in my arms, I felt an unfamiliar lump in my throat. I was glad she strode ahead of me, her strong figure cutting against the fading light, so she couldn't see the tears that had begun to blur my vision.

I remember vividly the day when everything changed for me at Bradbourne Manor. Perhaps, the seeds of this change had always been there, lying dormant, and all I was meant to do was look close enough. It was a Sunday morning, and as usual, I woke early to get a head start on the day. Drawing back the curtains, I found it too dark to read indoors. I picked up my unfinished essay and decided to work in the garden until it was time to wake Elizabeth. As I tiptoed down the stairs, a muffled thud and the sound of suppressed sobbing froze me in my tracks. The noise was coming from Lord Stanley's study.

Moving cautiously closer, I heard a woman's voice, faint and unrecognisable. I wished for the door to open, so that I could make out the words. Then a second voice broke through—heavier, deliberate, cruel. It was unmistakably Lord Stanley.

"It's not the infernal charities and balls you squander your time on," he thundered. "It's your refusal to let the child of this house be educated as she should be. I'm glad you can't bear me any more children—I'd hate to waste a *son* on this mollycoddling."

I stumbled away, horrified to have overheard such a private exchange. My heart pounded as I darted up the stairs, reaching the next level just as the study door flew open. Mrs Stanley burst out, tears streaming down her face, while Lord Stanley's voice boomed from within. I didn't wait to hear more.

Back in my bed, I lay still, gripped by an unfamiliar, sickening feeling. Mrs Stanley, crying and being yelled at? The idea was incomprehensible. She had always seemed larger than life, untouchable. Perhaps all couples fought like this and patched things up later? After all, I'd never lived in a house with a married couple before.

From that day on, it was as if an undercurrent had suddenly made itself known to me, and I could see things I must have been blind not to have seen before. Mrs Stanley was often away, and when she was home, she was often unwell. She would still come into the schoolroom and play, though her eyes seemed tired until she lit them up with a smile. She'd get fresh flowers fixed in Lord Stanley's study by the parlour maid, she'd pay special attention to her husband's afternoon tea or evening whiskey. She continued to appear like a dutiful wife in love.

The episodes became more frequent, and soon there were whispers among the staff that there was "once again" a strain in the Stanleys' relationship. I didn't have anything to say. It was unbearable to think about participating in the gossip about someone whom I realised I'd come to love very much. Yet the stories came relentlessly, washing over me like waves over a rock. Some deemed Mrs Stanley "flighty", too preoccupied with frivolous pursuits for the dignity her station required. Others admired Lord Stanley's legendary temper, sharing tales of his anger with a strange kind of reverence. Among the staff, Betty, Holly, and Dora sided with him, along with some very old retainers who had known Lord Stanley since the time he had lost his parents in his childhood. Nally remained aloof, while Mrs Kensley, shaking her head in quiet disapproval, would only mutter, "It's a disgrace that a woman so good should be bullied like this."

One day I found Mrs Kensley in a sombre mood, all by herself in the kitchen on a rare occasion when most of the staff had taken leave to attend a fair in a nearby marketplace. She seemed sad and somehow smaller, abstracted from the context of the crew she bossed over. We stood at the window watching the rain come down, over a glass of sherry she chose to confide more in me.

She told me that while Lord Stanley had always been a man of few words and colder manner, the fissures in his relationship with Mrs Stanley had appeared shortly after Elizabeth's birth. It had been a gruelling labour, one that nearly claimed Mrs Stanley's life. The doctors had warned that another pregnancy would be fatal. What should have been a moment of gratitude for life became a bitter reckoning for Lord Stanley, his disappointment in a daughter compounded by the certainty that no male heir would follow. He left the estate shortly after Elizabeth's birth, returning a week later, changed and crueller than before. The household teetered on the edge of disaster, but with time, things settled into an uneasy stability. Yet any warmth Lord Stanley might once have felt for his wife had vanished. And Elizabeth, never important to her father, became doubly important to her mother, who poured her love into the daughter who had became her singular source of joy. She channelled her social standing into charitable causes, immersing herself in the work as if to fill a void. There were hints, Mrs Kensley suggested, of even darker shadows that loomed over their marriage, though she refused to say any more.

I looked at the rain undulate in silent streams across the glass of the window, obscuring the dim grassy fields beyond, and wished that it could wash away these past few days and my knowledge of these events concerning my brilliant, beaming Mrs Stanley.

I paid closer attention to Elizabeth and felt relieved to note that she seemed unaware of the tensions between her parents. As her friend, I was determined to keep it that way. I believed children found their sense of security in the illusion, if not the reality, of their parents' love for one another. Growing up, I had clung to the idea that my father had adored my mother, even though I had no memories of them together. The thought that they might have despised each other would have been devastating.

One Sunday, I set out for London to visit the Ayah Home. Mrs Glasse had taken Elizabeth out for a picnic to make the most of a sunny morning. I needed to inform Mrs Stanley before I left. I walked to her room and knocked softly. A long pause followed before I heard her faint voice.

"It's open."

The room was dark as night, the heavy curtains drawn shut against the morning light. A sour mix of alcohol and smoke lingered in the air, an unfamiliar and disconcerting scent in a space that usually carried Mrs Stanley's vibrant energy. I hesitated on the threshold, unsure whether to step in.

"I have a terrible headache, so the room needs to be dark," came her weak, muffled voice from somewhere near the bed. Through the dimness, I could barely make out her figure, still clad in her nightclothes. I imagined how mortified a woman like Mrs Stanley might feel to be seen like this.

"I'm sorry to disturb you, ma'am. I'm heading to London for the day. Would you like me to ask Bethany to bring you some tea?"

"That won't be necessary," she replied exhaustedly. "I'll just sleep a while longer. Good luck on your trip. Please give my regards to Mrs Upton, won't you?"

"Of course, ma'am," I said, gently closing the door behind me.

The journey to London was a blur. My mind was consumed with the troubling image of Mrs Stanley. How must someone feel to lock themselves away in a darkened room on such a glorious morning, numbing their pain with alcohol? It unsettled me deeply, the contrast between the radiant, unshakable Mrs Stanley I had come to know and the shadow of her I had seen that morning.

After this, incidents of Mrs Stanley being unwell and refusing to leave her room for an entire day became more frequent. On some days, she'd make an effort for her daughter, putting on a thin smile, but she seemed distracted and withdrawn. There were whispers amongst the staff of her drinking. The fights continued. One day, her maid Bethany spoke in hushed tones about an ugly bruise she had glimpsed, hidden beneath the long sleeve of Mrs Stanley's gown. The image struck me like a blow, my blood running cold as I tried to make sense of it. The household felt like a storm was gathering—quiet and ominous, its full force still unseen. I couldn't have known then that events were inching towards a devastating climax.

One lazy afternoon, I was yawing my way through some fractions beside a napping Elizabeth when Mrs Glasse walked in.

"Asha? A moment, please?"

We walked to the far end of the nursery and entered the schoolroom. Mrs Glasse looked serious, in a way that made me worry. Mrs Glasse leaned against the bookshelf, closing her wrinkled eyelids, looking shockingly old.

"Is everything alright, Mrs Glasse?" I asked hesitantly.

She sighed deeply. "The inevitable is here, my dear. Every good thing must end. Lord Stanley and … possibly Lady Stanley too have decided to send Elizabeth to a residential school. Very soon, they will no longer need me here."

"What? That cannot be!" I blurted, the words escaping me in disbelief. "Does Mrs Stanley approve of this? She can't possibly agree—she can't live without Elizabeth!"

"Mrs Stanley, Asha, is a mature woman, but one out of choices. She has held off the Lord's decision for as long as she could, keeping Elizabeth here with you and me. But the toll has been immense. There is nothing left in this house for her except the child. And now, she is going to lose her too. All that will remain is ... the cruelty," she paused, her words heavy with unspoken pain. "I wish she could change her destiny. But women must be patient, Asha. Sometimes, that is all we are allowed."

I shook my head, unable to process it. "Is there something else, Mrs Glasse? I swear there's more. Elizabeth is thriving under you. Why would they send her away?"

Her piercing gaze met mine over her glasses. "If you are even half as perceptive as I think you are, you know what's going on. And perhaps, you know what to do when I'm gone."

I felt my throat tighten. "But if Elizabeth is leaving, why would they keep me here?"

"Lady Stanley insisted. She said she would find you a placement and until then, keeping you here is no great expense to Lord Stanley. He agreed."

I tried to let that sink in. The thought of joining a new family so abruptly felt disloyal, even if at Mrs Stanley's suggestion.

"Listen," Mrs Glasse continued, "Elizabeth leaves in three weeks. I was meant to stay until then, but my niece is travelling to America next week. At my age, it's best I leave with her."

"Next week?" My voice cracked. "That's too soon, Mrs Glasse. I don't know how to stay here without you."

For the first time, she reached for my hands and held them tightly. "You've come a long way, Asha. And you still have a long way to go. I am fortunate to have been a part of your journey. Now, off you go into the world and make me proud." She smiled gently over her glasses, but her words felt like a goodbye I wasn't ready to accept.

I stood there, stunned. I had admired Mrs Stanley's strength and grace, but Mrs Glasse had been my anchor. Her counsel, her presence—they had become essential to me. The thought of navigating life in the manor without her felt like being thrown into the world once more, unprepared.

And then there was Mrs Stanley. Was this really her fate? To be punished by being separated from her daughter, in the guise of better education? Could it be that, despite all her poise and privilege, she was no better off than me?

I did not sleep well through the week. Mrs Glasse, despite having to pack up, insisted that our schedule be the same as earlier. She would conduct school for Elizabeth until lunch and take my help with the packing in the second half of the day. Elizabeth and Mrs Stanley had a long conversation about her schooling and the big change. Mrs Glasse convinced her that boarding school would help her grow into a great individual, and that our little home school wasn't enough to hone the talent that she had. As for Elizabeth, she seemed quiet and uncomplaining about the upcoming changes.

"Are we never going to meet again, Asha?" she asked one night as I tucked her into bed.

If she had been four or five, I might have given her an easy reassurance. But Elizabeth was too old now for comforting lies.

"That's possible, Elizabeth," I said gently.

"Well, I refuse to accept that," she declared firmly. "You and I can both write. Promise me a letter every month or two? Please? I don't want to lose you." Tears welled up in her eyes, her deliberate composure dissolving into a torrent of sobs. My heart shattered.

I held her tightly, pulling her close, and realised I too was crying. She clung to me, burying her face in my shoulder, and neither of us tried to stop the flood of emotions. There was a peculiar relief in surrendering to our feelings, in letting the sorrow flow freely. Out of all the jobs I had ever taken, this one felt the least like work, and Elizabeth felt the least like my charge.

When our tears finally subsided, she asked in a trembling voice, "What lies ahead for you?"

"Maybe another family," I replied. "I'm not sure yet. Lady Stanley will let me know. If not, I can always go back to the Ayah Home. I'm grateful for how life has unfolded so far, and I trust that good things will come my way."

"Are you happy even about being abandoned by your previous employer?"

"In some ways, yes. If not for that, my life wouldn't have taken this path, and I wouldn't have met you all. I am grateful for the opportunities that came out of it."

"So everything happens for the better? And it always ends well?" she asked, her voice barely above a whisper. I knew she wasn't asking about me any more.

"It's like a story," I said after a moment. "You don't always get to control what happens, but you can persevere through what others might see as a tragic ending. Eventually, if you keep going, the story turns happy again. And I don't believe our stories are over yet."

As I left her room that night, a sudden realisation hit me. Elizabeth knew far more about her parents than she let on.

Mrs Glasse, Elizabeth and I spent the next few evenings strolling through the estate or sharing picnics in the garden. Mrs Stanley made an effort to join us at least once a day.

Beneath the laughter, a bittersweet awareness lingered: these moments were finite, the last we would share together.

The evening before Mrs Glasse's departure, we decided to take the boats out on the estate's lake. Elizabeth insisted on riding with Mrs Glasse, leaving Mrs Stanley and me to share another. The lake was still, its surface reflecting the fiery hues of the setting sun. Mrs Stanley was quieter than usual. For the first time in a long while, it felt as though she wasn't wearing a mask. I rowed gently, glancing at her now and then, offering a small smile in case she needed it.

"I know you probably don't agree with my decision to send Elizabeth away," she said, her voice heavy.

The lake stretched out before us, like a sheet of molten gold, its surface rippling gently as the oars dipped and rose in rhythm. I studied it for a few seconds before replying.

"Perhaps ... but I don't sense a 'but' there, ma'am." I was emboldened by the closeness we had developed and by the impending end of this chapter in our lives.

Her eyes widened slightly in surprise. "Are you being unkind to me, Asha?" she asked, turning her gaze away.

I froze, regretting my words. "I'm sorry, ma'am. I didn't mean it that way. I'm sure you must be justified in your decisions."

"These aren't ..." she began, her voice faltering. She paused, then swallowed hard before finishing, "These aren't my decisions."

I stopped rowing, the oars resting idly on the water. Her face was pale, paler than the delicate ivory of her gown, and her eyes seemed hollowed, weighted by grief. Unloved and deeply unhappy, she was still Claudia Stanley, the same woman who had brought me here to be her daughter's companion.

The same woman who had sought out Mrs Glasse to ensure Elizabeth's education. She had been nothing less than a brilliant mother, fiercely attentive to Elizabeth's needs. Of course, she didn't want to send her child away. How had I ever believed otherwise?

She dabbed quickly at her tears with trembling fingers, glancing nervously towards the other boat to see if Elizabeth had noticed. The instinct to protect her daughter, even in her own sorrow, was evident.

"I never thought I'd see her leave before her seventh birthday," she murmured, her eyes fixed on the horizon where the sun kissed the treetops. "I imagined … everything would be different. That there would be more time."

"I am so, so sorry, Lady Stanley. I cannot imagine how hard this is for you," I said, my voice soft with sympathy. My heart ached for her. I wanted to remember her as the bright-eyed, confident woman I had first met at the fund-raiser, the woman who radiated strength and composure. It was difficult to reconcile that image with this person before me, so out of choices, so weary.

She looked away to hide the tears now streaming from her eyes. Her voice wavered, "And … and I can't talk to anyone about it. I'm trapped, and now I'm going to lose my daughter!"

I locked the oars and knelt carefully, the boat swaying slightly beneath me. I couldn't move closer without risking us tipping over. Instead, I stayed steady, watching her as the weight of her despair spilled forth, breaking through her usual restraint. "I'm going to lose her," she repeated, her voice cracking into desperate sobs. "And I can't stop it!"

Here, surrounded by water and the fading light, we were utterly alone. Had she brought me to this secluded place for a reason? She needed to speak, to unburden herself to someone who would listen without judgement. At that moment, I wondered: Was I a friend to her? Was I the only one so alien to her world and her country that she felt free to talk to me? As we shared that moment, something changed between us—we were no longer simply mistress and servant.

Suddenly calm, I found myself balancing easily on the boat, and I reached out to hold her hands. "Lady Stanley? Please look at me."

She wiped her tears and waited for me to speak, still not meeting my eyes.

"I can't possibly know what it is to live your life," I began, my voice earnest, heartfelt. "But I do know this: Sometimes, to leave a bad situation, you have to take a hard step. And you should take it. You should take it *now*, before it's too late." I hesitated, feeling the weight of my words, but pressed on. "I may be out of line saying this, but … he doesn't deserve you."

She looked up, her red-rimmed eyes wide with surprise. I took a deep breath and continued, "You're too special, too capable to be treated this way. Look at everything you've done. You've been a devoted wife, running this estate and this house flawlessly, even under impossible circumstances. You've been both father and mother to your daughter. You've given her an education that no school could match, and you've nurtured her brilliance. You don't deserve to live a life where you're abused, forced to send away your daughter, or punished for something beyond your control. You deserve better—for yourself and for Elizabeth."

I was entirely out of line, perhaps I risked immediate dismissal, but I couldn't sit by any longer. With Mrs Glasse soon gone, who else could speak to her frankly?

She was silent. I quietly resumed rowing, the oars slicing through the water in a steady rhythm. When we reached the bank, she remained seated, gazing at me with an unreadable expression. "I don't know how you know what you know," she murmured. "I can't promise I'll take your advice, Asha ... but you make a compelling argument." A small, watery smile touched her lips. "And it felt good to hear something kind about myself."

I bowed my head slightly, unsure how to respond. She stepped out of the boat, her movements deliberate, and walked away towards the house.

Shortly, Mrs Glasse and Elizabeth reached the shore. Elizabeth bounded up to me, her eyes bright. "Did Mama leave?" she asked.

"She said she needed to lie down," I replied. Satisfied with the answer, Elizabeth ran ahead towards the picnic spot.

Mrs Glasse lingered, watching me closely. Her sharp eyes seemed to search my face for answers, and after a moment, she gave a slight nod. I nodded back in silent acknowledgement, and she turned slowly to follow Elizabeth. Silence hung heavy over the lake, as I stood watching the mist curling like whispers over its surface, lost in thought.

And just like that, Mrs Glasse was gone the next day, leaving Mrs Stanley and me to our solitude. Without her steady presence, the strained atmosphere of the house seemed even dourer. Mrs Stanley clung to Elizabeth's company as if holding her might keep the inevitable at bay, but it was clearly difficult for her to be around Elizabeth without shedding a tear.

They shared every meal together, wandered the estate arm-in-arm, and spent hours sitting in the garden, often in silence. At night, Mrs Stanley abandoned her grand bedroom to sleep with Elizabeth in the children's room. Meanwhile, Lord Stanley carried on unaffected, indifferent. He lingered in the study, ate his meals alone in the grand dining hall, and rode his horses every evening for pleasure. From what I had seen, it had been weeks since he so much as acknowledged his daughter's existence. How could someone stop loving their child, I wondered. How could he continue as if his family were mere shadows in his life, nothing more than quiet shades in the background?

One morning, while I was helping prepare breakfast in the kitchen, the conversation turned to him.

"What's so surprising?" Ada said, stirring a pot of strawberry jam. "He obviously doesn't care much about them. Years of marriage does that to couples."

"Well, I wouldn't do that to the woman I marry", said Patrick. I couldn't be sure but I thought I saw Ada blush through the steam over her pot.

I ate my breakfast in the kitchen garden, kept company by worrying thoughts. What was my future going to be like once Elizabeth left? Mrs Stanley might keep me for a while longer, but sooner or later, my time here would end. My heart heavy, I took a bite of bread, barely tasting it. Would I ever meet someone special, someone who could help fill the undefined spaces of my life? What kind of jobs would I do, what could my options be? These questions might have seemed less daunting if only Mrs Glasse was still around to guide me.

A faint cough pulled me from my thoughts.

"Just me," Patrick said, leaning casually against the closed kitchen door. He crossed the garden languidly, and sat beside me on the grass, stretching out his legs. "You don't look like knowing what you're eating, missy."

I glanced at my half-eaten toast and shrugged. "I really don't. Where's Mrs Kensley today?"

"Discussing pantry supplies with Mr Nally," he replied, waving a hand dismissively. Then, tilting his head to look at me, he added, "What's on your mind?"

I sighed. "You can guess, can't you? With Elizabeth leaving, I'll have to think about my future now. I can't stay here forever."

Patrick frowned thoughtfully. "How long has it been since you came?"

"Closer to three years," I said, the words heavy with disbelief. "Time flies when you're … well, I don't know what I've been doing."

"And what do you think you'll do next?"

"I don't know," I admitted with a wistful smile. "I'll probably imagine Mrs Glasse asking me this, and then write down my strengths, and see what fits."

Patrick grinned. "That does sound Glasse-approved. You're right—why stick to being an ayah when you've clearly learned so much? I bet working with Miss Elizabeth taught you plenty. I envy you a little, you know. In these changing times, you've got options.

"You probably shouldn't envy me ever," I said lightly. "You're the deputy chef, and you're good at what you do."

He smirked, leaning back on his hands. "You're right. I shouldn't envy anyone. I am a very lucky man."

I raised an eyebrow, giving him a knowing look. "You really are, aren't you?"

His expression flickered with alarm before he laughed. "What do you mean by that?"

Before I could answer, the kitchen door creaked open, and Ada stepped out, her cheeks pink and her hands dusted with flour. "Patrick, what are you—oh, Asha," she said, a little too brightly.

I turned to Patrick, stifling a laugh. "You're both very lucky, in fact!"

Patrick dropped the pretence, his grin turning sheepish. Ada dropped down beside me, her face a blend of guilt and sheepishness. "Asha, I was going to tell you, I swear. It's just … well …"

"You didn't have to keep it from me," I said gently.

Ada sighed, twisting her hands. "It wasn't you we were worried about. It's Mr Nally. If he found out … well, you know how he is about staff fraternising."

I nodded. Mr Nally had made it clear that such relationships were forbidden, even among the most trusted staff. "I'll keep your secret," I assured them. "I think it's wonderful. You both deserve this happiness."

Ada's eyes filled with gratitude. "Thank you, Asha. Truly."

Patrick grinned, his earlier tension fading. "I knew we could count on you."

"You did not," I teased, and got a shove from Ada in return. The three of us sat there, laughing, and the garden suddenly felt a little less lonely.

I went to wake Elizabeth at the usual time, only to find her and Mrs Stanley snuggled together on the bed. The sight struck me with a wave of tenderness. It reminded me of how parents and children slept together in India, sharing a bed. Mrs Stanley's face looked marginally less strained as she gently stirred and spoke.

"We're up a little early because we've decided to visit my mother, Asha."

"My apologies, ma'am, no one informed me. I'll start preparing for the journey at once," I replied, already turning towards the door.

"There's no need," she said. "We only decided early this morning, and I've asked Bethany to ready my things and see to the car. Just help Lizzy get ready. We'll only be gone for the day."

I nodded and set about the task. The change of scenery might do them some good, and the day to myself would give me a rare opportunity to reflect. Perhaps I could finally begin to make sense of my future.

Patrick had asked if I was ready to leave this line of work behind, and though I hadn't answered him, the question had lingered. I still took pride in my role as an ayah. I felt fortunate to have supported Lily, Poppy and Elizabeth in my short career. Even more, I was glad to have shielded Joanna from her mother for as long as I could. And yet, I couldn't deny the changes in me. The Stanleys had spoiled me with opportunities I knew most ayahs would never have—education, respect, and a degree of independence in the way that I did. Was it possible to go back to being someone else's silent shadow? Moreover, times were changing in this country. From my glimpses into the world of Bradbourne Manor and beyond, I knew people still needed servants but not necessarily ayahs. The English had their own ways of raising children, and I would never fit neatly into their mould. My time here had made me yearn for something more, though I wasn't sure what that was yet.

After they left, I took a moment to draw up a list. It felt strange to reduce my hopes and desires to ink and paper, but as Mrs Glasse used to say, "It's all there in your head, my dear. You just need to see it."

So, I sat down and noted in my diary:

Things I Like Doing

1. Having a job I can do well
2. A little mathematics
3. Embroidery
4. Travel
5. Meeting new people

Things I Want from Life

1. Respectful treatment
2. Money to spare for travel
3. Spare time for reading and embroidery
4. A cosy home
5. Love/Marriage (?) [I hesitated, then erased the '/' and replaced it with '&']
6. Beautiful sights and walks every day

It wasn't as hard as I'd thought, once I started. I tore the page from the diary, folded it and placed it neatly on the desk, feeling a sense of clarity, even if only for a moment.

I thought of writing to Mrs Glasse. She would understand these restless thoughts better than anyone, but I couldn't write to her for another few days, and it wouldn't do to burden her so soon after she'd left.

I had an idea. For the first time ever, I sought out the butler, Mr Nally. He was hunched over a book in his chamber, his baggy eyes moving from one end of the page to the other. The room smelled faintly of pipe tobacco and polished wood. I knocked softly on the partly open door.

He glanced up, startled, and let out a deep "Yes?" before setting his book aside.

"Good afternoon, Mr Nally," I said politely.

"Good afternoon, miss. What brings you here?"

"May I have the newspapers for the last three days, sir? The ones Lord Stanley is done with?"

He raised an eyebrow. "For extra reading?"

"It is," I replied. "Mrs Glasse always encouraged me to keep reading."

"Oh. Remarkable lady," he said disinterestedly. "Perhaps too much of a visionary."

I murmured my thanks as he handed over the neatly folded papers.

Back in my attic, I spread the newspapers across the floor and lay on my stomach, sifting through the job advertisements. Most of them were predictable: requests for sober, religious young women, or specific roles like "parlour maid" or "cook". Amid the listings, one caught my eye:

> Waitress required for small hotel; must be intelligent, energetic, have a pleasant disposition and good appearance; willing to work long hours; good prospects for a suitable person; non-national considered. Apply to Hotel Viscount, Oxford St., London.

I imagined myself waiting tables, scrubbing surfaces, working long hours, and meeting strangers who probably wouldn't care to exchange more than a passing word. Would I have the energy for reading or embroidery after such a job? I marked the ad for later consideration.

The next batch of ads featured the usual fare: "Nurse to the Infirmary", "Single and widowed women wanted as cooks", and "Women of religious character needed as parlour maids". I skipped over roles like "Label Puncher (female)" and "Cleaning lady" without much thought. Then I saw: "A female caretaker-companion needed for elderly widow. Should be well read and well travelled, willing to do household work when needed. Handsome pay for a suitable candidate. PO Box S 5382."

It piqued my interest. I'd never applied for a job before, but after reading through three days' worth of advertisements, I felt I could write a convincing letter.

Dear Madam,

I hope this letter finds you well. I write in response to your advertisement seeking a female caretaker-companion.

I am presently employed with a prestigious family, assisting in the care and education of their daughter. Without disclosing details, I can assure you that my references are exceptional.

I am well read, with a particular passion for history and literature, and have aided in the education of a young child. I have also cultivated skills in arithmetic and would gladly assist with household accounting, if needed.

Additionally, I take pride in my embroidery skills, for which I have received compliments from all my employers. To demonstrate my skill, I have enclosed a small cutting of a handkerchief I embroidered myself.

I must also share that I am Indian by birth. I have adapted well to English customs and language, and I believe my diverse experiences could bring a unique perspective to our work together.

Should you wish to meet, I would be delighted to discuss how I might contribute to your household. I can provide glowing references upon request.

Yours faithfully,
Asha

I enclosed the embroidered handkerchief sample, carefully folded, and wrote Ada's address in the village as my contact. With the letter sealed, I felt a small flutter of anticipation.

I also responded to "Girl for inspecting work wanted. Must be experienced. Write Box 7482, News Chronicle, E.C.4." In my head, I had found a suitable position with the elderly widow from PO Box S 5382.

By evening, the Stanleys returned, looking slightly more cheerful than when they had left. Mrs Stanley headed to her room to freshen up, while I unpacked Elizabeth's belongings and helped her change into something comfortable.

As I brushed her hair, I asked, "Was it a good day for you?"

"I think so," she replied, a touch of hesitation in her voice. "I wish Mama could enjoy it more, but she never does when it's Grandmother. But I don't blame her. She makes Mama feel small, even when Mama does everything right. It must be hard being Grandmother's daughter."

"Hmm ..." I murmured.

Elizabeth disclosed that they had visited her grandmother, who was leaving for the United States soon, to a faraway estate she had recently purchased. In all my time with the Stanleys, I had barely encountered Mrs Stanley's mother. She was an affluent marchioness, aloof and acerbic. The few times I'd seen her at the grand parties at Bradbourne, she kept to herself, paying little attention to anyone, not even her own daughter.

"I'm sorry it wasn't very pleasant for her," I said softly, brushing Elizabeth's hair. "But at least she got to say goodbye before her mother left?"

Elizabeth grew quiet. I could almost hear her thoughts stirring. Finally, she said, "I don't like that Mama will feel lonely after I'm ..." her voice wavered.

I put the hairbrush down and gently rubbed her shoulders.

"... And I don't think Papa is enough," she sobbed, burying her face in my arms.

I held her close, silent. She was right to be concerned for her mother. Truth be told, I was worried too, perhaps even more than I was for my own uncertain future.

Once her sobs subsided, I led her to bed and tucked her in. Kneeling beside her, I watched as she stared blankly at the ceiling, her small face etched with worry far too big for her years.

"You're a good daughter, Elizabeth," I said quietly, breaking the silence. "Your Mama knows that. And she'll always have your back, no matter where you are. You've given her more joy than you realise."

A faint smile flickered on her lips before she closed her eyes, exhaustion finally overtaking her. I stood by the window, staring into the dark, rain-soaked night. The occasional flash of lightning illuminated fleeting glimpses of the drenched garden, casting jagged shadows that danced and vanished in a flicker. I shut the window reluctantly when I heard the thunder. It was getting quite late and Mrs Stanley hadn't joined her daughter, so I decided to settle in the armchair, pulling a shawl tightly around me. Sleep came in fragments, though I tried to remain watchful, ready in case either of them needed me.

17

The days crawled by, oppressive and thick with an unspoken dread that had seeped into every corner of the house. The staff didn't laugh as much, footsteps were softer and voices lower. Mrs Stanley seemed stretched thin, her usual grace fraying and unravelling at the edges. I couldn't shake the uneasy feeling that something was very wrong, and that the entire household was waiting for something terrible that was about to happen.

Just two days before Elizabeth was supposed to leave for boarding school, I got slightly late in waking up—but it was just in time to dress her for breakfast.

Ada entered the room carrying a tray laden with food for two. She leaned in and whispered, "Where's the mistress?"

"I don't know. She must have slept in her room."

"That's odd. She hasn't done that in over a month. If she doesn't sleep here, she's always in the spare room."

I shrugged. "She just didn't come here."

Ada looked worried and lowered her voice even further. "She hasn't emerged even yet. And here's the strange part—

Bethany hasn't shown up in two days, and the mistress won't let me dress her."

"What's wrong with that?" I asked, puzzled.

"What's wrong?" Ada's eyes widened. "She would never do that unless she was hiding something, Asha!" She motioned me to follow her out of the room.

Ada's voice turned urgent. "Look, I know you're younger than me, and maybe it's unfair to ask, but you have to find out what's going on with her. She'll talk to you."

"Why would she?"

"I don't know ... You tell me. You're the one who's a servant but never gets treated like one. She talks to you the way she used to talk to Mrs Glasse."

Whether it was a compliment or a complaint, it was true.

"Now listen," Ada continued. "Lord Stanley left late last night. Mr Nally went to Staffordshire for a funeral and won't be back until noon. Lord Stanley won't return before then either. You've got time. Please, Asha. I'm worried. You have to make sure she's alright."

Ada assured me she would stay with Elizabeth and help her pack, so I made my way to Mrs Stanley's spare room.

I knocked on the dark wood door and waited.

"Bethany?" Mrs Stanley's voice called from the other side, surprised.

"It's Asha."

"Oh ..." A strained laugh followed. "Is everything alright with Lizzy? I fell asleep here. I hope she was fine."

"Don't worry, Lady Stanley. I stayed with her."

There was a pause before the lock clicked, and the door opened. The room was shrouded in near darkness, and Mrs Stanley's pale figure stood silhouetted in the dim light. Her delicate nightgown clung to her, and her shoulders drooped as though carrying an unbearable burden.

I stepped inside as she retreated, her movements hesitant. The faint smell of alcohol hung in the air. My eyes landed on a glass abandoned in the corner, though the bottle was nowhere in sight.

Mrs Stanley walked to the bed, her back to me, her steps heavy. I carefully navigated the darkened room, drawing the curtains open just enough to let in the grey morning light. She sat, her posture crumpled, her head bowed.

"I don't know what I did to deserve your concern," she said, her voice thick with emotion. "I'm touched, Asha, that you stayed with Lizzy."

I approached slowly, my heart sinking as I took in her face. The lively, mischievous eyes I had once admired were now swollen and rimmed with dark circles. And then, I saw it—a deep bruise blooming angrily on her shoulder, the purplish hue standing stark against her pale skin. I froze, unable to mask my shock. She caught my expression and gave a hollow laugh, before turning away to sit on the edge of the bed. I remained silent, trying to busy myself with tidying up odds and ends around the room while trying to process everything.

"Asha ..." Her voice cracked. "I should have listened to you. To Mrs Glasse. She hinted at it for months, but I was too afraid. And now ..." Her words faltered. "Now I have no choices left."

I knelt beside her, unsure whether it was appropriate to watch her cry. "That's not true," I said softly. "There's always a way."

She shook her head, tears spilling freely now. "There isn't, Asha. My money, every penny of it, is locked away with him. I have no friends I can speak to about this. The only living family I have is my mother, and she's left for the United States. Even if she were here, I don't know whether she'd welcome me. Do you know what that feels like? To be completely, utterly alone?"

Her words pierced me, and I had a vivid flashback to a rain-soaked little girl huddled on a metal trunk. I did know. I felt sympathy ache in my chest, washed with anger. Anger at the world that had done this to her, that had overwritten everything wonderful that she was with this dejection.

I gathered her in my arms and unexpectedly felt her hugging me, like I was a pillar. The last time an adult hugged me like this, it had been my father on his deathbed. I was no protector, but destiny had placed me here. She needed my help, and I must do what *I* thought was right.

"You're not alone," I said firmly. "You have Elizabeth. And you have me."

She looked away, crumpling as fresh sobs overtook her. I reached for her hands, holding them tightly. "Lady Stanley, you don't have to face this alone. You can take charge of your life. You've survived so much already—you're stronger than you know. But you don't have time to wait. Your husband won't return until later this afternoon, and Mr Nally is still away. This is your moment to decide. You could live a different life, somewhere far away with Elizabeth. Tell me how I can help you."

For a long moment, she said nothing, her gaze unfocused.

"We'll figure it out together," I said, my voice steady despite the whirlwind of emotions coursing through me. "But you have to trust me. You have to trust yourself."

She nodded faintly, her grip tightening on my hands. At that moment, I realized just how much strength it took for her to even consider hope. And I vowed silently that I wouldn't let her down. Not now, not ever.

In no time it began to rain, mirroring the sudden chaos Mrs Stanley's decision brought about. Within thirty frantic minutes, we flew from room to room, gathering and cramming essentials into as few pieces of luggage as possible, keeping them light enough to avoid suspicion. I made a few phone calls with my hands trembling, my voice urgent and desperate. Ada worked silently alongside me, her resolve as steady as mine. We swore to keep this between ourselves. A bunch of instructions were given to all servants to keep them occupied with something or the other. The kitchen was to prepare an elaborate dinner of Lord Stanley's preference and it was declared that the family would be dining together. It was announced that Mrs Stanley would be taking Elizabeth to London and that they'd need the car.

Nally's young understudy arranged for the car to be brought out. Ada, ever resourceful, had the car parked outside the estate's gates, hidden from view. We used a side trail to personally carry the luggage and load it into the vehicle unobserved, avoiding the main entrance, where years ago, I had stood with Mrs Upton.

"Miss? I could have brought the car inside," remarked the plump old driver from inside the car, trying his best to be heard despite the rain.

Ada cocked her head inside and said, "You wouldn't want your car to get stuck in the mud, do you?"

He wasn't done. "But miss? Why do they need luggage?"

"Change of clothes. It's raining, in case you can't see!" Ada barked, putting an end to it.

Acting on a sudden impulse, I darted back to my room and rummaged in my luggage for something I hadn't thought about in a long time, something I wanted Elizabeth to carry with her today of all days, when she would need all the luck she could get. We hurried to Elizabeth's room, where mother and daughter waited, their faces pale. For the first time in days, I saw a glimmer of the fierce resolve that had once defined Mrs Stanley. "God bless you, my dear," she whispered.

Elizabeth stood beside her, composed but visibly scared. I knelt to meet her gaze, mustering a smile to steady her.

"May you always be happy, Elizabeth," I said softly, brushing a strand of hair from her face. I wrapped my peacock-blue stole around her, my eyes welling up. "Keep this with you. May it always bring you luck."

She hesitated, her voice almost inaudible. "Thank you, Asha. I'll write to you."

I pressed a folded note into her palm. "Yes. This is Ada's address. Letters sent here will find me."

Elizabeth nodded, clutching the note tightly. And just like that, my favourite Stanleys stepped into the storm, leaving behind Bradbourne and a life that had too long held them captive.

Ada and I had no time to talk about it. We had to keep the show running. She prepared dinner with everyone else and I phoned Veeraswamy again at the number Kasim had proudly mentioned in one of his letters. I was counting on him and praying that he would remember and carry out my instructions perfectly. Ada and I spun a tale for Nally's anxious understudy, claiming that Lady Stanley had been driven to walk to the gate by her impatience at his delay in arranging for the car. The young man, embarrassed by what he perceived as a failure in his duties, wouldn't be rushing to report anything out of the ordinary. It wasn't my proudest moment, but we did what we had to do.

Ada swore that this would be the last time she'd hide something from Patrick and we exchanged worried glances every time we saw each other. Mr Nally and Lord Stanley arrived together at about 5 p.m. By now, Kasim would have collected my savings from Mrs Upton, who had responded to my frantic requests with surprised but unquestioning compliance. To her enduring credit, she asked me no questions and agreed to hand over the money to the boy when he came, if I was sure I trusted him. Kasim would then have helped Mrs Stanley and Elizabeth reach the station and board a train to Scotland, and loaded her luggage separately so as to avoid arousing suspicion if they were to be spotted by anyone else. The guest log at the restaurant they had lunch at mysteriously recorded that a Mrs Stanley and her daughter had indeed spent the afternoon there and checked them out well after the train's departure time. It wasn't a perfect alibi, but it would complicate any effort to trace them. Beyond this, I could only hope and pray that Mrs Stanley's letter for help would be answered, as I hoped it would. Scotland was no sanctuary, only a pause in her flight. My meagre savings could buy her a few days, nothing more. I hoped the answer would arrive before time ran out.

Ada and I watched furtively as the conversations at home turned into inquiries and suspicions arose with every passing hour. The poor understudy was the first to be summoned and questioned. He stuck with the story that the females left in the car for lunch. A phone call to Veeraswamy's confirmed reservations. But the trail went cold there. The car had been released by Mrs Stanley with instructions to meet her at her tailor's. Investigations into Mrs Stanley's social circle and possible whereabouts began to take place the next day.

I barely slept that night. My mind was constantly occupied with Mrs Stanley. I wondered if Lord Stanley would figure out that she had fled for good and have authorities trace her down. I wondered if my savings had been enough to tide her through. Would Mrs Stanley's mother answer to her letter for help?

At the break of dawn, there was loud knocking on my door. I jumped out of bed and happened to peep out of my window to find Ada vehemently gesturing a warning with both her hands. When I opened the door, I found Mr Nally standing there, lantern in hand, his face flushed and glistening from the climb. He was breathless, but his sharp eyes held a peculiar mix of urgency and suspicion.

"Miss Asha," he began, his voice low but firm, "a word with you, if you please." He stepped inside uninvited, setting the lantern on a small table near the door. The flickering light cast long, unsettling shadows across the walls. He looked at me, his eyes narrowing slightly, as though weighing my reaction.

"There's been a troubling development," he began. "Lord Stanley is deeply concerned about Lady Stanley's extended absence. He's asked me to account for every member of the staff. Where they've been, what they've seen, what they might know." He leaned in slightly, his voice dropping to a near-whisper. "And your name came up."

I blinked, forcing a confused expression. "My name? Whatever for?"

Mr Nally folded his arms, studying me carefully. "It seems you were seen speaking with Lady Stanley quite a bit before her departure. Some of the maids mentioned you running errands for her." He paused. "The Lord wonders if she confided in you. Did she?"

"Mr Nally, I ... I wish I knew anything about that evening. They had both demanded to be left alone so often. I assumed they wanted to spend some time alone and say their goodbyes in peace, sir. What other than that would a girl like me think? I didn't even know something was wrong until late evening when they did not return."

He stepped closer, lowering his voice to an almost conspiratorial tone. "You're going to be summoned by the Lord in the morning. Now look, you're but a migrant young girl. Should the Lord find you guilty of abetting this disgraceful affair, you cannot imagine what will happen to you." His gaze sharpened, his words cutting like a blade. "Child, if there is anything I should know, now is the time to tell, and you have my word—you will be safely sent back to your homeland with enough to spare. I have come all the way here to give you a chance to be smart and do the right thing for your future."

He leaned in further, his voice dropping to a harsh whisper. "Tell me, did Lady Stanley force you to help her abduct little Elizabeth? Where have they gone?"

I summoned all my effort, and started to cry. Hot tears spilled down my cheeks, and I buried my face in my hands. I sobbed, "She left me! She just ... left me here. No reference, no job, no way to go back home. How could she do this to me?"

Mr Nally stiffened, clearly taken aback by my outburst. "Now, now," he said, his tone shifting to something almost resembling concern. "What do you mean, she left you?"

I sniffed, dragging a sleeve across my face. "I don't know where she went. All I know is that I've been left with nothing. What am I supposed to do now? Who will hire me without a reference? How will I even survive?"

He frowned. "You're telling me Lady Stanley didn't take you into confidence? Not even a hint?"

I shook my head. "Not a word! She's gone, and I'm here, abandoned, without any idea of what happens next. She didn't care what would happen to me. I'm just a nobody to her. How would I know where she went? She didn't trust me with anything!"

He paused for a few moments, and then gave a curt nod and left, his footsteps heavy as he descended the stairs. I stood in place, listening to the sound fade before rushing to the window. Ada was still there, her hands clutched to her chest, her face pale with worry.

I gestured for her to leave and quietly sat down on the bed, closing my eyes for a moment. Mrs Stanley and Elizabeth had to be far away by now. They just had to be.

We both assumed we would be watched for several days, so Ada and I decided to minimise our interaction, speaking mostly to others and keeping our movements routine. On the third day, Lord Stanley dismissed Ada without explanation in an open fit of rage. She left the manor with her head held high. Lord Stanley stormed around the grounds like a man possessed, his fury palpable, while policemen arrived to interview the staff. I managed to feign ignorance, playing dumb when questioned, my heart pounding with every answer.

With Ada gone, I was utterly alone, holding my breath for any news, any sign that Mrs Stanley and Elizabeth had made it safely. Several times, I caught Mrs Kensley giving me a probing look, but I avoided her gaze, burying myself in tasks to avoid suspicion. Each night, I prayed fervently for their safety.

A week later, there was a knock at the back kitchen door. Ada's brother stood there, his face unreadable as he handed me three letters. He slipped away without a word, and I took the bundle to my room, my hands trembling as I unwrapped it.

The first letter bore the name 'Scarlett'. My lips curved into a small smile as I read:

> Dear Ashley,
> You were right, the queen did answer the missive. The troops are moving soon to answer her summons, before they can be sieged.
> The road so far has been smooth. Thank you for everything.
> Yours,
> Scarlett."

The second letter was a scrappy little note from Ada, written in her familiar, hurried scrawl:

> "Hope things are going okay for you there, Asha. Stay put. They're sending me away to London to my sister's for a bit while Dad is unwell. Lots of love. Meet soon."

The final envelope was from a Mr Hardinger of London who wrote to me on behalf of the old lady from PO Box S 5382. I was summoned for an interview that week.

On the day of the appointment, I packed my meagre belongings. Mr Nally, true to his word, had provided me with a modest but respectable letter of recommendation. My tenure at Bradbourne Manor was very clearly over. I was not told I was expected back, and my room was cleared before I left. If this position didn't work out, I knew I'd have little choice but to return to the Ayah Home.

As the cab pulled away, I looked out at the sprawling fields, Bradbourne shrinking in the distance. I felt a strange mix of relief and sorrow. Whatever lay ahead in London, it was the start of something new. The manor, with all its secrets and tragedies, was now a chapter I had to leave behind.

As it happened, God continued to be kind to me. PO Box S 5382 turned out to be a lady named Mrs Taylor. She was a writer, and many people read her books and writings in the newspaper every day. She was well travelled, and now lived alone in London after her husband had passed away. She still travelled and needed a companion as she had started feeling her age.

Mrs Taylor was a wonderful person, keenly interested in my life, my travel to England and my days as an ayah. She continued to be a prolific writer under a famous pseudonym. I had an eventful life with her. As the years and decades flew by, I continued to visit the Ayah Home and its successor organisations and contributed to them in every way I could. Through the World War, through the chaos, the building that gave me shelter that cold night, kept on giving shelter through the toughest, darkest times, to others. I like to think I helped.

Mrs Upton and I met many times over the years. Though we never became what one might call friends, there was a quiet understanding between us. Ours was a bond forged in necessity, tempered by trust. I always knew that if the world crumbled tomorrow, I could count on her, and she on me.

EPILOGUE

22 June 2000
Marlow, Buckinghamshire

Asha smiled, and leaned back in her chair. The interview was clearly over.

"Did you ever meet Scarlett…Lady Stanley…again?" Rashmi asked, her voice low, her eyes eager for a final piece of the puzzle.

Asha smiled faintly, her gaze drifting towards a framed photograph on the mantelpiece. It captured a young woman in a wide-brimmed hat and a sundress, sitting on a stone bench in a garden, an English foxhound by her side.

"No, we didn't," Asha said softly. "But I like to think she remained beautiful until her last day."

Rashmi stepped closer to the photo, her fingers grazing the glass. "Did she ever settle in the United States, with her mother?"

Asha shook her head slightly, her smile bittersweet. "She did settle in the United States, but not with her mother.

She always spoke of her mother with gratitude, of course, for helping her escape. But Lady Stanley was never one to stay in anyone's shadow. She built a life for herself. She wore many hats, and found her calling in the war efforts during the World War—a world away from the one she'd known, but it suited her."

"Lady Stanley became who she was always meant to be. A free spirit, unbound by anyone's expectations. She wrote to me for years. When she got married again, when she had children, and when she became a grandmother herself. She never forgot the small part we played. Elizabeth…she grew up knowing she was loved, and found a loving family, which was my greatest hope for her. That's what kept me going, Ms Rao. Knowing that even in the smallest ways, we can change someone's life for the better."

"And … you kept helping the Home? The ayahs?"

"It so happened that I was at the home in its final few years. But the need for help continued, for ayahs, and others who needed what the home gave us. I gave all I could, and I never became a rich woman." Asha paused for a moment here, with a sudden tear in her eye. "Yet, when Mrs Upton passed away, I found out that she'd willed this house to me. A house that she built from her life's savings. It meant everything to me."

"You've had such an extraordinary life," Rashmi murmured. "And yet, you speak of it as if it were ordinary."

Asha smiled wistfully. "Because it *was* ordinary, in many ways. I worked, I struggled, I learned, and I grew. But I was lucky … luckier than most. And I had help. From people like Mrs Upton, Mrs Taylor, and even Ada. It was only right to pass that help along."

Rashmi leaned forward, taking Asha's hand in hers. "Thank you for sharing this with me."

Asha patted Rashmi's hand with a smile.

As Rashmi left Asha's little house which Upton had bequeathed to her, she felt a pit in her stomach. She found it difficult to fathom why was it that Asha's story had affected her so much. The entire way home and then to India, Asha's story crashed around Rashmi's head.

She thought back to that final question she had asked.

"So when did you finally decide not to go back home at all?"

"I don't remember the year, or the age I was, or whether it was after the war, or which war. I just remember being young, and wandering around the English countryside one sunny afternoon. I was missing India. My attention wandered, and I walked through a bush only to find my hands suddenly stinging and numbing.

"I had walked into the common English nettle! Somehow, that thought brought me to my knees, and I sat down and laughed, thinking about how a pahadi girl like me could overlook this cousin of the Bichchhu Ghaas of my childhood.

"Life had come around in a strange circle. In the end, this nettle and the Bichchhu Ghaas, which I had left behind, held no difference. I had chosen a path and stuck to it throughout the adversity I faced, and though my life now looks nothing like what I had imagined, it wasn't a life I would ever regret or change. There was no home to go back to. I was home already."

It didn't matter any more what the Bagchis or the managements of the world had to offer. The more Rashmi thought about it, the clearer it became—all that mattered to her was telling stories, stories of ordinary lives that defied the odds, stories that would inspire people to achieve the extraordinary. She poured every ounce of herself into the essay on Asha, which quickly evolved into a report, and then a full-fledged piece. Within a day of her return to India, the article was polished, ready, and sent off to her editor. She didn't have to go to work for another two days, and planned on sleeping the whole time. If need be, she'd switch to a place that let her write what she wanted to write. She was done living the intermediate stages of her dream. It was time to do only what brought her joy.

Her phone started buzzing early Sunday morning, the voice on the other end sharp and urgent. "Rao!" It was Bagchi, hissing in her ear. "The big boss will call you soon! *The National Standard*! Take the good news and please behave yourself! Don't screw this up!"

"Rashmi Rao?" the voice of *The National Standard*'s editor came through the phone, warm but authoritative. "I read your piece on the ayah story. It was good. I didn't know it carried such potential."

Rashmi blinked, momentarily stunned. "Thank you, sir. But did you really like the piece enough to call on a Sunday? What's this about?"

The editor's tone shifted, a hint of excitement breaking through. "I shared the article with the other editors of *The National Standard*. It won't run in *Interludes* tomorrow, as planned. We want you to do a series of reports, dig into this a bit more, and run it in the editorial page of *The National Standard*. We're thinking perhaps four or five reports for the series would be good."

Rashmi's heart raced. She had barely even thought about a follow-up. "I … I can get those ready, sir," she replied, trying not to let her emotions show.

"Good to hear that, Rao. I'm looking forward to reading more from you soon."

And read they did. It caught the attention of several newspapers, including two British ones. Rashmi made the most of her spark of fame, and belted out article after article, choosing her subjects carefully. Though she failed many times, the foothold that she established for herself in the world of journalism was undeniable.

The cut-out of the first article, as it was first published, adorned Rashmi's desk amongst her awards and recognitions. She looked at it often, and it never failed to bring a smile to her lips. It reminded her of a remarkable woman who never gave up, and who never let her tragedies define her. It reminded her to keep her head down and keep working away, and to always look out for that ray of hope.

Asha.

ACKNOWLEDGEMENTS

Writing this book took passion and an unhealthy number of browser tabs open at all times. I owe a deep debt of gratitude to those whose own passion fuelled my research and helped bring this story to life.

Rozina Visram, a historian and educationalist of staggering importance, whose books *Ayahs, Lascars and Princes* and *Asians in Britain: 400 Years of History* made the past feel vivid and urgent, and who keeps a wonderful history alive and accessible.

Nicholas Messinger, archivist of maritime history of the P&O Steam Navigation Company at the British Library, whose meticulous research allowed me to imagine Asha's journey at sea with a depth I could never have achieved otherwise.

Arunima Datta, historian and scholar on women labour migrants in the British Empire. Her wonderful work *Waiting on Empire: A History of Indian Travelling Ayahs in Britain* provided invaluable insight into the journeys, struggles and resilience of these extraordinary women.

Farhanah Bello, whose tireless efforts in securing the long-overdue blue plaque for the Ayah Home brought this beautiful subject to the forefront of public discussion. From the moment I began writing, I found myself rooting for her, just as I did for the women in my story.

Hackney Museum for their tireless efforts at keeping the history of the borough alive. Thank you for the wealth of knowledge and for shining a light on a history that deserves to be remembered.

My editor, Sakschi Verma, whose warmth and insight have been a gift to this book. Jyotsna Mehta and the entire team at Om Books, thank you for making me feel at home in this publishing journey.

To Sujoy Datta, who has quite literally lost sleep over this book—thank you for being my first reader, my patient soundboard, and my biggest cheerleader. This book may have my name on it, but your unwavering support is written into every page.

To my son, Devavrat—thank you for sharing your mother with a book that took far too much from our time. I promise soon to tell a story just for you.

To my parents and parents-in-law, who were always there with their encouragement, child-minding superpowers, and a readiness to celebrate even the smallest victories—thank you for making this journey lighter.

And finally, to the ayahs neglected by history—this book is, in many ways, yours.